SPEECHLESS

ANNE SIMPSON

SPEECHLESS

Freehand Books acknowledges the financial support for its publishing program provided by the Canada Council for the Arts and the Alberta Media Fund, and by the Government of Canada through the Canada Book Fund.

Canada Council for the Arts Conseil des Arts du Canada Alberta Government Canada

Freehand Books
515 – 815 1st Street SW Calgary, Alberta T2P 1N3
www.freehand-books.com

Book orders: UTP Distribution
5201 Dufferin Street Toronto, Ontario M3H 5T8
Telephone: 1-800-565-9523 Fax: 1-800-221-9985
utpbooks@utpress.utoronto.ca utpdistribution.com

Library and Archives Canada Cataloguing in Publication
Title: Speechless / Anne Simpson.
Names: Simpson, Anne, 1956– author.
Identifiers: Canadiana (print) 20190214058 | Canadiana (ebook) 20190214198 | ISBN 9781988298627 (softcover) | ISBN 9781988298634 (EPUB) | ISBN 9781988298641 (PDF)
Classification: LCC PS8587.I54533 S64 2020 | DDC C813/.6—dc23

Edited by Naomi K. Lewis
Book design by Natalie Olsen, Kisscut Design
Cover photo © Sean Locke / Stocksy.com
Author photo by Kate Waters
Printed on FSC® recycled paper and bound in Canada by Friesens

For the strong women in my life.

1

ARE YOU THERE?

Yes.
I can't see you.
I'm right here. I'll kiss you and then you can go to sleep.
I'm not going to sleep. Not the whole night.
It'll be a long night.

Are you still there?
Yes.

If you stay there I'll go to sleep.
I'm here. Don't be afraid.

2

AT HER TRIAL, the fans overhead slowed and creaked and stopped when the electricity was cut, and people fanned themselves with pieces of folded paper, but A'isha, seated on the wooden bench, was entirely still, and soon her neck, arms, and thighs were damp. She was used to holding Safiya, used to her exact weight, but Safiya wasn't there.

The judge returned and took his seat on the platform, holding out his robe, a riga, so it wouldn't get bunched up underneath his legs. A'isha couldn't look up; she waited in that dense, stifling quiet, gripping the edge of the bench.

She heard her name – A'isha Nasir.

She heard the verdict without hearing it; she heard the word zina.

When she rose from the bench, her lawyer Fatima took her arm, and the other lawyer, the young one, the man who had spoken in court since Fatima was not allowed to speak, followed with the briefcases.

It'll be appealed, Fatima whispered in A'isha's ear.

What did it mean to appeal something? How long would it take to appeal it?

Unfortunately, Fatima continued, I won't be here to lead the appeal since I'm taking up a fellowship in Pennsylvania. But Gambo will appeal. She motioned to the young man.

A'isha heard the word won't. She heard Gambo. She heard the long, drawn-out syllables of Pennsylvania, and wished she could say it in the same easy way. Pennsylvania, in the United States of America. A'isha would never go to Pennsylvania. Life was short and full of difficulties; she would be dead soon. At that moment, she wanted to go back to her uncle's, where she was allowed to stay until Safiya was weaned. She wanted desperately to hold Safiya in her arms.

Fatima was asking her something, and A'isha looked at her, but saw only that her lips moved.

A'isha simply nodded. Fatima wanted some sign that A'isha had understood, but she didn't understand. She walked to the door as if she were sleepwalking, but she could see the reporters waiting for her, and half-turned, hesitating; there was the junior lawyer behind her, blocking her way. Gambo, that was his name. Gambo Ibrahim. She turned back to the door and Fatima tugged her by the arm.

Come, said Fatima. We'll get you to the car.

The reporters were everywhere, pressing close, jostling, shouting; they wouldn't let her through, but Fatima pulled her.

A'isha, said one reporter, a white man with a face as sharp as a machete. A'isha, were you expecting this verdict?

A'isha, cried another. They say you will be buried up to your shoulders and –

A'isha!

They were like flying termites. She wanted to reach out and swat them, but instead she found herself separated from Fatima. She stood still and didn't look at them. Could there be any dignity in silence? There was hush among the crowd; she knew they could see she was of two minds, that she might be persuaded to talk.

A'isha, tell us.

She found that she did want to speak about her fate, a fate that was now out of her hands, even though Fatima had told her, repeatedly, that it was better not to speak.

I'm – began A'isha.

She scanned their faces, so many ready to take her words and toss them out to the world, and found she was unable to go on. What did they know of pain? Her mother knew pain, and in thinking of her mother A'isha was pierced, as if someone had taken a sharp knife, thrust it between her ribs, and twisted it. She put her hand on her breast and bowed her head, because it was impossible to speak.

I will say something on behalf of my client, interrupted Fatima. Her thoughts are for her daughter.

But were you expecting this? A'isha Nasir, were you –

Tell us how you feel, said one of them. He had pushed himself into the front ranks and now he shoved a microphone in her face. It had begun to rain, a spattering of drops, but the others gathered beside the first man. One of them scratched her cheek, pushing to get close.

Soon the rain would be more than a light drizzle. How could she put into words the way she felt? It was beyond her.

A'isha, don't you think capital punishment should be abolished, especially this particularly brutal form of capital punishment? We're living in 2004.

A'isha Nasir, tell us your –

A'isha, when you compare your case to that of Halima Hassan, the one who received one hundred lashes for adultery, do you think –

One of them playfully smacked the other over the head.

This girl does not read or write, he said, and you are asking her about the case of Halima Hassan? She has probably never heard of Halima Hassan.

He was speaking of her, of A'isha. He was really saying that she was stupid because she couldn't read or write. But she could. She could read a little, write a little. The slow burn of fury. She knew nothing of Halima Hassan? The fourteen-year-old girl who had been sentenced to a hundred lashes for adultery though she had told the authorities she had been raped, or maybe because she had told the authorities she had been raped? *That* Halima Hassan?

A'isha, what is it like to be sentenced to death?

Are you angry?

You will have until the child is weaned, but why is the court not specific about the date for your execution?

The man, A'isha, the father of your child –

The fury turned to a drumming in A'isha's chest. Or maybe it was the rain, now beginning to pelt down.

That is all, said Fatima firmly, putting up her umbrella and taking hold of A'isha. That is all.

Somehow they made it to the island of the car, the cool, air-conditioned shelter, where A'isha was safe from them, even though they were all around her, buzzing, flying, landing – hundreds of termites.

WHEN A'ISHA RETURNED from the courthouse with her uncle, her auntie had asked him to explain what had happened, since A'isha was under the protection of her uncle and auntie now, as was her mother, Nafisa. A'isha had to stand beside her uncle while he went over what had happened.

There will be an appeal, he concluded. They will make an appeal soon.

Her auntie turned her face away and spat juice from the kola nut she'd been chewing. The reddish fluid landed on the ground not far from a chicken that squawked and scuttled off.

A'isha went to her mother, waiting outside her hut, while the hot, chubby body of Safiya squirmed in A'isha's arms, wanting to be fed. A'isha sat by her mother on the worn bench outside the hut, bracing herself against the wall and unbuttoning her blouse for Safiya, welcoming the breeze that lifted the leaves of the acacia tree. There, she could rest; the child had latched on to her breast.

You are tired, said Nafisa.

A'isha nodded. It was easier not to speak.

It took many hours, said Nafisa.

Safiya sucked and sucked, sating herself. Occasionally, there was a soft gurgling.

Her mother's feet were worn, A'isha saw. She still went out to work as a trader every day, though she was growing thin and gaunt. A'isha hadn't noticed, had been too taken up with her own problems; it was only later, much later, that she realized her mother must have been sick for months. Nafisa didn't mention the blood in her stool, and by the time she did mention it, and went to a clinic in Paiko, it was too late. It was most likely bowel cancer, she was told. A biopsy would give definitive answers, though it could not be done at the clinic, and she was instructed to buy pills for pain. She didn't buy them.

This isn't the end of it, she told A'isha now.

They will appeal, said A'isha dully, repeating what her uncle had said to her auntie. It didn't seem that an appeal would work. Nothing would work. The lawyer was leaving for the United States.

They will surely help you, said Nafisa.

A'isha watched the leaves of the acacia, as they lifted up and fell gently down. Up and down, as if they were breathing.

Nafisa put her hand on her daughter's arm.

A'ISHA COULDN'T SLEEP, and then she dozed because she was exhausted, but it wasn't the same as sleeping. Night after night, she would see it happen, how she would feel the rocks: the first, the second, and each time her eyes flew open into the blackness, deep black, blacker than a black-crowned crane. And the way it would come, in jolts, in shocks. A rock on her shoulder, a rock at the back of her head, a rock breaking the bones of her cheek. No one should have to die in such a way. Yet she couldn't stop herself going over it and over it, dying so many times. When it finally came, she knew she would want them to get it over with quickly, and there was no way of knowing exactly when it would come, which made it worse. It would come sometime after the weaning of Safiya, and so, if Safiya refused her milk, it might be sooner rather than later. Or it could be drawn out, month after month after month.

Now she was thirsty; she got up, drank water, lay down, turned to one side, then to the other and back again. It rained hard, then abated. She could hear the music again from the bar down the road, a singer howling, unendingly and raucously, about getting love and losing it. *Whyyyyyyyy?* cried the singer. *Why did you leave meeeeeeeee?*

Are you angry? they'd asked.

She wasn't angry; she was frightened. She'd been frightened the whole time the prosecutor had asked her questions.

She lay on her sleeping mat with Safiya beside her, Safiya sleeping the sleep of infants, that long, uninterrupted sleep that A'isha could only imagine. How she longed to drop down into that well of quiet, but then Safiya would wake, wanting milk, and A'isha would feel the draw of another human being, as if she were being pulled inside out. Yes, it had all happened because of Musa, but A'isha could not prevent herself from loving Safiya. She'd wanted to at first, but Safiya was too small, too innocent. If anything was pure in this world, it was Safiya. Sometimes, feeding her, A'isha couldn't help thinking that this child, so newly part of the world, had no say in any of it. It was because of Safiya that A'isha was frightened. A person could die, could die any which way, whether people threw rocks or whether they didn't, but Safiya was the one who would suffer.

I am A'isha Nasir.

I am A'isha Nasir.

3

FELIX TOOK SOPHIE AWAY for a few days. He said it was because he wanted to mark eight months of living together, but Sophie thought it was because he needed a holiday. They flew from Lagos to Lomé, in Togo, where Felix had booked a hotel room on the fourteenth floor of an elegant tower with a swimming pool encircled by women from France, or maybe from other countries, too, but to Sophie they were Frenchwomen. When she parted the curtains on the doors that opened to a small balcony, she could look down on them from above as they lay topless on their chaise longues.

You don't really like it here, said Felix.

With the oil slathered on their bodies, the women made her think of chickens roasting under heat lamps.

He was lounging on the bed, and she went over and climbed on top of him.

It's a big bed, she said. A football field. She settled herself and sat up. There, she said. That's better.

That *is* better.

I don't want anything to happen to us, she said. I want it to stay like this, just like this.

He pulled her down to him and kissed her.

Nothing ever stays the same, he said.

She got off the bed, took off her loose blue blouse, her skirt, her underwear, leaving them on the thick, patterned carpet.

He sat up and she helped him unbutton his shirt, but he was trying to kiss her at the same time, and she started to laugh. She rolled over, laughing. He laughed too and couldn't get himself out of his pants.

You're stuck, she cried, still laughing. You really are stuck.

I am, he said. But he stood up and unzipped his pants and tossed them aside.

We're crazy, she laughed.

Why are we crazy?

She stopped laughing. We can't stop ourselves.

He kissed her face, her hair, her closed eyelids. I can't stop, he whispered. I don't want you to stop.

And –

No, he said, don't say anything.

They made love quickly, hungrily, and then lay close together, exhausted.

Let's do that again and again, she said. While we have time.

There's no time limit.

No, I'm just happy.

He laughed, rolling over to stroke her sternum. This freckle, right here.

It's my third eye.

I love this freckle. And this one, and this one on the inside of your arm. Look at your leg over mine, he said. He fondled her ankle, the curve of her foot.

Felix, she said. How did I find you – out of all the people in the world?

Mmmm. It's the heart's work.

Heart's work, she said softly.

Trust the heart, not the head. The head says here's a black man and here's a white woman.

And there might be trouble. She bit a tag of skin on the side of her thumb. But do you think we'll stay together?

He turned to gaze at the ceiling. We live together now, and, who knows, we might even stay together. Neither of us knows for sure. For now, we're two people taking a holiday in Togo.

Lucky people.

Yes, he kissed her. Very lucky.

THEY FOUND A MODEST HOTEL they liked better near the beach, a low, white building with a tiled roof, and though there was air conditioning, they didn't feel sealed in by it. There was a pool, and a scattering of guests around it. A woman in a purple caftan and a wide straw hat, a man wearing shorts, a few children laughing in the shallow end.

This is more our style, don't you think? he said.

In the evening, they walked the beach, different than those Sophie knew at home in Nova Scotia. Here the waves roiled in, monstrous curls of white that cascaded on the sand with a roar.

You wonder how the boats go out in those waves, but they do, said Felix. Every day, they go out there. And what can they catch, with all the trawlers hauling in so much before they get there?

Sophie could see the high prows of the wooden fishing boats, with inscriptions carved and painted on their sides, and yellow, red, blue, black, and white in patterns that had faded from the saltwater. The words guarded the fishermen against the dangers of going to sea.

Jesus Comes, she read.

Star of Hope, said Felix. There's a French one: Lumière de Dieu.

Splendid Angel. Imagine having a boat called Splendid Angel.

A man sat with his back against the hull of a beached boat, mending a net. It lay in folds all around him like the blue skirt of a giantess. His face was golden in the evening light.

Sophie found Felix's hand, and they swung their arms back and forth for a few moments.

I was supposed to interview you, she said. Back then –

You had a list of questions. You were so serious. I was watching your mouth to see if you were the kind of person who could let go. I mean let go of being serious.

I just wanted to listen to you.

The Lady Sweet Café.

I thought, here's someone who knows what he's talking about. He actually works in the industry; he writes the screenplays.

Yes, I know that stuff inside and out. It doesn't make it interesting.

It was to me.

I felt like I could talk to you all day long. You listen to people, Soph. You hear them. You go right inside their lives.

I don't listen to everyone. You're not everyone.

You were taking down notes, actually writing notes. You were recording what we were saying, but you were writing down notes.

That's because I was afraid to look at you. She stopped and turned to the waves, pounding hard against the sand, and he put his hand at the nape of her neck, stroking it.

I don't want to leave, she said.

They circled around and went back the way they'd come. You know, she went on, my father told me a poem once, and I only remember bits of it.

I don't know many poems, said Felix.

My father did. He could recite the whole of John Donne's

"The Sun Rising." He could stand in the kitchen, drinking his coffee, and the whole poem would pour out of him. Who does that anymore?

I wish I could have met him.

You'll meet my mother soon, when she comes.

Sophie picked up a crushed plastic bottle from the sand. That poem, she said. There's a line at the end.

She poured out the water from the bottle. A line about the sun. Shine here to us – Shine here and you'll be everywhere.

The sky was growing dusky blue, and the sun had set. It would be completely dark soon.

Shine here to us, something something, she said. And then the bed becomes the centre of the universe.

Felix leaned over and kissed her hair.

IN THE MIDDLE OF THE NIGHT she woke, thinking of what he'd said. He lay with his back to her. They were together now, but it might all come apart. She got out of bed, went to the bathroom, came back. He turned over, facing her, and his breathing was slow and reassuring. The length of curtain at the window seemed almost ghostly. She might not be able to sleep now. Drawing her finger up her sternum, she rubbed the slightly raised bump of the freckle.

It frightened her to be so close to another human being. Liam, Noah. No one like Felix. But how well did she know him? How well did anyone know anyone else?

That was the head talking. Not the heart.

She touched his half-opened lips, running her finger across them. He shifted, opened his eyes, and she slipped her finger between his lips. He caught it, held it. Then he reached for her and kissed her, his tongue inside her mouth.

ON THE PLANE BACK TO LAGOS, Felix put on his headphones and closed his eyes. But Sophie wanted to talk.

He shifted the headphones so he could hear. They were misshapen knobs on his head.

Felix, what would you do if you weren't doing what you're doing?

Screenplays about people who are conveniently rescued as they hang from bridges – that sort of thing? He considered. I'd do something with a bit of substance.

Like what?

I don't know. I can make a good living doing what I do.

You could do serious stories on the side, she suggested.

The seat belt sign flashed on. We are beginning our descent into Lagos, a voice intoned.

Through the window, partly obstructed by the wing, Sophie could see the endless sprawl of the city below, a sweltering labyrinth. But she loved the labyrinth.

What about you? said Felix. He took off his headphones and put them around his neck, a collar.

I'd like to do something serious too, but no one lets me do the challenging stuff. It's because I'm on contract.

Give it time. They will.

They just want me covering the arts.

You did that great story about the artist who recycles tires to make sculptures. And he's really good.

And there's another one who makes things out of recycled flip-flops. She laughed. I could do a whole series.

The plane bumped onto the runway and sped along its length before coming to a stop. It would take a long time before their plane was directed to a gate. Felix turned on the fans above their heads.

There are times when I think I should go home, she said.

Is that what you want?

No.

No?

I want to find the story that speaks to me. You know? It's almost as if the kind of story I can write has to meet the right person, the right circumstance. It's only then that I'll have an impact.

Having an impact isn't all that it's cracked up to be.

But I'd like to go outside my comfort zone, I really would. There's so much I'd take on if people had confidence in me.

You can't expect people to have confidence in you unless you've done the work.

How did you get to be so wise?

I'm not wise, just practical. My father died when I was having the time of my life in the States, he said. That's when I came back here – I told you about that. I had to think about my mother, my sisters, my brother. That's why I make the crap I make. Or at least that's what I tell myself about the crap I make.

I didn't have to look after a family when my father died. I didn't have to think about anyone besides my mother, whether she was all right.

Maybe not, but you took a leap of faith because of her, because of your father. Not everyone would have come here.

The plane jolted forward, paused, moved forward again.

You must think I'm so young and impetuous, she said.

You *are* young and impetuous. Kind. Ambitious. Sensitive. Smart. Umm ... kind of wild too.

She reached over and touched his cheek, drew her fingers down the side of his face.

A buzzer sounded, and people snapped off their seat belts and got up. Felix helped a woman with a suitcase in the overhead bin. It was a heavy piece of luggage, but he pulled it free and gently put it down. She thanked him and he flashed a smile at her. Sophie could see how the woman softened, became a little flustered, smoothed her dress. Sophie dropped her eyes so the woman wouldn't notice her watching. Had she been that woman herself, when she first met Felix? She got up from her seat as the passengers disembarked ahead of her. What would it be like if she went home? She thought of winter, of a north wind sniping at her face.

He stood back now so she could get into the aisle, and she went forward, haltingly, held back by others pulling down their carry-on bags. She didn't want to think of a life that didn't have him in it.

4

SOPHIE AND HER MOTHER passed under the high-walled, roofed gate of the old city of Kano in a taxi and came to an abrupt halt because of a bottleneck. In the narrow space it was impossible to get around the vehicles, and after a few minutes some people got out of the minivan in front of them. One woman took a green orange out of her purse and began to peel it with a small knife.

They built it centuries ago, said Clare.

What?

The kofar. The famous gate of Kano. It's remarkable, isn't it?

Sophie concentrated on the long twirl of orange peel as it hung from the woman's knife, before she broke it off, dropped it, and wiped the blade on her bodice – all of them, including Sophie and her mother, could have been stuck in time, centuries back in time, where a woman was eating cool, sweet pieces of orange.

The driver held up his hands and let them fall on the steering wheel. *Kai!*

Fumes, honking, a twanging Hausa song on the radio, an old man begging at the window. Sophie wanted to turn the radio down, but the driver turned it up, and the singer wailed and wailed. Within the furred shadows of the kofar was a place as intimate as a bedroom, the one where Sophie had slept as a child, her father switching off the light, his hand tousling her hair.

I love you.

The old man at the window tapped, tapped with the head of his cane: his fingers, with their uneven, cracked nails, could have been tree roots. Past him, beyond the gate, rain clouds massed together in a dirty pile though the sun was white hot over the market, which was spread out in infinite variations, stall after stall, each one a small theatre: blue, turquoise, magenta, white, and green of hijabs on the heads of mannequins, a man sorting washing powder, soap, matches, and batteries in a cart, emerald green limes in a basin on the ground where a woman bent over a child, holding him firmly by the arm. An elderly man was being shaved by a younger man, his front covered in a plastic sheet, and the younger man turned to laugh with his friends over something one of them had said, razor in hand.

I love you, said her father. Go to sleep.

The minivan in front of them moved into the shock of daylight and the taxi followed, past the man holding the razor and the woman berating the child, until the left front wheel of the minivan plunged into a pothole, splashing up rainwater. Sophie and Clare could see the passengers being jostled as it listed to one side, poised there before it jerked back onto solid ground.

This was the first time Sophie had ventured into the north of the country. Her mother had flown into Kano and Sophie had made her way there from Lagos to meet her at the airport, as if Sophie were the parent and her mother the child, looking a little lost as she waited, one hand on the handle of her small suitcase, the other clutching her knapsack. Her mother, who was always so assured, so capable: here she was, alone. Sophie felt this acutely, a pang in her chest, as she went forward to hug her. When had they been together last – her mother, her father, and Sophie? Three and a half, almost four years ago. Sophie was planning to go to Nigeria on an internship back then, but in the end, she'd put it off and the internship opportunity had dissolved. That time they'd been together was only one day in Cape Breton, but so much was pressed into those hours.

Now, the taxi pulled into the Kurmi Market behind the minivan, and Sophie and her mother got out into the searing afternoon.

They walked slowly, looking at the wares; at one stall, Clare paused to finger a calabash with its black pattern on a bone-white ground.

Did you imagine it like this? Clare asked. This place?

Well, nothing's what you expect.

The stall was full of towers of calabashes, each calabash cupped together with the one below. Madam, come now, said a woman. Small small naira.

You couldn't have gone farther away, said Sophie. When you left.

I left and came back, left and came back. Strange to think I was born in this place, said Clare. There's no other country like this one; nothing else seems vivid or lively after you've lived here, but after that last time your father and I – well, you know how it went. We didn't see your uncle unless he came to us.

And Aunt Monica.

Yes, and the children, but I hardly know the children.

THE DAY BEFORE her father died in Cape Breton, Sophie sat in a lawn chair beside her mother, father, and grandmother watching a baseball game, sun warming her neck and shoulders and the sour-salt coolness of an onshore breeze riffling her hair. The young man swung the bat a little off kilter, but with force, and the ball cracked against it and shot up in an arc. It was slow, effortless – the ball glided, almost hovered – before it dropped. It had gone too high; a teenager in the outfield was already racing toward it, body tilted, glove outstretched, willing the ball to punch down into the leather.

It must have been lonely, said Sophie.

Sometimes, said Clare.

Sophie was watching the game, but at the same time, she was far above the patch of green, the ball diamond and the people gathered there, the village, and the roofs of the houses and gas stations and motels spread out along the coast, the tarnished silver ocean, the vast array of hills turning blue, bluer, deeper blue in the distance.

Your father used to quote Milton to me, said Clare. The mind is its own place, and in itself –

Sophie missed the outfielder catching the ball with a *thwack*, whipping it to the first baseman. The batter was out, but he shrugged his shoulders, grinning, and walked over to his teammates, members of the Volunteer Fire Department of Cheticamp. The score, kept by two men at a wooden table just outside the wire fence, was thirteen to eleven, and one of the two popped his words, leaning too close to the microphone. Sophie held up her phone and her father wiggled his hands by his ears and made a face when she took a picture. He didn't look as though he'd had a stroke, not when he was sitting down, anyway, in his white T-shirt and old khaki trousers. Her mother leaned closer and put her arm around him, and Sophie took another picture. Clare and Gavin. His seamed face, close-cropped hair; her tanned skin, strong bones. Her mother was still lovely in her late fifties, though she waved her hand dismissively when people told her so.

What was the rest of it? said Sophie.

The rest of what? said Clare.

What you said about Milton.

Something about making your own heaven.

Sophie's mouth was tinny, as if a ball of aluminum foil were crumpled at the back of her throat. She wasn't in Cape Breton; she was in Kano, at the Kurmi Market, the oldest market in the Sahel, standing on a patch of claggy earth where a child was twisting a wire hanger into a new shape as he sat on an overturned basin.

Dad knew things like that, Sophie said, wiping sweat from the back of her neck. I was saying that to Felix.

Felix, said Clare. Tell me about him.

He's wonderful.

He must be, if you're so taken with him.

The child was making a sort of car out of the hanger. It was so hot that even the goat next to him seemed flattened against the ground, unable to get to its feet; even with the piled clouds above, there was no relief. Nothing was shielded from the sun, a steaming iron flattening all that lay below, the corrugated tin roofs, the faded umbrellas, the woman who was fanning herself where she sat by a pile of yams. Only the children didn't seem to mind, and Sophie was encircled by them as they giggled, covering their mouths with their hands. Several of them pulled on her skirt and followed her and Clare past a stall full of enamelled dishes bearing the portraits of politicians, a stall full of detergents and laundry powder and mops, a stall full of rugs. The heavy, tumid air pressed down on them.

Come, said a man. Come and look.

Sophie smiled, drifted past.

I have all you want, he persisted. Low price. You look now.

When I think of home, it's so far away, said Sophie.

Sometimes I wonder about home, about the notion of home. I've spent my whole life with a foot one place, the other foot somewhere else, said Clare. This is my country and it's not my country. I'm an outsider.

They walked along the damp ruts of the track, avoiding the mud.

You're preoccupied, said Clare.

There's a story I want to do at work, said Sophie. But they've given it to someone else. She won't do justice to it.

They turned to a man yelling protests as a yellow and green taxi rode over a tarpaulin on which he'd spread his cooking pots.

Wallai!

Immediately, a cluster of people gathered around the man with the cooking pots, who listed his grievances loudly, poking at the air in the direction of the taxi. A girl selling sandals encrusted with fake jewels gazed at the man with indifference, and beside her, a pregnant woman slept under a rack of brightly coloured caftans.

Abdullah, called someone.

Not far away, in a shed covered by a rusted tin roof, several butchers were gathered.

Abdullaaaaaaaah.

The stink assailed Sophie. A slaughtered goat hung from a makeshift gambrel: ropes were tied around each hoof, so the body was spread apart. Nearby, a boy turned over a pan full of blood and it ran into a ditch, a slippery creek of dark red. A man rinsed his hands in a bucket of water and then slit the animal's hide from its hind ankle to its anus with a sharp knife. He made a slit in the other hind leg, smooth and fast as the first.

Maybe you just *think* she won't do justice to it, said Clare. Maybe that's not fair.

Maybe.

The man made another slit from the goat's belly to its neck. Now he was able to take the hide off slowly and firmly, as if it were a tight piece of clothing, pulling it down and over the neck stump and hanging it up with care.

Clare put her hand on Sophie's arm. Careful. You have to stop yourself from rushing in.

At work on another carcass, a boy was yanking on a goat's intestines. They slithered through his hands in slim ropes.

It's not like I'm wanted, Sophie said ruefully.

The boy's hands were covered in blood as he pulled out the slick intestines, more and still more.

Sophie turned away from the butchers. It had finally begun to rain, and the wetness felt like relief. But soon they'd be drenched. They found a tiny café with benches in the shade and bought drinks from the cooler that took up most of the space against the wall. Sophie sipped on sugary juice that tasted of strawberry, but Clare didn't touch her drink; she was fiddling with a seam in her skirt. She looked older, Sophie thought. There were lines around her mouth.

You must miss him, Sophie said.

Clare looked up. The rain clattered on the roof.

He thought he failed, she said. At the clinic. I mean, we all failed, all the time –

Sophie sipped some more of the strawberry drink to get rid of the taste of metal in her mouth.

That little boy, said Clare. His parents brought him to the clinic and there was nothing your father could do, nothing I could do.

Clare's fingers went over and over the place in the seam that needed stitching.

THEY GATHERED AT Caroline and George's house that evening for a dinner in Clare's honour. Sophie's Uncle Thomas and Aunt Monica had come from Abuja. Thomas raised his glass, smiling.

To my sister Clare, he said.

Yes, said George. To Clare. And to the memory of Gavin.

George didn't speak; he announced. He broadcasted. Sophie wondered if it came of his work for the United Nations, the first Nigerian to coordinate public health policy for West Africa.

The champagne was a gift from Thomas and Monica, who had arrived late, putting the dinner behind schedule, but no one minded the delay: they'd eaten cheese imported from France, water crackers from England. Now they were all around the table in the dining room, where the sky beyond the window at Caroline's back had darkened into deep blue, almost indigo, making her blond head shimmer. Thomas was seated next to his sister, Clare, but they could not have been more different: Clare was white, her reddish-brown hair threaded with silver-grey, while Thomas was a brown-skinned Nigerian. When he spoke English, it was with a touch of a Scots accent.

Oh, we're one short, said Caroline, rising. She went to the cabinet, but there were no more flutes, so she took a wine glass instead.

Sophie was seated beside a journalist for the BBC, Fabian Beck. He listened to her talk about her work at *The Daily Leader*, and he asked one question after another, genuinely wanting to know more. There were tiny, scattered pockmarks on his cheeks, but when he smiled and his irregular features aligned – long nose, high cheekbones, deep-set eyes – he seemed less forbidding, not as old as he'd seemed at first.

Are you working on a story? asked Sophie.

Ah, he said, almost curtly, as if he didn't want to talk about himself. It's about a controversial verdict in a case –

A'isha Nasir, said Sophie.

Yes. That's the one.

There must be something that can be done for her, she said.

It's our job to tell the news, not change it, he said.

She can't just be abandoned.

It was strange that Fabian Beck looked like exactly like the place he came from, thought Sophie. A field, blanketed in new snow, at the edge of the North Sea: white, blue, and slate grey.

She'd picked up her salad fork absently and was pressing the tines into the palm of her hand. I'd like to cover that story.

And so – ?

They've given it to someone else, someone senior.

George broke in. The Nasir case? Are you covering that one, Fabian?

I'll be going there.

Paiko? said George. It'll be a feat if you can get someone to talk to you. I mean, I'm Yoruba and I'd have a hard time. They're all Hausa there – a reticent bunch. And A'isha Nasir would be protected from people like you, I imagine.

Fabian shrugged. I'll have to try.

There's been a great deal of talk, said Caroline. We're wondering if this is a watershed moment. I cover up from head to toe when I leave the house now, she went on. Maybe soon I'll never go out.

Sophie clenched her salad fork. It's different for A'isha, she burst out.

Clare looked at her daughter.

Well, it *is* different, Sophie said. She drew in a breath, put down her fork. I'm sorry, she said to Caroline.

Caroline shook her head and her bright curls bobbed. She waved her hand.

I don't know about this case, said Clare.

A Hausa girl in Paiko, Niger State – Thomas began.

Yes, I know Niger State.

This girl, A'isha Nasir, has been given a controversial sentence for adultery.

Sentenced to death, added Fabian. There's to be an appeal.

I don't know what sort of appeal it will be, said Thomas. The lawyers have dropped it like a hot potato.

You see? said Sophie. She has no champion.

Imagine waiting until the child is weaned.

I don't understand, said Clare.

A'isha Nasir has given birth to a child, Monica explained. Evidence of her adultery, apparently. They're allowing her to nurse it, so they're waiting until the baby's weaned before the sentence is carried out.

Clare looked from one to the other.

Her case was tried under shariah law, said Thomas.

For so long it's been one set of laws, explained Monica.

Yes, said Clare. Nigerian common law.

The British came and gave us the Great Gift of Law, Monica went on. Honestly. But now many of the northern states have instituted shariah law. Thomas has been studying shariah law for quite a few years now, just to understand it, but it's completely foreign to me, all this. Anyway, the North is a country unto itself. As for Ibos – well, I truly believe we should secede from Nigeria.

Thomas laughed. You'd have to secede from me, in that case.

Monica smiled.

He fingered the edge of his plate. It's because my birth mother was Hausa that I want to understand shariah law. How will these two systems of law play out over the long term: Nigerian common law and shariah law?

It remains to be seen, said George. I suspect there will be violence.

Caroline stood up, brows furrowed, and went into the kitchen to see about the shrimp salad.

But in this case, there's a child, said Clare quietly. Doesn't that change things?

THE SALAD PLATES had been taken away and the main course of meat was set down before them, grilled to perfection, lightly drizzled in sauce.

The eyes of the world are on this girl, said Fabian. I hope she is able to stand the attention.

Indeed, said Thomas. By the way, it looks delicious.

Good beef is hard to get, said Caroline. The price has gone up.

Sophie pushed her rice into a hill, eating and prodding, eating and prodding, though the julienned carrots were tender and the sautéed mushrooms velvety. Carrots were grown in Nigeria, but they weren't always easy to find in the markets. Mushrooms made her think of cool, damp forests. She hadn't seen such an array of vegetables since she'd left Canada more than a year before.

You're a journalist now, Sophie, boomed George. Surely you'll write something about A'isha Nasir.

Sophie gathered herself. I'd like to, she said.

She might relate to you, said Fabian.

The conversation moved in another direction. Thomas told them a story about his friend who had been learning Swedish while going through his divorce.

Swedish? said Caroline.

You can imagine what he sounds like, laughed Monica.

Ditt jävla ålahuvud, Thomas said, looking at Clare. Everyone at the table burst out laughing.

What? said Clare.

THEY WERE PREPARING TO LEAVE the motel in Pleasant Bay when Sophie saw her father fall, and she ran to him where he lay sprawled by the car. She pressed her hand to his neck trying to find a pulse, she shouted for help, but he'd walked out of his life into the blaze of morning. Her mother came outside, sank to her knees and called to him, called him back.

Gavin. *Gavin!*

He was going grey.

Sophie got out of the way, standing up to see her grandmother at the open door of the motel room, small and frail and white, with the shadowy, boxy forms of the twin beds behind her, and on the wall the pale oblong of a mirror, which exactly outlined her form.

Grandma, said Sophie.

Her grandmother didn't move, as if imprisoned in the silvery liquid of the mirror.

My goodness, said Monica. Such food!

A feast, said Thomas.

Sophie went to her grandmother and put her arms around her, but all her grandmother did was to lift her waxy face to Sophie's.

We'll get him to a hospital, Sophie whispered.

A soft, strangled noise from her grandmother. Tears on her lined skin. Exactly like his father, she murmured. Like Malcolm.

Oh, Grandma.

Sophie held her grandmother like a child. She kissed her cheek, or tried to, and kissed her ear instead.

She returned to her mother, who was sitting back on her heels, rocking slightly. Clare wiped her face on her sleeve, and kept on with the compressions, counting them under her breath.

Now she'd tell Sophie what to do.

I can't begin to thank you, said Clare. You've been so good to us.

5

SOPHIE SCANNED THE LOBBY of the hotel, draped in white curtains, glittering with an oversized chandelier, and sighed.

We're doing this for Simon, remember. Felix took her arm.

But they're all so – that one in red. Can you see her heels? Does she have feathers on them?

None of them hold a candle to you.

Sophie laughed. She smoothed the navy-blue material of her dress. I'm the only woman here who doesn't have foot-high heels.

You're the only woman who won't fall on her face.

I could. You could skate on that floor.

The floor was glossy green marble with white streaks snaking through valleys and mountains, as if another country existed below their feet. A fountain in the centre of the lobby was made of the same marble, topped with a statue of a voluptuous woman holding a pitcher, out of which no water poured since the fountain wasn't working.

Don't look at your phone – your mobile – okay? Sophie said. And don't leave me too long.

I won't.

But a woman in a creamy gown had already taken note of Felix, and she extended her neck the way a swan might, rising out of water.

Felix. She didn't waver on her heels as she approached; she balanced beautifully, spreading her arms. Oh, *Felix!*

Sophie left them. Oh, *Felix!* she muttered, stepping outside.

On the patio the mild air was thick with the musky fragrance of flowers: the pale shapes of lilies were almost invisible in the shadows. Tables had been covered with white cloths, small lanterns shed a soft light at the base of almond and banana trees, and the trunk of an acacia had been wound around with strings of diamond-bright glimmerings. A few of the hotel workers were busy putting chairs at the tables, and a man was methodically setting out cutlery at each place.

Madam, said a crisply uniformed woman polishing glasses. It is not yet open for the awards banquet.

I'd just like to sit. Do you mind?

The woman nodded at a young man, who put a chair near a banana tree, out of the way of the tables.

Sophie? Is that Sophie?

Yes.

It was Charles Oluwasegun, the editor at *The Daily Leader.*

Oh, she said, jumping up.

No, no. Stay where you are. I'll get you a glass of wine – would you like something? White or red? White?

He spoke rapidly to a young man, the same one who had got a chair for Sophie. Charles lifted a chair by its delicately wrought back, and swung it into place beside her, and within moments, the young man returned with two drinks. He gave a goblet of wine to Sophie and a tumbler of Scotch to Charles.

Now I'll be out of the way while my wife does her rounds. Charles unbuttoned his white jacket and relaxed against the chair. She likes these events, but I don't.

I don't either, admitted Sophie.

But you're young. Young and –

Young and – ? She laughed.

Young and full of ideas. You should be mingling.

A waiter had gone beyond his orbit and discovered them. He offered fried scallops wrapped in prosciutto.

Ah, said Charles, snatching up several of them, together with a small square of napkin.

I do have ideas, said Sophie.

Charles quickly ate the scallops and leaned back. He pushed his glasses up onto his head where the light caught the lenses, turning them into miniature moons.

Yes, young people always do, he said. They have many more ideas than middle-aged people like myself. Perhaps I should say old people like myself. He glanced around for the waiter. This dinner will not begin for hours, you know, and then there will be speeches that will make us fall asleep. He turned back to Sophie.

My mother used to say that where you sit when you are old reveals where you stood when you were young, he went on. A Yoruba saying. She was reminding me that I could go away to college in Washington, but not to forget. He laughed, a deep bass laugh. First and foremost, she wanted me to remember *her*. The waiter passed by with more fried scallops and Charles beckoned him.

Yet if we do not have those who love us, what do we have? He took a heaping portion of appetizers from the waiter, and now he tried to contain them on his small napkin. Your own mother and father, he said. Tell me about them.

My mother's visiting Nigeria for a month. She grew up here.

And your father?

My father died a few years ago.

He smoothed his jacket. I am sorry. My sympathies.

Sophie felt a stinging in her eyes.

They sat watching a young woman hitch up the tablecloth skirt at the head table with a gold decoration, measure off a few paces and fasten another gold decoration, between which the white cloth drooped in a pretty arc. Another waiter, or perhaps the young woman's supervisor, came along and twitched the cloth loose in one place, and spoke in her ear so she laughed as she fixed it.

My own mother passed away, Charles said. She was full of joy, full of good humour. Many, many people came to our village for her funeral. In Nigeria funerals are significant events, you see, like weddings, or naming ceremonies. Everyone appears at funerals, even those who hardly knew the person, he laughed.

He sat for a while without speaking. My mother died of cancer, and she was in pain, but the way she died didn't make me a pessimist. If anything, she showed me how to die well.

He ate the remaining scallops, one by one.

I always think of my mother, and her good life, even though her husband had abandoned her to raise six children by herself. I hear her laughing – a big laugh. She'd cover her face. She couldn't stop laughing.

Sophie's own mother sometimes laughed until tears ran down her face, rocking backwards and forwards mutely.

He stood up, settling his glasses back on his nose. So I can't believe we should live without hope.

He held his glass tumbler by its rim, as if it were a ball he was going to drop and kick. I must leave you to look for my wife, who feels she must talk to everyone.

Mr. Oluwasegun. Sophie leaned forward.

Please, call me Charles.

Charles. Mr. Oluwasegun, I have an idea.

Oh ho, an *idea!* He put down his glass on the table, his gaze fixed on her. I am all ears. He cupped his hands on either side of his ears.

She laughed.

I will be serious, he said. Tell me your idea.

I would like very much to do the story on A'isha Nasir. Sophie's words spilled out in a rush.

That assignment has been given to Maryam Maidoya, as you know. Charles became formal. She is one of our senior writers. And, of course, she speaks Hausa, which –

Yes, I know, Sophie faltered. But A'isha and I are both young women. Maybe I could talk to her.

He gave her a penetrating look. Do you think so? He swirled the remaining Scotch around the bottom of his glass.

Sophie sipped her white wine, but her hand was trembling.

Let me be blunt, he said. You came here from Canada on a plane. A'isha Nasir will probably never travel in a plane, not now, anyway. She is Muslim. You are not. You're white; she's black. You are worlds apart. He held up his empty glass as if to mark the close of the conversation.

So you think –

I think that your life is very different from A'isha's.

Does that mean I can't do anything? I'm a woman. Surely I could do something on her behalf? You just said you didn't believe we should live without hope, she said.

You think you can give her hope?

I didn't mean that.

You are young and idealistic. However, I will talk to Maryam. Maybe she will let you accompany her.

Thank you, sir. Mr. Oluwasegun.

He straightened his jacket, which was a little tight across his middle when he buttoned it.

It's not merely a story, you understand. It's someone's life.

Sophie nodded.

It was his white jacket that moved away from her through the gloom, as if the jacket did not belong to him and had floated free. Then he came to the lit doors and stepped inside.

SOPHIE HAD LISTENED TO too many speeches and indulged in too much rich food, so that later, when she lay in bed, she felt nauseous. She lay straight and still as Felix slept beside her, and she waited for her stomach to settle. It was all she could do to turn her head so she could look at his back, solid as a wall. He was so worldly. He'd lived in the United States for years; he'd learned how to make films in California, and he'd become quite good at film editing before he turned to screenwriting. He'd lived in Paris for a while, and he spoke French, but he told her he spoke it badly. She was sure he spoke it well. He said things women wanted to hear, and she was certain he'd had women coming out his ears.

She was in an unknown country, and it made her think of the marbled green floor, with its rivers rushing white. It was strange to be here, altogether strange, but by coming here she had met Felix.

And she trusted him. She'd moved in with him.

After they'd returned from the banquet, Felix had taken off her dress and let it slide to the floor, the slippery navy-blue dress. He held her lightly by the shoulders and she shivered.

Let me look at you, he said, as she made to bend and pick up the dress. Your shoes seem just right without the dress.

No –

Shhh. Perfect shoes. They don't need feathers.

She laughed.

He touched her hips with his hands, gently, moving them up and down the curve of her waist. He traced the lacework that edged the top of her panties and messed her hair so it fell in front of her face, and then he put his hands on her buttocks and slid them down her thighs. He got down on his knees and let his hands travel down to her ankles. He unbuckled the straps of her high-heeled sandals. She watched him with the small buckles: his large hands. Left, then right. She stepped out of them and he stood up.

Mmmm. He brushed back her hair and kissed her forehead.

Sometimes I don't know where you stop and where I start, he said. I disappear, you disappear.

I don't think I want to disappear.

What I'm trying to say is that it's larger than both of us.

She felt it too, the largeness of it, the overwhelming sweetness of it. And she knew what he meant, though she couldn't say it the way he could. It was vast, a galaxy, no end to it.

He sighed and took her hand. I know it can be kind of thorny sometimes. Simon had something to say about it.

He did? Tonight?

Not tonight. He just asked if I knew what I was getting into.

And what did you say?

I said I thought I did.

They'd talked about her. She moved away from Felix, got into bed. He got into bed, flicked on the lamp on his bedside table, and picked up his book. The tender moment between them vanished. She lay still on her side of the bed, arms at her sides.

Tonight I talked to Charles, she said. You know, the one I've been working for.

He put down his book.

I said I wanted to do the story on A'isha. He said I was worlds apart from her.

You *are* worlds apart.

Sophie propped herself up on her elbow.

Does that mean that it's impossible? Is that what Charles meant?

It's harder, but not impossible. Don't hold it against him.

It just feels as though there are things I'm not allowed to do.

Later, she could hear him brushing his teeth, flushing the toilet. When he came to bed, he lay on his side facing away from her and fell asleep quickly.

She wanted to talk; she wanted to ask him things. She reached over and let her hand hover just above his arm, but she couldn't bring herself to wake him. How could she be so direct and impetuous in some things and so fearful in others?

SHE ROLLED OVER in bed, waking. It was already light. When she groped for her phone, she saw it was later than she thought; Felix would be gone. She glanced at the face of the phone again and groaned. There was a voice mail. She wanted to sleep.

The voice mail was from Charles Oluwasegun. Please give me a ring this morning, he said.

She sat up. Give me a ring. Charles Oluwasegun had never called her; it had always been an underling of his who had asked her to meet with him at a specific time at his office, never the man himself. Perhaps he hadn't liked her assertiveness in asking for the A'isha Nasir story – no, it was not merely a story, as he'd said.

She got up and showered, went into the kitchen where Felix had made coffee, opened the fridge, and reached for the half mango left on a plate. The cold, sweet juice of the mango slipped down her throat, and she stopped in the middle of the kitchen, eyes closed. Nothing else tasted quite like mango. The sweet slickness of it, as if she were eating sunlight. She leaned against the door frame, collecting herself before going back into the bedroom and picking up the phone.

Mr. Oluwasegun? she said.

No, it wasn't Mr. Oluwasegun. It was his assistant, the woman with the array of coloured hair clips fanned around her forehead.

Who is calling, please?

Sophie MacNeil.

One moment, please.

Thank you. Sophie twisted a curly strand of hair, trying to recall the woman's name.

Sophie? said Charles.

Yes.

Maryam Maidoya is not going to do the piece on A'isha Nasir. I wanted to let you know, since you showed interest. Are you still keen?

Yes, of course, yes.

I must also say that Maryam pointed out that she thought the subject was a touchy one. She comes from Niger State herself. The situation there has been tense, especially between Christians and Muslims.

I'm still very keen to do it.

Are you sure?

Yes.

You must respect her by doing your work well. In other words, don't flatter yourself.

Yes, sir.

Good. That's settled then. You'll go there before the weekend.

6

A'ISHA SAW THE VISITORS ARRIVE; a small, speedy car turned around and around in what seemed to be two loops, an unfinished figure eight, and stopped. A cranking of the emergency brake, and then the driver got out, a man she'd known when he'd been a boy, Ahmed, and a younger boy, and a woman. Ahmed was lean and full of confidence, with a loose-fitting shirt, jeans that fit his legs like skin, and leather shoes that looked expensive. She had heard that Ahmed had gone to Italy, and that he was studying there. Italy. The younger boy had no such confidence, and he half-hid behind Ahmed. And the woman, who was not tall, seemed inexpertly but compactly pressed together. Her wrapper and blouse were made of the same fabric, printed with every colour of the rainbow. She had a flattened face, all the flatter because of the hijab that framed it; she turned and looked quizzically at A'isha. It was Rahel.

On the other side of the compound, A'isha helped her mother over the threshold. Nafisa leaned against the frame of the door weakly, and, once inside, it was with difficulty that she lowered herself to her mat on the floor.

Aghhhhh, she breathed, the slightest moan, as if the wind had gone through her.

Rahel had been A'isha's neighbour when she was married. It was this woman who had come to her once; it seemed as though it was many years ago, though less than a year had passed. She had come with bean cakes, evenly fried, and A'isha and Rahel ate them together. A'isha was wondering whether she should stay in the house when all of her husband's family was trying to ensure that she left. The women of the family had been bullying her to get her out of the house, property that was hers by rights. The morning of the bean cakes, the family had settled on something new, and that something was Musa.

He caught her by surprise; the basin of warm water was pushed out of her grasp. The basin clattered, spilling the water, and she fell with Musa on top of her. He tore at her clothing and shoved himself between her legs, though she beat him with her one free arm. She wasn't strong enough to throw him off. He was already inside her. Hard, hard, hard – he hurt her with each thrust, so she shrieked, and he clamped his hand on her mouth. The liquid warmth from the basin slid under her body, a dampness under her shoulders and arms, her hips and legs, and she lay in that puddle after he left, thinking about what she'd have done if it had been a knife she held.

She lay looking up, at the underside of the corrugated tin roof that extended over the porch, listening to the sounds in the road: a motorcycle zooming past, someone yelling in a voice that whooped up, someone banging a hammer against metal. This was how it was, she thought. Why didn't she get up? She didn't care. But her dampened clothing grew cold, and she shivered, and then she knew she should get up. She would heat the water again, since the electricity was still on; she would heat the water and clean herself and then she could lie down inside. She thought of Musa, and how he would find her there, and determined that she would keep the door locked against him.

A'isha had cleaned herself by the time Rahel came with the bean cakes, but the shame had been the kind that did not allow A'isha to raise her eyes to Rahel's face, except briefly, as she was leaving.

A'ISHA FELT NAFISA'S HAND ON HERS. She came back to herself. There was Safiya, lying on her sleeping mat near Nafisa, having kicked off the brightly coloured piece of cotton that covered her. Her sweet, curled-up body, ripe as fruit. One part of A'isha was slipped inside this child, one part of herself was slipped inside her mother. Nafisa had given in to the luxury of sleep, and A'isha saw how her limbs, which had been knotted in pain, were relaxed. It was warm, too warm to do much of anything; it soothed A'isha just as it had soothed Nafisa, and she lay down beside Safiya. Just a few minutes, she thought lazily, just a few.

Nafisa snored, and this kept A'isha from falling asleep, a roll of sound, grinding and throaty, and then it diminished, water taking stones down a track. The sound comforted A'isha. Sometimes she woke in the dark and heard it and went back to sleep: the deep, guttural inhaling from the centre of her mother's chest, the loose exhaling.

AFTER THE BEAN CAKES, when Rahel was leaving, she said, That boy did something.

A'isha couldn't bear Rahel's large, downturned eyes fixed on her.

You think this was the first time for him? said Rahel.

A'isha and Rahel stood on the porch, nearly at the place where Musa had knocked the basin out of A'isha's grasp, made her fall. Five steps away, maybe four. A'isha could see through the openwork of breeze blocks at the top of the wall that Rahel had put clothes out to dry on the bushes of the compound that adjoined hers, draping them the way A'isha's own mother had done when A'isha was a child. The sheets, pink, were looped across her line of vision on the other side of the wall. Rahel must have done the washing that morning. She must have heard what Musa did to A'isha.

I will tell someone and he will beat Musa, said Rahel. Teach him not to do such things. My brother –

A'isha shook her head.

She thought it might be impossible to eat another bean cake, the succulent bean cakes that this woman had made with such kindness. Rahel had heard A'isha cry out. How much had Rahel heard before Musa put his hand over A'isha's mouth, his hand smelling of grease from fixing bicycles?

He will come back, Rahel said. She sighed and took her pan, feet slapping in her shoes. She was right about that.

A'ISHA COULDN'T NAP WITH SAFIYA. She got up and went outside, close to the hut, where she would hear her mother if she called. The visitors might still be there, and they were, taking cool drinks in the shade with A'isha's auntie and uncle. Ahmed was laughing about something, leaning back. He'd always had a smooth face, and he could contort it into grimaces, fold his lips under his nose and pull his eyes back to make himself look entirely different, as if he'd pulled himself inside out. It could be hard to remember that he was very smart when he could be such a comic. He was like his mother in the way he kept his intelligence hidden.

It rained in quick torrents, but A'isha was protected on the bench under the thatched roof. They had not come before.

Why were they there? To ask A'isha's uncle to pay the boy's school fees? But surely Ahmed, with his fancy shoes, surely he could help with school fees? Rahel stood up from the gathering. She was thanking them; soon they would leave and A'isha didn't want them to leave. She wanted them to remain in their chairs around the table so she could watch them. Rahel's boys didn't move, though the youngest was jumpy, not wanting to be with adults.

Rahel motioned for him to stay where he was, put up her umbrella, and made her way in the direction of A'isha, with an unhurried gait, as if she hardly cared about greeting A'isha, but was doing it because she knew she ought to. Halfway across the compound she paused to put down the umbrella, since the rain had passed over. She tightened the knot of the wrapper at her waist; the yellow and orange and red and green and purple made her a gorgeous butterfly, but her blunt, homely face was at odds with the rest of her. She was taking her time.

They greeted each other, and Rahel wiped her brow with a white handkerchief extracted from some secret place in her blouse before sitting down carefully on the bench beside A'isha.

You are well, A'isha?

Rahel looked in front of her as she spoke, not at A'isha, as if they were in a car, side by side.

I am well.

Your mother? asked Rahel.

She has been ill. Her colon is making her unwell.

I am sorry-o.

And your family, said A'isha. All are well?

Rahel made a sound of assent. Your child?

A'isha nodded.

I am sorry for all that has happened, said Rahel. I am sorry for you. My brother could have done something.

No.

Rahel clutched and unclutched the white handkerchief.

Musa is there, in that house. The house where you lived with your husband. Musa has taken a wife.

A'isha knew Rahel didn't expect her to speak.

Rahel jerked her head toward the group. Those are my sons.

They are fine.

Yes, they are. Ahmed has no wife, but he has need of one. Rahel laughed, a laugh that cascaded out of her throat. Today Kojo needs help with a scholarship, and so – She spread her hands and laughed again. We come begging for the elders to help him. Your uncle is a good man; he has helped many.

Yes, sighed A'isha. Her uncle barely acknowledged A'isha's presence, let alone Safiya.

Rahel mopped her brow. The sun had come out and it was oven hot where they sat against the wall of the hut. No birds moved or sang, and there wasn't even a breath of wind to lift the leaves of the trees.

He came again to you. Musa. Didn't he?

A'isha had closed her eyes. She opened them. Yes.

He waylaid you.

Even Rahel, who was forthright, would not say what Musa had done.

I did not know when he would come.

Every day?

He thought I was his property; he thought the house was the property of his family. He made use of me. And he knew what I would do.

Mmmnn.

He knew I would give in, and I did. Maybe he knew I'd get pregnant. I thought I could be stronger than Musa.

You are.

A'isha laughed, a brief laugh. He got what he wanted. He wants no part of Safiya, no, but he has the house and now he has a wife.

You will see, said Rahel, stuffing the white handkerchief into her blouse. A tip of white stuck out, a feather tip.

What will I see?

You are stronger. Rahel stood up.

A'isha shook her head.

There will be an appeal? asked Rahel.

Yes, they tell me so, but I do not know who will represent me, or when it will happen. The head man has told my uncle there will be a lawyer for me.

He will help you, certainly. Alhaji Hassan.

Rahel adjusted her hijab, as colourful as the rest of her attire. There were wet half circles under her sleeves as she raised her arms. You must tell them.

Of Musa? A'isha's voice was hard. Musa? I told them only that he was the father. I will not say that I thought of ways to cripple his good leg, that I imagined stabbing his chest right through to his heart. I thought of carrying the kitchen knife around with me, but Musa would have used it against me. I will not tell them what he did to me. It is like the knife. It would be used to cut me.

Rahel readied herself to endure the baking heat of the compound, which lay in the full flare of sunlight. The puddles glistened. Then I will tell them, she said.

No. A'isha stood up. You have a good name, as does your husband. Your sons, you must think of them. It will come back to your family, as this disgrace has come to my family. You must not speak of it. It will be your word against Musa's.

She took up her umbrella. But it is not right.

Musa will have his punishment. At some time, he will have his punishment.

Rahel turned quickly to A'isha as if she had a sharp rejoinder, but she stopped herself and didn't speak.

7

SOPHIE HELD HER HAND HARD and flat against her mouth because of the sweetish, rank smell. It wasn't A'isha's mother Sophie had come to see, but A'isha had asked Sophie to greet her mother, to come into her mother's hut, the last one by the cashew tree, and Sophie went with her, wishing selfishly that she could take something to defend herself, anything at all: one leaf among the densely crowded leaves of the cashew tree, a curled flower newly fallen on the swept earth, the vivid pink of a child's head scarf as she hooted and broke free from the grasp of another child, sprinting away.

Sophie entered the slow twist of warm honey, morning into afternoon, but there was the car that had brought them from Lagos that morning, and there was Felix, talking to one of A'isha's uncles, and there was A'isha, holding back the frayed curtain at the door of the hut, through which Sophie went, pausing on the threshold to close her eyes and slide into a darkness pricked with claw-sharp points, trying to escape the stench, the inescapable stench.

She swayed for a moment at the door and when she opened her eyes it took a few moments before she could make out what lay before her. A woman's body, a bundle of rags, a body. A'isha knelt and Sophie followed her lead, composing herself and trying to focus on the uneven floor under her knees. But she could also make out the woman's eyes, their shine, as they shifted from A'isha to Sophie and back to A'isha, eyes that burned under the shelf of her brow.

My mother, Nafisa, A'isha said softly. Very sick, but not – She hopped her fingers through the air.

She meant contagious, Sophie thought.

Hello, Nafisa, said Sophie.

The woman didn't reply, or maybe she spoke and Sophie didn't hear it.

Nafisa, Nafisa, that was it. Sophie clung to the name, as if it would help her.

A'isha took a sponge and dipped it in a cup of water. She put it to her mother's lips, dampening them.

Sophie wasn't prepared for a woman lying on a dirt floor. It wasn't simply a dirt floor, though: now she could see how it had been dug out so that there was a space beneath Nafisa's body, where several mats had been placed. And there was a pan beneath her wasted body, but Sophie didn't see the pan until A'isha took it away and dumped it outside the hut, and came back in, wiping it with a rag and holding up her mother's legs to slip it under her body again, as if she were diapering a baby. It was done quickly, expertly, so as not to draw notice.

Sophie pressed her hands hard against her thighs, dug her fingernails through the fabric into the skin, willing herself not to move, not to get up and run. Down her back, under her cotton top, ran tributaries of sweat, rivers of sweat.

A'isha knotted the curtain loosely, and then the light came through the door, falling on her as she came close and knelt by her mother again. The stripe of yellow gold divided Nafisa's body into light and shadow. Except for the light – animated, vital – everything within the hut spoke of decay: the curtain, knotted so it looked like a bedraggled moth wing, the yellow and red and orange patterned cloth that lay over the body of the skeletal woman, revealing only her head and her narrow feet with their ridged toenails. Sophie put her hand over her nose and mouth again, wanting to gag. No, she would not. She placed both hands firmly against her thighs as if to keep them from straying. Instantly she wanted to vomit again; she could taste it, and it was all she could do to force herself not to turn her head and throw up in the corner.

The mother and daughter were speaking in low tones, and now, with the light coming in, Sophie concentrated on the mother's face, her hooded eyes and exposed teeth. Nafisa's skull was nearly visible under the taut layer of skin. A'isha gestured to Sophie and talked about her. She must have said that Sophie was doing an article about A'isha for *The Daily Leader*, that she'd arrived with someone who would record what they said, and that this woman, Sophie, had come to Nigeria all the way from Canada. Maybe A'isha was saying these things and maybe she wasn't, but Nafisa's eyes travelled over Sophie's face, her wild, curly hair, her foreignness, as if uncovering everything that Sophie didn't want to tell.

A finger formed itself into a hook, beckoning Sophie, and A'isha made room so she could shift nearer. This movement made the nausea rise again, and Sophie had to restrain herself, settling in place. Nafisa's hand knotted tightly around Sophie's own hand; she gestured to her daughter. A'isha translated.

My mother is glad you have come, she said.

All the while the hand that held Sophie's did not loosen, and if anything, it seemed to clutch more firmly; Sophie would never be able to free herself from such a grip.

What was she saying? It was as if Sophie was made to promise something in that half-lit room, stinking of bodily waste, of blood and urine and shit, a promise made to someone who was very nearly dead, but who held on to life. Or her hand held on to life. It was as if her hand rose independently of her body and grasped the first thing it found, fastening itself on Sophie's hand, and maybe dragging her down with it.

A'isha, please. Please, welcome, said Nafisa in English. She continued in Hausa.

Sophie understood that she must help A'isha. She nodded to Nafisa.

The hand slipped away and lay still on the patterned cloth. The woman's face was like a door swung shut; her eyes closed. A'isha got up and went to the door of the hut, motioning for Sophie to follow, but when Sophie came to the entrance – too much heat, too much light – she put a hand out to the wall and steadied herself as she had when she'd entered. Here the knives slashed her. Light, light, light.

She watched A'isha walk across the compound to wash her hands with water from a bucket. A'isha gestured to Sophie – why hadn't she followed? A'isha rinsed her hands with a cup and swung droplets from them as she went to the woman who held her baby, barely visible, clapped as it was against a huge chest by a broad hand, while the other hand picked through beans in a colander. A'isha took the baby, and in one smooth movement, bent over and put the infant on her back, gave a jog of her body to rearrange her, and rewrapped a length of material around herself to hold the baby tight.

The mountain of a woman paid no attention to A'isha. She didn't greet her; she simply went on sorting through the beans, picking out insects and flicking them into the dirt. This was A'isha's auntie, Felix had explained earlier, making some sense out of the stream of words that met them when they arrived. He'd mentioned her name too, but Sophie had forgotten it. Bundled in a red caftan and a white veil, the auntie was imposing. Sophie noticed her feet were cracked with dryness, especially around the heels. She allowed herself to stare at the woman's feet because she didn't know where else to look. The woman was keenly aware of the two of them, especially Felix, as if she were deciding how to exploit them for her benefit, not unlike a gigantic red spider languishing in its web.

The compound, with its house and the outbuildings grouped around it, with a hut for A'isha and her mother, its full-grown trees and bushes, and a contraption of wire that might have been a chicken coop once, and the uneven, but tidily swept ground, was comfortable, tranquil. A small girl with a bucket of water on her head, liquid sloshing in it, moved deliberately toward the house, one hand balancing the bucket. The woman in the red caftan stood up, easing her bulk to a standing position, but did not help the child take the bucket from her head and put it on the ground. The girl set it down on a tilt, making water stream out of it, and she ran away, her dress sliding off one slender shoulder as the woman berated her.

Felix waited by his car, eating groundnuts and spitting shells on the ground. He put up his hand, a sort of wave. A'isha's uncle had gone away, but another man came to speak to Felix now, greeting him in an elaborate way, so he quickly stuffed the groundnuts in his pocket and did the same. Sophie had never seen him do this. In Lagos, when he met one of their friends, he simply reached out to lightly grasp the man's hand and then held on to it as they talked, as if a person needed to touch another in order to speak to him. Now Felix put his hand loosely in this stranger's hand for a moment, and bowed and bowed again, until their hands seemed to become one single, complex structure. It seemed to Sophie that their handshake, which was not even a handshake by her standards, hovered in the air even after their hands had dropped to their sides. Her mind was playing tricks. She and Felix had woken far too early that morning to drive to Paiko.

Sophie walked across the compound unsteadily. The cup floated on the surface of the bucket, and there, on a plastic lid on the ground, was a bar of hard green soap. She scooped the cup into the bucket, deeper than she needed to, and let the water run over her hands: precious, cool water. She was using too much of it. She lathered her hands with the bar of soap until her hands and wrists were white with froth; she scrubbed them clean. When she had rinsed them, she saw how the flesh was reddened.

HER FATHER HAD TOLD HER she'd learn things in this place, things she wouldn't learn at home. This was when she was about to do an internship in Nigeria.

I thought I knew it all, he said. A smart young doctor, off to do some good in the world. *Pfft.*

Sophie and Gavin were in the kitchen at home, doing dishes.

Things will happen to you there, he said, washing the muffin tin without paying attention to it. You'll change. That's what Nigeria will do; it'll work a kind of magic on you.

I'll just be doing an internship.

You need to watch and listen. Nigeria has had its share of white people quick to impose themselves –

The British, the whole colonization thing, the chiefs who were persuaded to sign their lands away even though they couldn't read the treaties. It was a monumental scam. So yes, Dad, I know.

It's one thing reading about it. Anyway, the country would have been better off without any of us meddling in its destiny.

You think I shouldn't go?

No, I think you should go. Learn as much as you can. But as I said, it's a place that will change you.

I'm open to that.

His hand emerged out of the dishwater and he pointed to the poplars behind the house. Think of a tree, he said. For a long time there's nothing, and then you look and you see that there are leaves where there were no leaves. It explodes from the inside out. I met your mother there, and I fell for her. I exploded from the inside out. He put his arm out, dripping hand and all, and waggled it, as if he saw new green leaves sprouting from it.

We worked side by side, the two of us. Then a family brought their little boy to me. Joseph. He had rabies, and by the time they got him to the clinic I knew he was done for. You can't imagine what rabies does to a person.

He wiped his hands on a towel.

There's an expensive cure if you get it soon enough, but this happened in rural Nigeria. That family carried Joseph for a day on a path that led from Obudu to a place where they could get public transport. On top of that, it had been about two weeks since the bat infected him.

He spread out the damp towel to dry on the rack. Her father who was invincible, who knew so much.

Obudu is like a place of myth, high in the hills in the east of Nigeria, he said. It's near the border with Cameroon. I went hiking there, and I found a place that could have been enchanted, with a river coming down through a rocky cleft. I believed I had found a part of the world that was like no other, a dream place folded into the clouds. Could there be anywhere in the world as wonderful? I got stuck trying to get down from the waterfall, and then I almost fell, but I never thought I was in any real trouble. The river, the sound of water pouring down. I knew I was in some kind of otherworld.

He leaned on the counter. Obudu – that's where they came from. Joseph's family, he said. Their son's death broke them, but they accepted it. I couldn't. I always felt I'd let them down.

Then he smiled. But I met your mother, didn't I? I met your mother and she agreed to come here, and we had you.

A'ISHA WAS A JUST A GIRL cradling a baby; at most, she was nineteen or twenty, with smooth skin and deeply set eyes and a hijab of pale turquoise. When Felix took a photograph of her, one that A'isha herself asked for, most of her face was hidden. Both A'isha and the baby were feathered by the afternoon light that came through the branches and leaves of an ancient neem tree. Just as Felix took the picture, Sophie's quick, sweeping hand reached out to steady A'isha's arm because the chair had shifted, so there was a blur where her hand had been.

Felix came close, trying to get the baby's attention. He squeezed up his eyes and waved his hands. The child watched him, fascinated, her head almost too heavy for her neck. Her skin was velvet brown, and already she had a crop of tiny black curls on her head. But he must have felt Sophie's impatience.

So, said Sophie. Are you ready, A'isha? You don't mind Felix recording us?

Felix had set up the old tape recorder.

Only you will have it?

Yes, I'm the only one.

I'll be writing an article for a newspaper. This one. Sophie handed her a copy of *The Daily Leader.*

A'isha nodded. She handed the paper back to Sophie.

Felix will translate for us if we have trouble in English. He knows Hausa.

I will try in English, said A'isha.

Say anything you like, A'isha, said Sophie. Felix will just test the sound, see how it's working.

Good afternoon, said A'isha.

That's good, said Felix.

You are A'isha Nasir, said Sophie.

Yes, I am A'isha.

And you were born in Paiko, in Niger State, where you still live.

A'isha nodded. Yes.

How old are you?

Seventeen or eighteen. A'isha switched to Hausa and told Felix something.

There aren't always birth records, he told Sophie. That's why she doesn't know for sure.

You have a beautiful baby, said Sophie.

Safiya.

Safiya is a lovely name. My parents gave me my name because it meant wisdom, but my mother said it doesn't mean I'm wise.

A'isha looked as if she didn't understand and Felix translated for her.

Wisdom, said A'isha. Safiya means pure heart.

She'll have a pure heart, said Sophie.

A'isha drew up her blouse and rearranged the cloth expertly over her shoulder, so it covered her breast. The child's head was now hidden by the pink and yellow cloth, but she could be heard suckling. One small bare foot was visible.

She knows – she will know – I gave her this name, said A'isha. To make her strong.

Sophie was about to ask another question when A'isha added, This is no fault of Safiya.

No, said Sophie. She cast about for something else to say. Almost two years ago you were married. In 2002. Is that right?

Yes, my marriage was set by my father.

Tell me about that, said Sophie.

A'isha looked puzzled.

Tell me about your husband, about your marriage.

My husband was an alhaji, given respect by everyone in this place, said A'isha.

She turned to Felix and spoke in Hausa.

Felix said, Her husband told her that he would pay for her school uniform and fees.

A'isha continued. I was young and I wanted to go to school, but I did not want to marry an old man.

You were just a girl, said Sophie.

I said yes to marriage with him. This is what my family wanted.

A'isha put the baby on her shoulder and patted its back gently.

I went to carry water with other girls before I was married, she said. They told me that the man lies down with the woman. They laughed. I did not know a man, I did not understand.

A'isha kept her eyes down. She spoke in a rush. She kept the baby against her shoulder, but she rocked back and forth in her chair.

The alhaji was older than my father. There was a book in

English and he showed me the words to tell me the meaning. I liked the book. It had stories about children.

And your husband died soon after you married? said Sophie.

On that day, in the early morning, I was getting peppers that I put on the ground to dry. He fell on the door.

Against the door?

Yes, she said, moving her hand to indicate he had fallen down. When I went to him, I knew he was dead. There was no breath. I could tell by his eyes and the touch of his skin. I went to my father after it happened. She turned to Felix and spoke rapidly in Hausa.

She went to her father's compound and told him that her husband was dead, said Felix. Her father told her she had given bad luck to her husband. It had only been five months, he said, that they had been married, so she must have thrown bad luck his way. That's how she put it.

But he was old. He could have died from a heart attack or a stroke, said Sophie, turning back to A'isha.

I did not know what to do, said A'isha. I wanted to be in the home of my family. I went there, but my father said for me not to stay. I went back to the home of my husband. I had nowhere else to go. Everyone thought I gave my husband bad luck. I did not want to be married to him, but it was worse after he died.

The baby burped loudly. *Uh-ha!* said A'isha, holding the child against her shoulder and patting her on the back.

They said I had put juju on him and caused him to die, she said. I did not try to go to school after that. I was learning to write many words and I was reading books, but I could not stay there. When I left the house to fetch water, people said I gave bad luck to them. Children ran away from me.

It was a witch hunt, that's what it was, said Sophie quietly to Felix.

I thought to go away to Lagos. But I was afraid. My husband's family tried to take the house from me. First the women cooked food there. My husband's brother lived nearby, and his son, Musa, he came to sleep there. In the day, he went away, but he came back.

Safiya was beginning to fuss, and A'isha rocked her. One leg of Musa's is short. This leg. A'isha touched her left leg.

Sophie waited, but A'isha didn't elaborate.

Maybe these questions –

I prayed, said A'isha. Then I stopped. I felt something in myself, and I knew. I thought I will kill myself and the child. It was a bad thought. Because of this I began to pray again. So Safiya was born. After she was born, I took care of her and I did not want harm to come to her.

Mmm, murmured Sophie.

It was a time of many things. My father died, and my mother came here to live in the home of my uncle. Now my mother has been told at the clinic that she has a cancer.

Can she be given chemotherapy? asked Sophie. Radiation?

She does not want to go to a hospital. And I must not leave this compound, unless I am told I can go.

There are only a few places in Nigeria where people can get chemotherapy or radiation, interjected Felix. Treatment is just not available for most of them.

Sophie wiped her neck. Most people probably suffered with untreated cancer, like Nafisa, she thought.

I have heard that men came for you, said Sophie.

They came in the night. They shouted. A'isha used a corner of Safiya's baby wrapper to wipe her forehead.

They took you to the police station.

Yes, they took me there. They were pulling me.

Dragging you?

Yes. A'isha explained more to Felix in Hausa.

She was arrested on the charge of adultery, but she didn't know what that meant. She had to name Musa as the father of the child, and she was asked if she had consented for Musa to father Safiya.

A'isha said, Musa said to them he was not the father.

Musa was not charged, said Felix. Only A'isha was charged.

Where is Musa now?

He sells bicycles on the main road.

I think we might have passed that shop, said Sophie.

All is good for Musa, said A'isha. For me, things are not good. But my uncle tells me to come here with Safiya to the home of my family.

You were allowed to come here after you were sentenced, said Sophie. After Musa assaulted you, though he was not charged or sentenced.

A'isha looked at Sophie.

Did he assault you? asked Sophie. I mean, did he force himself on you?

She dropped her gaze to Safiya.

I'm sorry, said Sophie. I will not mention him. And so now you wait.

I have the baby and when she does not want my milk –

How long will that be?

A'isha moved her head.

They haven't determined that, I guess, said Sophie. But maybe now you can get assistance from those people at the Spreading Acacia? That non-profit for legal aid – surely they can help?

A'isha brushed away a mosquito from Safiya's arm.

Felix, I think we should stop, said Sophie.

A'isha pulled one end of her hijab across the baby's face so that she would be covered with shade as she slept. She watched Felix putting away the tape recorder.

Beyond them, near the kitchen, some girls were pounding yam. They were working hard, pushing the long-handled pestles up and down, up and down; they had a rhythm to the work. A'isha's auntie was sitting on a low stool, knees spread wide under the caftan, shelling groundnuts and giving advice in her loud voice. Up and down, up and down went the pestles. The girls were sweating; they stopped, ran their hands over their faces. They giggled and leaned on their pestles until A'isha's auntie said something to them and they started again.

Three boys walked around Felix's car, holding hands. One of the boys was very small, and sometimes they hoisted him up. They laughed when they looked in the driver's mirror.

Sophie rose and ran her hand over her forehead. These boys cared about a car. They hardly cared about A'isha.

Thank you for talking to me, A'isha, Sophie said. You have helped so much.

I want you to speak for me, A'isha said.

Yes, I will.

Sophie saw how A'isha's eyes were hooded like her mother's eyes. They were the same eyes, mother to daughter. Safiya might have them too.

Felix went to the car and opened the trunk, taking out two yams, heavy things, like logs, each covered in bark, holding one in each hand. Sunglasses up on his head, where he'd put them to get them out of the way. Hum of sunlight, guinea fowl scratching across the swept yard. Clouds full and billowy, but there was blue sky; it wouldn't rain. Felix was smiling, playing a game with the three boys.

Who can take the yams? He held them up high, laughed.

Because he laughed, with his sunglasses up on his head, sliding down, and the yams held in either hand, Sophie wanted to go him and be folded into him, yams and all, but that wasn't done here, especially here, in the compound belonging to A'isha's family.

Felix had yams and Sophie had pain medication in several packets. She had learned that it was useful to take it with her, especially if people couldn't afford much. A'isha took the pills, gratefully, the red and the brown ones, but Sophie wasn't sure they would help now that she had seen A'isha's mother.

Felix offered one yam to the girl who wore a yellowish dress that was too big for her, the same one who had let the water splash out of the full bucket of water when she'd taken it from her head. He gave the other yam to the smallest of the three boys. The biggest boy asked Felix for his sunglasses, but Felix shook his head.

Nagode, nagode, said the boys.

A'isha's uncle came to say goodbye to them. He was tall, poker thin. Sophie waited as he spoke to Felix in Hausa; even if Sophie had understood Hausa, he wouldn't have spoken to her. But the little girl with the big dress, the one to whom Felix had given the yam, came and stood next to Sophie. She'd already deposited her yam beside A'isha's auntie, and now she twined her hand into Sophie's and stood with her, touching her skirt, the silky material, with the other hand. Sophie looked down on the child's head, the corn rows neatly dividing her hair. Gleam of black hair, skin between, gleam of black hair.

Felix started the car, the air conditioning. A'isha's uncle had some parting words. Felix thanked him.

Sophie glanced at the neem tree as she got into the car, but A'isha had vanished, and except for the chairs grouped companionably together, it was as if she had never been there.

ON THE WAY OUT OF TOWN, Sophie asked Felix to slow down. She wanted to buy juice.

A line of stalls and shacks stood at the edge of the road, tires in heaps, hubcaps adorning the trunk of a scrawny tree.

Could you stop? she asked Felix.

Here? If we go farther we can get some cold juice.

Could you get it and come back? Sophie was already out of the car.

After she got out, the black car went steadily on, nosing along the road. She watched as Felix parked it, got out, and went to a stall to buy drinks.

Then she went directly to the shack with the bicycles. A man squatted over a bicycle turned upside down, working on the derailleur. His two thin legs, bent, made a V; his jeans had holes at each knee.

Are you Musa? asked Sophie.

You are English? he asked. American?

Are you Musa?

I am not the one. The man stood up, wiping his hands on his T-shirt. It was hardly a T-shirt. He called out without turning his head.

Musa, he is coming. See him.

A man was running toward them along the road. He loped in an odd way, as if one leg was shorter than the other. Yes, the left leg. This was Musa. He was too young to be Musa.

And when he stood in front of her, heaving because he'd been running, with sweat beading on his upper lip, on his forehead, the anger went out of Sophie.

Madam, he said. Because he'd been running the word sounded like *maw*.

Sophie stared at him. Was this the Musa who had fathered A'isha's child? And what was Sophie going to say to him?

You are Musa?

Yes, he nodded vigorously. Yes, Madam. Again, it sounded like *maw*.

Musa, the one who repairs bicycles?

He spread his arm. Behind the stall were bicycles of all shapes and sizes. Bicycles with bent wheel rims, bicycles with no seats, bicycles without handlebars, parts of bicycles, bicycle tires, bicycles that would never be ridden again. Behind the shack were heaps of them, upended, and with wheels sticking up, wheels over wheels over wheels. Red bicycles, black bicycles. It was a kind of cemetery for bicycles.

I repair all, said Musa proudly. I sell all.

She felt faint, just as she had coming out of Nafisa's hut earlier.

He brought a chair for her. You sit, Madam. Sit.

No, I –

Yes, sit. You are ill.

No, said Sophie. She rummaged in her bag for her water flask.

Up the road she could see Felix coming out of the stall, bottles in his hand. He glanced around for her, got into the car, and circled back along the road.

You want bicycle, Madam? asked Musa.

No, she said. No bicycle.

Felix parked the car. He got out.

This is your husband? asked Musa.

He is not my husband.

Sophie, said Felix.

You want buy? said Musa. I have. He limped over to several bicycles hanging from hooks in the ceiling of the stall.

Sophie shook her head.

They are good. All working parts. Musa waited, wiping his face on his sleeve.

Sophie.

You do not buy?

No, we do not buy, said Felix.

But see now. Musa took down a black bicycle from the hook. It is working, this one. It is good.

No bicycle, said Felix. Thank you.

Sophie stood up. All the fight had gone out of her. She no longer wanted to hit Musa, slap him, punch him, batter him with her fists until he sank down on the shop floor, where she could kick him, kick him again.

Felix touched her shoulder.

This is Musa, said Sophie to Felix flatly, as if it explained everything. She realized she was trembling.

Felix nodded to Musa, put a cold bottle of juice in Sophie's hand.

Come on, he said, steering her away. Time to go.

Tell them.

Who will tell them?

8

FELIX WAS READING THE PAGES Sophie had printed.

She busied herself in the kitchen, cutting the papaya that had become soft. She cut the orange-red fruit into small chunks. Then she took the pineapple, cut off the crown of leaves, and sliced away the bark. He was still looking at the pages, but was he reading it? He hadn't shuffled the papers, hadn't shifted position on the couch. He was staring at it. She cut the pineapple into slices, rings of yellow, then cut the slices into chunks, and got rid of the pieces of pineapple bark, the hard, spiky leaves. She washed her hands.

Felix? she said softly.

Hmmm?

Tell me what you think.

He leaned back, the pages in one hand above his head.

She pressed her hands against the counter, damp with juice from the pineapple. It's awful?

No, of course it's not awful. Anyone would want to write the way you write. I mean, there are some things, but there always are. The long and short of it is that you shouldn't be wasting your time with *The Daily Leader*.

He was looking across the room at the blank television screen in a deeply focused way, as he did when watching football – though Sophie knew it as soccer – clusters of men moving a ball in fits and starts across unnaturally green turf.

He noticed the strategy, the improvised moves made on the fly; he saw what she couldn't see no matter how hard she tried.

But? She wiped the counter.

He got up, the pages held loosely in one hand. You won't like what I have to say.

She could deal with it. Felix, she sighed. Just tell me.

You're a woman standing up for another woman who is more vulnerable. The odds have been stacked against her. She's powerless in this.

She waited. He rolled the pages into a tube, unrolled them.

That's laudable, he said.

She could feel herself wanting to tap her fingers on the counter. Why didn't he come to the point?

I'm not sure you should publish this.

What? she said. Why?

You come from Canada, and you can't help but be a little naive –

She slid the knife and cutting board into the sink.

Because I'm white and naive, she repeated.

She tried to think, but things moved around in her head like insects, a swarm, and she had to wait for them to settle. She didn't wait. Because I'm white and naive, a bleeding heart, not to mention a bleeding heart who is an outsider, I can't speak out when I see a miscarriage of justice? I can't have a voice? Why didn't you say all of this before, when we were with A'isha?

I didn't know what you'd write.

What's so wrong with what I've written?

There's a way to do this, but you've got strong ideas on the subject. That's really what I'm saying. I'm not accusing you of anything.

I'm just going to pull some other article out of the air? Something else that maybe you'll think is good enough?

My advice, for what it's worth, is that I think you need to find a way to tone this down. Maybe it will work if you do that. He put the pages on the high ledge of the counter, where they put drinks for guests when they came for dinner, but he'd curled the paper by rolling it and none of the pages lay flat.

She swiped the board with a cloth and put it in the rack. What do you want me to do? She picked up the knife, rinsed it, smacked it down beside the cutting board. This is the *truth!* What I wrote is the truth.

Entirely unable to stop herself, she wheeled around to grab a small purse off the shelf and slammed out the door.

SHE WOULD GO TO THEA'S. Maybe she could sit on Thea's balcony, in the shade, sipping a drink with her. A break from Felix and his – what? It wasn't even criticism. It was totally unfair. But she didn't get as far as Thea's, and her tatty blue and white striped chairs, her old patio umbrella casting its deep shade over them. Thea from Brighton, forever an expatriate. What would Thea say? Maybe she would say something snide about Felix. Maybe she would say that Sophie should get over herself. Thea had her snippy opinions. No, Sophie couldn't go and see her. It was the hottest time of the day and here she was, stepping into the street with barely a glance at the traffic, so that two motorcyclists had to avoid her, one nearly grazing her as he passed.

Laudable, she said.

The anger rose up, hotly, and she knew her cheeks were flushed with colour. Nothing would stop her: not the heat, not the dampness of her blouse against her skin. The clouds looked ominous above, but on she went, striding forward. She'd forgotten her umbrella; it was bound to rain. After a half hour of strenuous walking, she resorted to taking a minivan that slowed, stopped for her, and she had to find a space to sit as it continued to rock and tilt forward, making her jerk to one side and crush the mint-green finery of a woman who was probably on her way to a wedding.

Sorry, Sophie said. Sorry.

It *was* because she was white, wasn't it? He hadn't said that; he would never have said that. Sophie had said it.

The driver's boy was asking where she was going, but she had no idea. She had got herself in the minivan so she wouldn't have to walk anymore. Victoria Island. Victoria Island, and onwards to the Lekki Conservation Centre. No, all of that was in the other direction. Anyway, she didn't want to go to a place full of expensive condos, one building after another. She paid and got off the minivan along with the woman in mint green, as if her sheeny head wrap were lighting the way. Now it began to rain. The woman put up her large umbrella and walked quickly ahead, but Sophie would have to find shelter. Just ahead was the entrance to a market where Felix had once taken her.

Outside the market, women were rushing to protect their wares: baskets upon baskets of shiny-backed tomatoes and okra, so she could almost taste the slipperiness in her mouth, and purpled eggplants, slick smooth, piled one on top of the other. On the other side of the lane, market women under umbrellas were grilling corn, and one laughed with her hand over her mouth. *What-o?* cried someone. Sophie walked into the main portion of the market, where the rain was buckshot on the roof. Gunny sacks filled with chillies, and beyond, every sort of spice imaginable: cardamom, cumin, and pudgy, splayed thumbs of ginger root. She went on to the fish market, with pots of live crayfish, basins of enormous snails, rose-pink shrimp. Catfish in a tub, red snappers in another. Brine-thick smells. She kept moving, kept shifting from one table to another.

Why you go now, lady? cried the shrimp seller. Oyinbo, come.

There was no place for her to stop, and she simply wanted to rest. A shadowy, cool cave was what she wanted. She kept walking, wishing the rain would stop so she could go back, take a shower and put on fresh clothes, speak calmly to Felix as he had spoken to her. Fish heads were stacked in a pot. She was compelled by the round, unshimmering eyes of the dead fish that had once been living, once been in the water, flashing their tails. She bumped into a woman carrying a bucket on her head, then someone collided with her: a man in a dirty T-shirt that said *Let's Jamboree.*

Why did she want to tell the story of A'isha Nasir? Someone else could do it. Anyone else could do it. This was what Maryam Maidoya had probably thought. But hadn't Sophie been asked? Hadn't Charles asked her? Would she say no, say that she'd given it more thought and that she couldn't do it? A'isha herself had said, I want you to speak for me. Nafisa had said, Please.

Sophie's phone fell from her purse and she reached for it, bending past a basin of eels, gliding and gleaming over each other. When she stood up, the market had darkened, and she put out a hand to a table edge. She faltered, fell. Something crashed with her, maybe the thick black ropes of eels in the basin. All she knew was the falling, a wobbled buckling, as her knees refused to bear her weight. Her body came undone, as if she had no spine, no bones to hold her in place.

The market women lifted her, a press of women, bringing the musky smell of their aprons, slithery with fish guts. They propped her on the stool that had held the basin of eels, which several of them were scooping up in handfuls. A child came with a pail, and Sophie watched the silvery water pouring into the basin. It wasn't real; it couldn't be. Her head was throbbing. She should leave, take public transit, go home to Felix. But a woman put a restraining hand on Sophie's wrist as she tried to stand, spoke quickly in Yoruba.

Stay seated, said a man. I have called. Someone is coming.

Sophie shut her eyes. All she had to do was obey and wait for the fainting spell to pass.

He is coming, said the man.

Who? said Sophie.

The deacon of St. Bartholomew's, the church, there, across the road. See him now!

But –

The deacon came, escorted by a trail of children. His jacket had been soaked by the rain.

He put his hands over Sophie's head, not touching her. Something dripped down her neck.

What are you doing? asked Sophie.

It is the devil that needs to come out.

There's a devil?

She saw the button of his wet jacket straining in its buttonhole and had to cast her eyes on the slick of tangled eels. Why did it all make her want to laugh?

I will bring it out, he said confidently. I have done it many times before.

The market women began quarrelling with the man who had asked for the deacon to come. An ambulance is needed, said one, in English. Not this man.

See now, said the deacon. The Lord God will vanquish His enemies.

SOPHIE RETURNED HOME. She'd meant to buy a few things at the market, but she'd simply fled. All her wet clothes would have to be hung up. Now she wanted to talk to Felix, wanted him to put his arms around her.

But the rawness was still with her, and even after she showered and changed, she could not free herself from it. He was making a curry with vegetables and chicken. He'd make rice to go with it. If she were in a mood to be helpful, she'd have cut vegetables for him.

You were gone for hours, said Felix. I went out looking for you.

I was at the market, the one with all the fish.

I thought you'd be upset. I wasn't sure you'd come back here. I knew that what I'd said hurt you.

You didn't hurt me, she said, looking at him levelly. You said I shouldn't do something that I have every intention of doing. I'll do it for A'isha.

You'll do it for Sophie.

What?

She left the kitchen. Her damp hair was in ropes and she towelled it dry. Yes, she would publish it. It might not be brilliant, but she had to try. She would try, yes, she would. She marched along one side of the bed. Yes. But then she heard him saying you'll do it for Sophie. She marched along the other side of the bed, and paused at the window, covered by blinds.

The heat of her anger. She had to grip her hands to stop herself from ripping down the blinds. She kicked the bed instead, and hurt her foot, so she had to sit down, take the impatient foot in her hand and rub it, knead it, fool the pain out of it.

Felix was at the door. That was uncalled for, what I said. I'm sorry.

He came and sat down beside her on the bed and took her foot in his hands.

She shut her eyes.

Sophie, it's because I care about you. I wanted to warn you.

He rubbed his hand slowly up and down her instep and it felt good.

You can't tell a person what to do. I can't say to you, don't do this, don't do that, he said. I just worry that they're going to point at you. They're going to say, she's outside this. She doesn't count.

Maybe that will happen, she said slowly. Maybe you're right.

He waited.

I've been exorcised. Of demons, or just one demon, I couldn't tell.

You went out of here and –

I didn't mean to get exorcised. I fainted in the market, and they told me to wait for someone who did that sort of thing. From St. Bartholomew's.

He stopped massaging her foot, and she tucked it under her leg.

Felix, she said.

What?

First, I'm sorry. I was ferocious.

He smiled. And second?

Well, she said, someone else could do it. It's true.

I just want to know why it has to be you. I want you to think it through. I'm no expert on this country, but –

You were born here, she said.

That doesn't mean a lot. Here, any little misunderstanding and people lash out at each other. This is the history of the place you're in. First there was the slave trade, then the abolition of the slave trade, though you can be sure there were always people wanting to profit off the backs of others. Now, thanks to the British, what's called Nigeria is really a patchwork of North and South, but the North doesn't understand the South, and the South doesn't understand the North.

Sophie thought of her trip to the Kurmi Market in Kano with her mother. Didn't Nigeria gain independence in 1960? Didn't that change things? she asked.

He laughed. Then he became thoughtful. There were great civilizations here once, he said. Before the British Empire, before the United States, there were strong and ancient cultures. The Empire of Oyo, of Benin. And long before that, the Nok made the most beautiful sculptures in terracotta. I saw some in Paris.

He was quiet.

So many things were taken, he said. Looted. But there's enough to know that the Nok must have had a sophisticated culture. No one knows exactly when these sculptures were made, they can only estimate that it was sometime between the fifth century BC and the fifth century AD. He drummed the fingers of one hand on his thigh. I had to go away to be able to see my country, you know? To *see* it. I hated being away at first, but then it gave me a kind of double vision. I could see in more than one way.

He got up from the bed. We should eat something.

I know, Sophie said, but she stayed where she was.

What I'm trying to say is that we take our countries with us wherever we go. We can't help it. When you think of A'isha, he went on, you fall back on your idea of justice.

But isn't it also your idea of justice that she should go free?

Yes.

Then?

It's like a nest of scorpions, her situation.

I don't care.

Sophie, that's what I'm trying to tell you. You have to care. She's been tried in a shariah court. You get in there and you might get your head bitten off.

But what should I do? I have to do something.

Why you?

Why not me?

He shook his head.

What?

This sense of being chosen for the mission.

She turned her head away.

Soph.

It's not that, she said. It's not a mission. At first, maybe it was. I wanted a story, especially one about a woman. Then I met her, A'isha, and I saw her mother, and it changed. It's that I can't bear it. I can't. Sophie faced him. If I see her and talk to her and don't lift a finger, then what kind of person am I?

He didn't say anything.

When we talked to her, she said, I got this sense of her being alone. Who will stand up for her? – that's what I thought.

Everyone is alone, ultimately, said Felix.

Alone, Sophie thought, lying awake, waiting for her father to come home. She could hear the sounds of the refrigerator downstairs in the kitchen, and outside, a couple of motorcycles on the highway, and in the trees between the house and the highway, the sweet piping of a bird she didn't know, maybe a wren. The sun had gone down long before, but the bird was singing. She felt the night opening up as if it were a peony, many-petalled, and she knew there were other people like her lying awake in their beds, waiting, so the world became large, then larger, then so big she could hardly hold the thought. Who were those other people and what were they thinking as they lay in their beds?

Her father's car rolled up the gravelled lane, the long curving driveway that brought him to the house, and there was the thump of his car door as he closed it, and his tread on the porch steps, and once he was inside, the sound of his keys being dropped into the bowl on the chest in the hall. She knew he would come upstairs and sit by her and tell her what had happened in his day. When he was there, she wasn't afraid of anything. She wanted him to sit on her bed until morning, telling her things, just so she could listen to the sound of his voice, but she had to get some sleep and he would leave the door open the way she liked it. He told her he loved her. Then he left and she could hear him talking with her mother in their room down the hall and the bathroom door and the flush of the toilet and the bathroom door and the thread of talk picked up and trailing off and after a while the house was still except for the refrigerator, and the train in the distance as it worked its slow way up the hill and then across the trestle and through town near the hospital. She thought again of other people in their beds, some of them the same age she was, without fathers to come and talk to them, some of them staring at the ceiling in the dark, though it was almost too dark for the ceiling to be seen. Some were afraid. She could feel them as if she were another person, in another bed, in a house somewhere else, alone.

Yes, she said.

9

FELIX WENT OVER IT WITH HER, paragraph by paragraph. Sophie wrote and rewrote it, but she was working to a deadline, and in the end it was rushed.

Charles approved the piece and it was printed. Nina called from the Spreading Acacia to say how much everyone there liked it, and other than that, a sprinkling of comments. Sophie was researching the kidnappings of foreign nationals in the Delta when Charles called her.

There's a problem.

What kind of problem?

Come to the office.

She went. It was late in the day when she arrived, and no one greeted her as they usually did. The woman with the coloured hair clips studiously avoided looking at her.

Charles came out of his office, beckoned her with a wave, and she went inside. Everyone was watching her, the "American" girl, the favoured one who'd probably bought her way into a job or slept her way into it, since she was the only foreigner working in the Lagos office of *The Daily Leader*. It didn't matter that she was on a contract, that she hadn't been given a cubicle, that she didn't work with the rest of them. Charles's office wasn't big, but his desk was huge, made of dark wood, mahogany, or wood veneer made to look like mahogany. The air conditioning was going full blast, and Sophie shivered. He took a stack of papers off a chair and held out a hand.

She sat.

Your article about A'isha Nasir, he said. I'm afraid we're into some trouble.

What do you mean?

The publisher has already spoken publicly on your behalf. He's had to apologize.

For what?

Maryam was right. It is a touchy subject.

Oh dear. But you approved it, you said it was all right.

I received word that the office of *The Daily Leader* in Kaduna was firebombed.

What? Was anyone hurt?

We don't know a great deal at the moment, but as I understand it there was no one working at the office. It happened the evening before last. No one was hurt, except that one of the protestors was involved in a scuffle, but I'm told he will be fine.

It was burnt to the ground? The whole office?

Part of the office, and a chemist's shop below the office. Charles took off his glasses and pressed his fingers under his eyes as if they hurt him. It seems they've taken umbrage to what you wrote. He put his glasses back on.

She couldn't absorb it. Umbrage, she thought.

It's serious, he said. Quite serious.

What did I say? I mean, it was an article about A'isha and the fact that she'd been sentenced to be stoned to death. Sophie's mind raced.

Charles reached behind him for the folded newspaper on top of the filing cabinet. He smoothed it out on his desk and adjusted his glasses.

This is really more of an op-ed piece, as you say in the US –

I'm not American.

He waved his hand. You ask about the man who committed adultery with A'isha. You ask why punishment should fall disproportionately on the woman. You mention that mercy should be shown –

But is it merciful to kill A'isha? Sophie pushed back the cuticle on her thumb.

He sighed. It's true we live in a world that upholds free speech as the ideal.

She waited.

Still, we have to be judicious. You're not from here, and so you have to be even more careful.

But you didn't come back to me with any changes except those few small ones, she said. Before we went to print.

I thought it was all right. I really did. But I misjudged the way things are in Kaduna, Minna, Kano – the North.

She pushed back the cuticles on her index finger, on her middle finger. She pushed hard, so it hurt.

He shook his head.

What should I do? she said.

He swivelled in the chair. We need a public apology. They want to see a contrite – Sophie, you must understand.

Maybe I was too forthright, she said. I guess it's something to keep in mind for other –

He shook his head. I'm going to have to let you go.

Let me go?

I'm sorry. It's for your own sake.

Her mouth was dry.

It's worse than you can imagine. It's not only you who stands to lose a job, but that's the least of it.

Oh, God. They're not going to fire you, are they?

She put her hand out to the shining surface of the mahogany desk, the heavy, oversized desk that was his pride and joy. His laptop, his printer. The ugly desk chair, split on the seat, in which he was leaning back, glasses on the top of his head, eyes shut.

I will make myself scarce, he said. It will be called a leave.

She'd had her interview with him in this same office, many months before. How nervous she'd been. And he made her feel comfortable, asked her how she liked Nigeria.

Oh, she liked it, yes. She loved the markets. One of her favourite things to do was to eat suya on a stick.

Bush meat. He laughed, the deep honk of a bass trombone.

She liked him right away. And now it was because of her that his job was threatened.

She wanted to flee, although she couldn't very well go running out of his office.

The only thing I'm concerned about right now, he was saying, is that we offer an apology, that we stop this in its tracks.

I'll go and do it now, she said.

No, I've written it. I want you to read it so you know what I've said.

He put a paper in front of her. This, he said.

She looked at it, but she couldn't read it. She blinked, but the words spidered up and down instead of staying still.

It looks fine to me, she said, trying to keep her voice even.

Good. He took the paper back.

I want you to go home and stay there. Go by taxi.

Now? She looked at him.

Sophie, he said. It is not safe for you. In fact, I have been warned that everyone in the office should go home this evening and stay put. We'll all have to lay low for the time being, but you're the one in the most danger.

She stood up.

If you get any threats, anything like that, I want you to get in touch with me at this number. Don't use your own mobile. He gave her a pink Post-it note.

Sophie took it from him slowly.

This will pass, Sophie. By next week, they'll be on to something else.

She knew she should go. He was already busy with papers on his desk.

What about A'isha? she asked.

Pardon me?

Charles was always polite, even when he wasn't really aware of her.

Sophie swallowed. What will happen to A'isha Nasir? she said. I don't want anything to happen to her because of me.

FROM THE COOL OFFICE, Sophie stepped into the blaze of late afternoon. She was not going to bother with a taxi. Two women sidestepped Sophie, who stood without knowing what to do. A yellow dog sniffed her legs. She began walking, barely avoiding a ditch filled with murky water. A man carrying a huge cooler on his head was nearly caught by the mirror of a passing taxi, but he moved nimbly out of the way, while the driver swung his arm out of the car, showering him with abuse. At every roadside stall, the faces of vendors were hidden in the dusky shadow of umbrellas, some so faded that their original colour could no longer be discerned: a woman selling soap, milk, custard powder; a boy selling phones; a girl with an infected eye, sitting on a wagon, begging, with a ripped cardboard sign that read, simply, *Plese;* a mother with a sleeping baby; someone selling limp green leaf. One man was laughing, bent over, and another man was slapping him on the back. Staccato of horns. A strong smell of fresh paint, the sticky, pervasive odour of sweat as she passed someone, the mouth-watering smell of shish kebabs, a wave of perfume wafting after a woman in a tight coral-coloured dress.

Sophie turned wildly when someone honked at her. When she moved out of the way of the car she walked straight into a nattily dressed businessman, banging against the rectangle of his briefcase. She bought some packaged milk with a picture of a mountain on it, snow at its peak, the stuff they filled with preservatives, and dropped it into her string bag as she threaded her way back to the apartment, working her way around a stalled car and men offering advice, avoiding a straggle of children in school uniforms. Girls with perfectly white blouses, dark blue skirts, and braids tied at the ends with ribbons.

She bought as many newspapers as she could find on the way home: *The Nigerian, The Nation, The Green and White, Newsday, The Record.* There it was, the picture of the rubble outside *The Daily Leader* office building in Kaduna, and the fallen corner of the structure, prominently displayed in every one of the papers. She stood in a doorway, quickly flipping through each article. Her phone rang and she ignored it. They called her by name in two of the articles. One of them said her article on A'isha Nasir was misguided; one stated that she had followed feminist ideology into perilous territory; one said that a white person had no right to discuss issues concerning Nigerians.

Miss Sophia MacNeil, a newly arrived expatriate on Nigerian soil, seems to possess no common sense —

Sophie MacNeil made it clear that A'isha Nasir is a hapless victim of newly instituted shariah laws in Niger State.

In the midst of the uproar, American reporter S. MacNeil has been keeping a low profile. *The Daily Leader* did not offer comments on the story, though its publisher, Franklin Ojukwe, provided an apology —

She leafed through them so quickly that sections fell away, and a boy returned them to her, crumpled. She thanked him, but her face must have shown her panic. Did the boy read? Had he seen what they'd written?

Despite the torching of the office of *The Daily Leader* in Kaduna, blame should not fall upon the shoulders of anyone but the thugs who caused the damage. Surely there have been enough outbursts? Let our nation be free of terrorist tactics!

SOPHIE DRAGGED HER WAY up the stairs to the apartment, her phone ringing its stupid drum roll. She turned it off and let herself inside, bolting the door behind her.

Where was Felix? Right, he'd gone to see Simon. He'd finished the screenplay about the wealthy young woman abducted from the hospital. Why didn't Sophie write screenplays about voluptuous heiresses?

She set down the box of milk on the counter, took her phone, and went into the bedroom. Curled herself into a comma on the bed. What was the sense of coming here? She picked up the phone. Where was her mother? She was in Abuja with Uncle Thomas and Aunt Monica, yes, but her mother didn't answer when she called and Sophie didn't leave a voice mail. She threw the phone down on the bed, pulled up the sheet, thrust it away. Hot, hot, hot. She would have to say, sooner or later, that she'd failed, that it had been foolish to try, that even with the best of intentions she'd done what Felix had been afraid she'd do. She had walked into the middle of a scorpion nest.

She closed her eyes.

A'isha was in a courthouse, a rustic building with no louvres in the windows. She was alone, without a lawyer, while the judge sat above her on a raised platform. A'isha Nasir. The judge had a fan made of white feathers, which he moved languidly in front of his face. Didn't he see? The court was on fire, yet no one rushed to leave the building. They continued to stare at A'isha, whose hijab was touched with flame, and Sophie realized that someone would have to roll her on the floor of the courthouse to put out –

The phone rang and she woke with a gasp.

Yes? Hello? she said.

A voice, a man's voice. She didn't know what he was saying. Hausa. A volley of words, shot at her. The voice switched into English.

I will come to where you are.

She sat up straight, listening to the voice. What was the matter with him? She couldn't understand him, couldn't do anything, couldn't turn off the phone.

I will kill you, American whore, daughter of –

She turned off the phone. Someone wanted to kill her. If someone wanted to kill her, she should hide, that's what she should do. She fitted her feet into her sandals. Why was it so difficult to get her feet into the straps of the sandals? When she stood up, it seemed that the floor was rushing up to meet her, as if she were on the deck of a ship. She sat down heavily on the edge of the bed, got up more cautiously. She found herself in the hall, and then in the kitchen, phone still clutched in her hand.

Someone was buzzing the apartment to be let in, she realized. She wasn't going to answer it. It kept buzzing, buzzing.

She wedged herself into a corner of the kitchen, and crouched down on the floor, staring at the strap on her sandal. There was her phone in her hand. She dropped it on the floor and put her arms tightly around her body. If she just stayed there she would be all right, a knotted tangle of herself. But someone could still see her, if he crawled over the balcony of the neighbour's apartment, leapt from there to the balcony –

Pounding at the door.

Soph, yelled a voice.

Felix?

Can you open the door? You've got the deadbolt on and I can't get in. I tried buzzing you downstairs.

She got up, slid back the deadbolt. Yes, it was Felix. If she let him in it might turn out to be someone else. She opened the door despite herself.

Sophie, what's wrong? said Felix.

She couldn't speak.

What happened? he pressed.

She was shaking now; her knees were made of liquid. They'd give way under her.

Felix came inside, dropped a bag on the floor, kicked the door shut, and held her.

Oh, Felix, she said.

THE TELEVISION NEWS was abuzz with it. The Lagos offices of *The Daily Leader* were bombed that evening with a home-made device, enough to blow out a few windows and scatter furniture. No one was inside.

I was just there, said Sophie in disbelief. I was at the office. I was there talking to Charles.

A reporter stood on a street corner in Kaduna as small, angry people marched across the television screen. Their posters blazed. Shariah – Just Laws for Just People. Go Home, American Whore.

Do they mean – Sophie broke off.

As they moved toward the camera the people loomed larger. Someone held up a white cut-out in the shape of a woman with a bull's eye painted in red where the woman's face should have been.

The reporter spoke of protests in Minna and Kaduna, and of the rumours that the protests could become riots. Violence could spread across Niger State, Kaduna State. A'isha Nasir had been moved out of fears for her safety after the publication of the article.

Will she be all right? asked Sophie.

I don't know. Felix jabbed the remote in the air, turning the volume on the television to mute. Shit, he said. He leaned forward, head down, not looking at the screen.

But Sophie couldn't turn away. Men gestured at the camera, bent pieces of rebar in their hands. Their mouths were open as though they were yelling. In the background, smoke lay in a grey pall over the buildings. It was almost worse without the sound.

I don't think we should stay here, said Felix.

He paced back and forth in the small living room, a large man in a confined space. We could go to my mother's.

She'd appreciate that. She doesn't even know me. Hi Mom, here's my girlfriend, Sophie, American Whore. She threw up her hands. We'd be driving at night. You always say it's a bad idea to drive at night.

It's not far, he said. Anyway, you can't use your mobile anymore. You'll have to use mine.

But, I mean, if it's Charles, I should –

You shouldn't use it at all.

Felix, she said, getting up from the couch.

He glanced at his watch, a big-faced circle on a gold band. We'll go first thing in the morning, he said.

Why don't I just go by myself? she said. I don't want to get you into this. It's enough to have it hanging over my head. I can go early in the morning to the taxi park and get a minivan to Abuja. My Uncle Thomas will pick me up.

He tapped the face of his watch.

Felix?

His eyes gleamed under his brows, and in the dim light of the lamp, he looked angry, though she couldn't be sure. His face could have been cut from rock.

How can you ask me that? he said.

What?

How can you ask whether you should go by yourself?

Well, I –

You can't take a minivan, he said flatly. He went into the kitchen, divided from the living room only by the counter, where she could see his hands busy with cups. The forks and knives clattered as he scooped them up. You can't take any kind of transport to Abuja, he said. I don't want you travelling by yourself.

She sat down heavily on the arm of his leather chair, gazing at the figures moving on the television screen.

Anywhere I go, anywhere I stay, I'll be putting people in danger, she said.

He stood looking into the sink. It won't be for long.

I don't want you to have to do things for me, she said.

That's what people do. People do these things if they care about each other. He closed the dishwasher.

Where had he gone? It was as if he'd pulled inside himself where she couldn't see him.

He came around the counter. Sophie, he said. We have to have a plan. The first thing is that you leave your mobile here. Call your mother but leave the damn thing here. Then we should pack, both of us. Maybe I should ask Simon about a visa for Benin if you need one. That would hold us up, but maybe it's worth it.

Benin? You mean I should leave the country?

Things were going too fast for her. She went into the bedroom, got her red suitcase out of the closet, and put it on the bed. He'd predicted something like this. Now they had to figure it out as they went along.

She thought back to when she'd asked to interview him, and he'd suggested a café. Hibiscus flowered near the table he'd chosen on the patio; he stood up when she arrived, pulled out the chair for her, made her laugh about his fake Rolex. She'd been told he was a good screenwriter. He'd studied the craft in the US, returned to Nigeria. No question, his friend Simon told her, Felix was one of the best in the country, if not *the* best. It made her nervous. His eyes were velvety black. He was kindly, gentle. They'd talked for two hours, ordered second cups of tea, and kept talking.

As smooth as water slipping over glass, the way it went from there. Dinners out. A club she hadn't much liked, so they left early, and walked through a night market, before he took her home to his place, which is what she discovered she wanted. This very bed, she thought, standing back and looking at the open suitcase, its black interior. She stuffed sandals into side pockets, one here, one there. Had she been drawn to him because of his differences? Was that it? She rolled up a skirt, a dress. No. It was because of who he was, how he was, what he thought about.

No, he had taken her face in his hands, carefully, as though putting his hands around a crystal vase, as if she might break. And then he kissed her, taking his time. Mouth against mouth, tongue against tongue. She didn't remember undressing, just kissing him and then her clothes on the floor. She reached out a hand to the sheet: not these sheets, the blue ones.

Let me look at you, he'd said, getting into bed beside her.

She was shy, but she pulled down the sheet. He ran one hand over her shoulder, down her arm, coming back to her face, putting his fingers under her chin to get her to look up, and moved his hand along her hip, over the slight bulge of her stomach.

She shivered and he pulled her close and whispered into her ear that she was like a painting. Did she know the paintings by Matisse? The ones of nudes? She was like that. She was one of those. They stopped talking. His lips on hers again, the merest touch of teeth. His tongue. His hands on her body, moving her, shifting her firmly, but gently, so she was on top of him, the way he did that so easily, and the way she opened to him, hands pressing hard into his chest.

She stopped putting things into the suitcase, found her hands on the wide brim of a sunhat. She punched it down so it would lie flat.

IT OCCURRED TO HER LATER THAT NIGHT, when she couldn't sleep, that the nude by Matisse that Felix liked best had been of a woman's back. Her back. *La Coiffure*. The pale-skinned back of a woman whose arms were in the air as she worked on her hair. Sophie wasn't like that woman at all.

She sat in the dark on the leather couch, flicking through the channels on the muted television. Scenes of golf, then fish swimming through a ghostly, whitened coral reef, then an evangelical healer at a monster church. She let the healer talk and move his arms. She called her mother again, but there was no answer and she left a voice mail. Nothing. She tried to calm down. She phoned her Uncle Thomas without thinking about the time; she woke him and Aunt Monica too. Yes, Sophie remembered now: an alternate universe existed in which they had given her a drive from Kano to Lagos, only ten days ago, and now they were back at home in Abuja. They'd all been together at that dinner party in Kano.

Sophie? said her uncle sleepily.

I'm sorry – I'm sorry to wake you. I can't reach Mom, she said.

Try again, but no, wait until morning. She is still in Kano, and she's coming to Abuja soon. Her uncle spoke in a muffled voice to her aunt and then returned to Sophie. Yes, she is coming here tomorrow.

Sophie explained, but her uncle had seen the report on television. He told her she should get herself to Abuja as soon as she could, and that she could stay with them.

Thank you, she said. I just don't know where we're heading or when.

Let me know when you decide, Sophie, he said.

In the bedroom, her suitcase was on the floor, half-full.

She'd left Felix sleeping, the way he did, deep in the cave of sleep, one arm draped over the edge of the bed. How could he sleep like that when she couldn't sleep at all? It was 2:43. Why hadn't she looked at the time before phoning Uncle Thomas? She turned off the television and went back to bed, careful not to wake Felix. Soon they'd be on the road and she wanted to make sure he was rested even if she wasn't. She lay wide awake. If she could just get her heart to be quiet, if she could just get all the flashing pictures in her brain to stop.

She felt his hand over hers. She hadn't known he'd woken. His hand was warm and heavy, and she lay with her eyes closed, feeling the good weight of it.

10

THEY HADN'T GOT FAR ON THE ROAD, only as far as Felix's mother's place in Ikeja, part of the great web of the city that stretched outwards, ever outwards.

Felix lay snoring in the other twin bed. Though the room was at the back of Felix's mother's house, Sophie had woken to the sound of the imam chanting before dawn at the mosque across the road, and woken an hour later to the garbage truck, a loud, singsong melody playing each time it paused, and then a boy started filling pails of water at a tap outside, all the while carrying on a conversation with someone at an upstairs window. The tap squeaked like a tortured animal as it was turned on and off.

She got up, went to the dim, unlit shower in the bathroom and poured water over herself with a cup from a bucket of water. Aside from the shower, toilet, and tiny sink, there were seven huge buckets in the bathroom, all covered with lids. Here, everyone saved water when they could, since it ran from the taps only a few hours daily. Again and again, the chill of the water sluiced down her skin, but she couldn't remember that shock of cold when she went back to lie on her bed, covered only with a light wrapper; she was immediately hot. Felix woke and sat on the edge of his mattress.

He reached over and passed his hand over her brow. Sleep all right?

She turned on her side to face him, shook her head.

Make a bit of room there. He got into bed beside her, a narrow twin, with space for one. It creaked loudly.

Someone will hear you, she whispered.

No they won't.

He kissed the wild hair that covered her turned-away face.

What are we going to do? she said.

We'll figure something out.

But your mother will think less of me. When she finds out what I wrote, what I did.

Felix laughed softly. He'd relaxed, coming here. Why would she think less of you?

Her body nestled against his and she closed her eyes. She slept.

At breakfast, she faced him across the table as he looked at his phone. Her arms, resting on the plastic cover, a design of blue flowers on yellow trellises, were already sticky. Felix's mother, Grace, didn't eat with them; she sat on a wooden stool in the shadowy room that served as a kitchen, pouring liquid into a pan. Sophie had glimpsed her there, hair bushy, a wrapper around her expansive breasts, flip-flops on her feet, a different person from the Grace she'd seen the evening before, birds emblazoned over her sea-green bodice. It was as if Sophie had caught a glimpse of the private Grace.

The girls, Felix's younger sister, Angelica, and his cousin Minta, ran to and fro bearing plates and cups, and then a heaping platter of pancakes, made specially for Sophie. Minta was too shy to speak, but Angelica talked to Felix without looking at Sophie.

Your mother should come and sit with us, Felix, murmured Sophie.

She almost never sits at the table, except at dinner, when she's worn out.

He called out words Sophie didn't understand, and his mother answered.

She says you are our guest, Felix told her. She wants you to feel welcome.

The pancakes were served with African honey, which was dark, rich, and thick. The cakes were crisped brown on top; Sophie ate two of them quickly and helped herself to a third.

Good cooking, hmm? said Felix.

She nodded. Each bite was light and airy.

Felix tied up the cotton curtains at the window to let in some air. Through the dirty glass of the louvres, Sophie could see people coming and going on the sidewalk above her. Felix's mother lived on the bottom floor of a house, tucked below a busy road with steps ascending from its front door. A goat, separated from the rest of the herd, clicked its hooves down the steps and stood looking in their direction, its ears pricked, nose high, having caught the smell of pancakes.

Yaa, cried the neighbour, clapping his hands at it. *Yaa!*

The goat skittered up the steps. A man on the sidewalk thwacked it on its rump when it reached the top.

Felix called to Angelica, who came to the threshold of the dining room just long enough for him to tell her something. She ran off and Sophie heard the door open and close; Angelica and Minta were on the steps outside, long-legged girls in purple and white gingham dresses, one taller than the other.

She'll get some milk for your coffee. He studied her. Cheer up.

Sophie was thinking of how she'd tried to reach her mother on Felix's phone, but there had been no response. All she could do was leave voice messages.

Felix flicked on the television on top of the bookcase, with the volume kept low. The anchor's eyes followed the prompts, noting that the Nigerian president, Olusegun Obasanjo, was in France for meetings, and there was a quick video clip of him with his entourage.

Always out of the country, said Felix.

Three foreign workers had been killed in Cross River State the evening before. And in other news, a fatwa had been issued by Alhaji Nuhu Mohammed, the deputy governor of Niger State, against the life of Sophie MacNeil, a reporter for *The Daily Leader*. A picture of the deputy governor flashed on the screen.

In other news, the emir of Sokoto State has –

Felix turned off the television. Well, that's not good.

It's like a bounty on my head, isn't it? Sophie's throat felt constricted.

We should still go to Abeokuta, as we planned, he said.

What about your sister?

What about her?

Wouldn't we be putting her at risk? What if I'm recognized?

They said your name, Soph, they didn't show a picture of you. Just the deputy governor.

But they *did* say my name.

Felix's mother came in with two brimming glasses. She'd made them the pineapple smoothies that Felix had talked her into making. American smoothies. She set down the glasses and wiped her hands on her wrapper, making a motion for Sophie to drink.

This is good for you, she said to Sophie in English.

Sophie raised the glass to her lips, tasted the foam. A fatwa against her life, she thought.

It's delicious, she said to Grace.

I went to visit Felix in America when he was living there, said Grace. I was scared all the way there, travelling on a plane for the very first time, stopping at Frankfurt. What if I didn't know which airplane to take? What if someone stopped me? So nervous! And what would I do when I got there and Felix was not waiting for me at the airport?

But I was there, he said. And you burst into tears when you saw me.

Oh, I'd been so afraid. But I went all the way from Lagos to Los Angeles and he was there.

And you wore a hat, that funny-looking hat, said Felix.

It was a fascinator, she said, turning to Sophie, hands shaping something on top of her head. Everyone in *Majesty* magazine wears hats. It was blue and –

It looked like a giant bug, said Felix. That's the first thing I saw, the giant bug.

It was not a giant bug. Maybe a bit like a butter –

Giant bug.

She flapped her hand at him, batted him on the side of his head, laughing. A happy laugh. Felix, you are a scoundrel!

She looked at Sophie. No one in LA wears hats unless they go to the beach.

The girls flew into the room. Angelica had a can of evaporated milk, and Minta hunted in the cupboard for a can opener. They poured coffee from the thermos into the waiting cups, and Angelica set the milk on the table and slipped under Felix's arm, where she stood, stealing glances at Sophie. He stroked her slender arm. Minta took away the dishes in swift, catlike movements.

You were beautiful. All in royal blue, said Felix.

He took me everywhere, said Grace. Drove me everywhere, even as far as the Hoover Dam and the Grand Canyon.

The Grand Canyon. Sophie was in one world with Felix and his mother, and in another world at the same time, one that could have been the slippery deck of a boat, tipping her into the ocean. I've never been there, she said.

You see? Grace pointed to a calendar on the wall, with a glossy picture of the Grand Canyon. Oh, my, she said, I'm getting too excited – I'd better sit down. It's my BP, you see, she explained to Sophie. It's high.

Blood pressure, said Felix.

Do you have to go to Abeokuta? Grace asked. I think you should rest another night here, at least one night more. Felix? She switched into Yoruba, still pleading.

We have to go.

Sophie came back to herself, finishing the last of the pineapple smoothie, Grace's treat. Sophie had been far away at the Hoover Dam, the Grand Canyon, but the deputy governor of Niger State had justified the taking of her life, and now anyone could kill her.

She got up from the table too quickly, nearly spilling her half-drunk coffee, and swayed in a room that seemed to be pinpricked with a thousand lights.

I'll get our things together, she said.

Too soon! exclaimed Grace. She put her hand on Felix's wrist. Angelica was still twined against him, a vine around a tree.

Well, anyway, I'll tidy up, said Sophie vaguely. Thank you for the wonderful breakfast.

But she sat on the bed in the guest room and didn't try to tidy anything, let alone pack. The tap outside made another anguished screech as it was twisted open and water gushed from the pipe under the window.

She put her head in her hands, wishing she could roll up in a ball and go to sleep. I can sleep when I'm dead, her father had once said. She stood abruptly, catching her hair in the clothesline that was suspended from one wall to the other. Again, blackness before her eyes, then a scattershot of light. She gripped the edge of the bureau and waited until everything took its place again: beds, small night table, lamp. Then she reached up, disentangled her hair, and dragged the red suitcase from under the bed, opened it.

She needed something to cover her head. Maybe the cream-coloured scarf printed with women in long dresses on old-fashioned bicycles. She drew it out, put it over her head, knotted it at the back. And here was the unflattering beige dress, the one that hung on her like a potato sack. It was cool and easy to wear. She slipped out of her fuchsia-bright sundress and into the beige potato sack, studying herself in the mirror. Now she wasn't nearly so conspicuous. A few corkscrew curls cascaded out of the scarf and she tucked them back, but there was no disguising herself. She pulled the scarf a little lower.

She took the prayer flag out of the suitcase pocket, balled it in her fist. Her mother had given it to her at the airport. For protection, she'd said to Sophie as she kissed her. Keep it with you wherever you are. She held Sophie's shoulders for a moment, then dropped her hands. Sophie went forward in the security line but looked back at her mother. For a moment her father appeared, looking pale, his hair thinning, with his arm around her mother. No, he was not there. He ghosted into air. Only Sophie's mother remained. She smiled, though her smile was a little unreal; she smiled for Sophie's benefit. It was as if she could be swept away by other people on their way to the security gate, the ones who were getting on airplanes, not the ones left behind.

Sophie waved. And her mother waved back.

WHEN THEY TOOK THEIR THINGS to the car, which Felix had parked at a friend's gas station across the highway, Grace picked up Sophie's red suitcase and put it on her head.

No, it's all right, said Sophie. I can manage it.

It's easier, said Grace.

The girls came with them, Angelica carrying a bag of food that Grace said they needed on the journey, and Minta carrying Sophie's knapsack. A boy appeared out of nowhere to hoist Felix's small suitcase onto his head.

Randolph, Felix said. Is that Randolph? You are such a big man now. He patted the boy's shoulder playfully and Randolph smiled, shuffling forward in a pair of sneakers that were too big for him.

Grace put out a hand to stop them as they reached the traffic lights. Slow, slow, she said. Even when the light turned green, and the policewoman signalled for them to cross, Grace took Sophie's hand so she wouldn't barge into the motorcyclist going the wrong way.

When they reached the car parked at the gas station, Randolph had something to tell Felix. Felix had to bend low to listen.

He wants to show me how he can read, said Felix. At the children's library.

Sophie wanted only to be gone, wanted only to be inside the cool car with its tinted windows where no one could see her.

Felix came close to her. No one here will know about you, I'm certain of it. And this won't take long.

But our things.

Francis will watch them.

A man sat on a stool under an umbrella at the gas station, and he raised his hand when she turned to look at him.

Grace took her hand just as she had when they were crossing the street. Randolph is my sister's boy, she said. And Minta is her daughter. She had three children, but Aloysius died.

Cars streaked alongside them on the highway and there was too much noise to talk. Randolph, minus Aloysius, walked with Felix just ahead. Then Angelica and Minta, and Grace and Sophie. Where were they going? Sophie felt she was back in her daydream of a tilting boat, except now she was on a sidewalk that would tilt them into the traffic, not blue-black water. She couldn't get out of the daydream; she'd be prevented from getting out of it; they had put a price on her head.

At the children's library, Randolph wanted them to leave their shoes on the racks outside. Then they had to wash their hands with soap in a basin of water and clean them with a pink towel embroidered with the words Ikeja Children's Library. They were asked to sign their names in a book by a man at a desk.

After school, hundreds of children come, the man told them. Not all are allowed to enter because there are so many. He had a long face and drooping eyelids, and Sophie had the feeling he was studying her potato sack of a dress.

Are you the one? he said.

Sophie's heart seemed to flop in her chest. No.

Yes, you are the one. You are an actress, he said. An American actress.

People tell her that all the time, said Felix, breaking in. You could ask her for her autograph. She'd give it to you.

The man laughed sheepishly, waved them on.

THEY WERE FINALLY IN THE CAR, on their way to Abeokuta. The detour to the children's library had taken much too long. Felix turned the wheel sharply to avoid a man on a bicycle.

Remember I gave Simon the key to my place? he said.

Yes.

Well, someone must have got in. Simon left a voice mail.

When?

It must have been last night.

But we've been gone such a short time.

Maybe someone watched us leaving. Anyway, I didn't want to worry you. There wasn't much damage. They didn't find your mobile because I gave it to Simon, but they did wreck some things. They wrote on the walls. It was just a way to scare us.

You should have told me. You can't go back there.

I will, but not right away. I'll stay with Simon.

You don't seem worried.

He wove around potholes. Muck from the lorry in front of them hit the windshield in splotches of reddish brown. I do worry. Try not to let all of this overwhelm you.

When I'm running away from the mess?

He was fiddling with the windshield wipers to get rid of the mud splatters. They made a mess across the glass, and he had to peer through the streaks to see where he was going. They paused for a man with a wheelbarrow on which he'd piled a heap of tires. Felix sprayed wiper fluid on the windshield as he waited, ran the wipers back and forth. But the man was having trouble manoeuvring the wheelbarrow across the road. It wobbled with the weight of the tires.

Sophie said, I'm just trouble for you. No one wants me here.

One of the tires fell off the wheelbarrow, and the man put out his hand in thanks to Felix for his patience while he set down the load and put the stray tire back in place. It was a busy road, and the cars streamed past on all sides. Nagode, cried the man, as a minivan brushed past him with the driver's helper leaning out the window to curse him.

Everyone would find out about it, Sophie thought. Maybe it would be on the BBC. There might be a link to that famous fatwa involving Salman Rushdie. She was young and white; she was a woman. Things would be said about her. Perhaps they'd say that she had provoked this, and that a fatwa was what she deserved.

Felix entered a roundabout and had to look in every direction. Once he was within the circle, the car was surrounded by a fast-moving river of cars and small trucks and lorries and people on motorbikes: it seemed to Sophie as if they were all caught in Dante's many circles of hell. Finally, Felix eased the car onto the Abeokuta ramp, but now they were stuck in traffic, three cars across, since no one paid any attention to how many cars could be on the ramp at one time. In the car next to them, a man delicately picked his nose. Felix pulled ahead of the other cars and shot forward.

You don't want me here, she said.

Beside them, at the edge of the road, a man without legs paddled forward on a contraption that resembled a skateboard. His gloved hands propelled him, but he scrabbled to stay clear of the cars. His legs were bandaged stumps.

Felix pulled over to the side of the road, and cars honked,

slanting past, as he took off his sunglasses to look at her. He left the car on so they'd have the comfort of the air conditioning, its whirring constancy. She wouldn't look at him; she gazed straight ahead, intent on the man on his skateboard, pushing himself forward, his gloves grimed with dirt.

Sophie.

What?

The whole thing is crazy. You're scared. Don't give in to being scared.

She took off her head scarf, stared at the women riding bicycles across the fabric.

I know, she said quietly. I am.

I don't want you to have to go, but wanting doesn't come into it, he went on. What I want, what you want.

When she turned to him, she'd softened. He had said what it was, named the jumpiness inside her. She didn't think of herself as a fearful person, but she had never been so fearful before.

You're a good person, she said.

You are too, Soph. You have a big heart.

For a moment they sat without moving, on the outskirts of Abeokuta, under the bloom of clouds and the pale blue softness of afternoon sky, the hot asphalt and gleam of cars and buses, the unharnessed rush of traffic. Then they went on.

11

THE GUARD AT THE GATE WAS FRAIL, and when he stood up from his small fire, his body seemed collapsible, his bones simply sticks dropped in a sack. His blanket was also his shawl, with which he covered his head. A second guard appeared, a huge man, strutting in his uniform, the sleeves torn at the elbows. He spoke roughly to the driver in a language Clare didn't recognize before they were allowed to pass, snicksnack of tires on the gravel drive.

Everything was new to her. Thomas and Monica had moved since she'd last visited them; this part of Abuja was more opulent, and now that the driver could see the compound, though it was nearly dusk, he would probably ask for more naira than she was prepared to give him. The car stopped and Clare got out, tottering from exhaustion while waiting for her luggage to be taken out of the trunk, no, the boot. Yes, of course, the *boot*. Smell of rain, and a haunting perfume of flowers that might have been gardenias. The hibiscus by the door swayed like phantoms, leaves dripping.

She fumbled in her purse for money.

Ah, welcome, welcome, Thomas said, coming down the steps. You've come. Welcome. No, put that away, he said to Clare, putting up a hand and unfolding some naira from a money clip.

The driver bowed obsequiously at the sight of the money,

and Thomas no doubt gave him more than he asked for, slipping bills out of the clip. There was a hurried offering of thanks, a slam of the car door, and the taxi sped away, as if the driver couldn't believe his good luck.

Thomas, said Clare, throwing her arms around him, breathing in the smell of his laundered shirt. She stepped back. What have you heard from Sophie? Anything? So much has gone on.

I talked to her, he said. I told her to come here.

Is she coming?

He spread his hands. She spoke to me from Lagos. She called again saying she might be going to Abeokuta. Can't you reach her on your mobile?

His glasses slid down his nose, and he pushed them back up, that old gesture.

Abeokuta, said Clare. Why Abeokuta? Yes, that's the last I heard too. She left a message. Anyway, I've tried to reach her – it's Felix's phone, his mobile. I don't know Felix. Do you? She's only spoken to me about him.

Come. Come inside.

In a daze, she was led into Thomas and Monica's house, with its thick carpets, their intricate designs folded into a central lotus, under Monica's high-heeled shoes, her slim ankles.

She embraced Monica. It seemed so long ago, the dinner in Kano.

Clare, said Monica. You must be tired.

Hortensia appeared from behind her mother. She was the youngest, the one Clare had last seen as a toddler, her hair in a bristle all over her head. She had a dimple in her cheek when she smiled. Clare smiled back, stooped and touched the child's cheek, and Hortensia's smile widened. Gavin had still been alive when she was very small.

Everyone told me you would be white, but you are whiter than I thought you would be, like the patio stones, Hortensia said.

Clare laughed. Patio stones.

Hortensia's face was a puzzle. My father was adopted, she said. So you must be his adopted sister. She looked at her mother.

Thomas bent down to Hortensia. I was adopted when I was a boy.

But what does it mean, to be adopted?

My mother and father died. I was taken into another family and Clare became my sister.

Doesn't that make you both adopted?

No. Only me.

If you and Mumma die will I be taken into another family?

That could happen, but we hope that it won't.

What you hope won't happen is called adopted?

Monica shook her head. Back to bed with you.

They could hear Hortensia's childish voice as she went with Monica. I don't want to be adopted. I *never* want to be adopted.

I must look a sight, Clare said, straightening up. There were riots.

You were caught in them? asked Thomas.

For a few hours, near the outskirts of Kaduna, the traffic didn't move, and then there was a commotion. A lot of people, some men fighting.

Her thin cotton sweater and dress were finely stippled with red dust, the dust of the sub-Sahara. She trembled, realizing how hungry she was, the way she felt lit up like a searchlight, and she touched a hand to the carved back of a chair to steady herself. All I can think about is Sophie, she said.

Come now, said Thomas. And he led Clare down the hall.

In Thomas's house, Clare knew there was no need to check for snakes in the bathroom drains, and she also knew there would be running water. She turned on the tap in the bathroom: yes, it was hot. The guest towels were thick and fragrant, and she had to resist the urge to bury her dirty face in one of them. After she showered, she wanted to lie down on the guest bed, sheets drawn smartly across it, as though it were a wrapped parcel without a wrinkle to be seen. For a moment, just for a moment, she switched off the light and sat in the armchair to let her burning eyes rest. Sophie, Sophie, Sophie. No, she could not rest, she must not rest. She stood up so quickly she had to put her hand out to the wall to steady herself; she was blind in the dark room, and it took time before she found the light switch. It didn't work.

Clare rummaged in her knapsack, found a small flashlight, switched it on and set it on the table. She got out her phone, called the number.

Hello, said a man.

Hello. I'm looking for Sophie.

Who is speaking, please?

I'm Clare, I'm Sophie's mother, I've been trying to reach her.

Oh, she'll be very glad, he said. One moment, please.

Mom?

Clare felt her throat constrict. Sophie. How are you?

Oh, she said, I'm okay. There was a rushing sound like a wave falling on a shore. I'm with Felix and we're at his sister's place.

In Abeokuta?

Yes. Where are you?

With your Uncle Thomas.

You got there. Mom, *The Daily Leader* – did you hear everything?

Yes. How are you holding up?

I'm all right. Felix and everyone – they've been looking after me.

Can you and Felix come here? To Abuja?

I don't know.

Clare was at a loss for words, but if she could see Sophie, if she could touch her, it would be different.

I guess I had no idea, Sophie said. It just exploded. I knew there might be a reaction, because A'isha deserves freedom, but not this – not this craziness.

You never know what will be said.

It's not what people say, it's what they do. They're fighting in Kaduna, and in Niger State. Well, that's what we've heard. I never meant for any of this.

We could come to you.

Well, but you couldn't go through Minna or Kaduna. You'd have to take another route. Why don't you wait?

But you're alone.

I've got Felix.

There was a roaring noise. She could see through the blinds that the outside lights had come on, illuminating a man leaning over a generator.

Are you still there? asked Clare.

We'll stay here in Abeokuta. If things don't work out here we might have to leave.

But you'll tell me?

Tomorrow, yes, I'll tell you.

Sophie –

Mom, I have to go now. I'm sorry. I love you.

Clare turned off the phone, set it down, and watched the man who seemed dissatisfied with the way the generator was operating. She took the flashlight and went down the hall. Where was Thomas? The road was not a road anymore, but a mass and spill of people, more than she'd ever seen, pressed together. Thomas, she yelped. *Thomas*. A face thrust in front of her, an old man's face with a dark hole of a mouth, and a set of teeth, rockhorned in a cave, before the mouth and teeth disappeared. She smelled dust and sweat, sticky and hot, but what frightened her was the push and shove of the wanting, the roar that took her with it, not letting her go.

Thomas had spread out papers on the dining room table. There was a battery-operated lamp on the table, but now the lights in the dining room wavered on again, off, then on. Seeing Clare, Thomas collected the papers, put them in his briefcase. At the other end of the table, a place had been set. The generator chugged to a stop outside.

I asked Veronica to make you a small meal, said Thomas. She managed it before the electricity went off, but see, now – it is on again. We don't need this. He turned off the lamp on the table. I thought you might be hungry.

He pulled out a chair for her. Did you speak to Sophie?

She nodded and sat down. She's in Abeokuta, as you said. She says she'll stay put unless there's a problem.

She'll tell you.

I guess she will. She didn't sound like herself. And it was rushed – she had to go and there were still things I wanted to ask her.

From the dining room, Clare could see Monica in the living room with two of the younger boys. On the television screen, Clare could see men getting out of a car at a police checkpoint.

There was some overly dramatic shouting; one man raised his hands, and another ran into the bush.

She is in good hands right now, said Thomas. That's the main thing.

I don't know anything about Felix.

A cracking sound from the television and the man with the upraised arms clutched his chest, which appeared to be smoking. He fell over. The other man, who had run into the bush, parted the leaves of a banana tree to look out. The alarm on his face was comical.

Monica got up and came into the dining room. Two boys peeped over the back of a sofa.

Jonathan? said Clare. Andrew?

The boys laughed and fell down on the sofa, their feet in the air. Their father called them, and they reappeared, one yanking up a sock.

Is this how you greet your Aunt Clare from Canada? said Thomas.

Hello, boys, said Clare.

How do you do? asked one of them. It was the elder one, Jonathan.

Very well, thank you. Clare smiled.

The youngest boy clutched his chest, closed his eyes and rolled on the floor. He started giggling, and Monica rattled off a volley of words.

He stood up, biting his top lip to keep from laughing. His brother nudged him.

Hello I am Andrew how do you do? he burst out, all in a rush.

On the screen, a young woman bent over the man whose chest had been smoking. He appeared to be dead. I beg you, cried the other man from between the parted banana leaves, and the woman backed away in fright.

I beg you, cried Andrew, imitating the voice perfectly, and Clare laughed before she could stop herself.

Boys, boys, said their father. Off to bed now. Goodnight.

Goodnight, they said, in unison, and careened down the smooth floor of the hallway, sliding in their sock feet. I beg you, they sang. *I beg you!*

Monica and Thomas sat with Clare while she ate her jollof rice. Nearly time for bed, Clare thought, and here she was, eating. Ice cubes clinked into a glass as Thomas poured her some water. Her hand had slid out of Thomas's hand. Her father had told her to hold his hand, because she was eleven and Thomas was only nine, but the man with the mouth like a cave had come between them. She clutched the change purse her father had given her, with the hard coins inside, but her head scarf came loose, and the dancers printed on it twirled away so she couldn't see them under the sandals and shoes. She was working out a problem and she couldn't work it out if she was being shoved forward. Beside her, a man in torn jeans slipped and almost fell down, but two people next to him helped him up and he laughed and started yelling again. The cook died and Thomas had been adopted, but how did that make him her brother? Someone's elbow or knee jammed into Clare's back, and she cried out. If she fell, no one would see. She was too small. They would keep moving and she would be slapped into the dirt of the street.

Clare!

She could hear her father, but she couldn't see him. She could see someone's worn shirt, buttoned up the wrong way. A politician's face printed over and over on a wrapper around the belly of a heavy-set woman. Splotches of paint on someone's arm.

Clare!

Her father found her. He gripped her wrist and it hurt when he did that, his fingers hard and tight around her narrow bones; he could have crushed them. But he'd found her, he'd managed to catch her, and he pushed away from the crowd, gasping. Then he picked her up and held her close, his chin scratching her cheek. Are you all right? He turned to a street vendor, a woman selling soft drinks. Thomas, he called.

A boy detached himself from the woman and ran to them. He turned up his face, open as the bowl of a spoon, and Clare's father took him by the hand.

Good fellow, Thomas, said her father.

Clare promptly turned her face into her father's shirt and burst into tears.

I wonder how Sophie's holding up, said Thomas.

When Clare finished the rice, and Monica offered her a dish of papaya, pulpy fruit so deeply orange, seeds like shiny, black eyes. She hadn't eaten papaya in years. She picked up the fork, set it down.

Do you like papaya? asked Monica.

Yes. Yes, very much. It's lovely here.

Your first time in this house. Monica smiled, in the same way as Hortensia.

I brought small things for the children.

That is kind. You didn't have to do that.

Clare nibbled on a piece of papaya.

Thomas got up, fetched a newspaper. He slid it across to her.

What is it?

But Clare already knew what it was. I just want to see her, she said. I want to go to her.

Maybe we should leave all this until you've slept, said Monica.

No, I have to know. You read it, Thomas. It's what Sophie wrote, isn't it?

I won't read the whole thing, he said. The act of adultery involves two people, and yet, in the case of A'isha Nasir, only the woman has been brought to trial. In this case, the woman is regarded as a criminal, dragged through the courts, and sentenced to death by stoning, while the man with whom she had relations is allowed to remain free. What justice can there be if this man is not brought to trial?

I'll skip the next part, he said. Here, yes: The essential fact of this case is that the woman is the one being prosecuted, and she is being prosecuted precisely because she is a woman, because she became pregnant and gave birth to a child. This is the sum of the evidence. The evidence that might reveal the man to be at fault, that of DNA testing, is not required by shariah courts.

Thomas jabbed at the newspaper. That's the point a lawyer would make.

That's the point a woman would make.

Thomas looked at her sideways and they laughed, ruefully. Monica didn't laugh.

What else did she say?

That's enough, Thomas, said Monica firmly.

He folded the newspaper and pushed it away from him.

I wonder what has happened to A'isha, said Clare.

She finished the last of the papaya. The lights of the chandelier were scattered, reflected in the polished table.

Today I saw one man hit another man with a crowbar, she said. Wanting to kill him, I think.

Uh-oh! exclaimed Monica.

First there were men fighting each other, punching and swatting, you know, like kids. And then one of them hit the other hard, and he staggered back. The third one had a crowbar.

Monica put her arm around her. It's all right now.

I could drive you to Abeokuta, Clare, said Thomas. Or wherever you need to go.

But the fighting, objected Clare.

We could take a circuitous route.

Thomas, now – said Monica.

Yes, we could go tomorrow after church. I'll talk to Jacob. He touched Monica's hand reassuringly.

After church? said Clare.

But now you need to rest, he said.

Clare wasn't ready to rest. You know, when I first learned about this case, I researched some of the cases of women who had been convicted of adultery around the world. In many cases, the woman was never stoned; her sentence was commuted to a prison term or something like that, but in certain cases, the stoning was carried out.

Monica made a sharp little sound.

They bury the woman up to the chest, I guess so her arms can't be free, can't cover her head.

I know how it's done, Thomas said, looking at Monica.

But we don't know, Clare went on, unable to stop. We have no idea. To feel the first rock hit your head, to feel it. And it's slow. It takes time to stone a person to death. There was a child, a thirteen-year-old child in Somalia who was gang raped and her family went to the authorities –

Clare, it is not good to speak of this, said Thomas. He was examining the surface of the table.

I think of that child, she said. Since I found out about her, I can't get her out of my head.

Clare.

I have to believe there's justice, she said. That wrongs can be righted. There are people like you, people who believe such things. You're a lawyer, after all.

That doesn't make me good. It only makes me strive for the good.

But isn't that what's needed here?

I work hard, but I don't take on more than I can chew. Don't get the wrong idea about me.

She didn't say anything.

Clare, don't imagine for a minute that I'm going to take up that case.

No, no, no, said Monica. Thomas is not going to put himself in the way of danger like that. He cannot do such a thing.

Thomas looked at Clare ruefully. I'm not a courageous man. I couldn't do it. Anyway, I do not believe it will go badly for A'isha. You will see: they will appeal it. In Nigeria no such sentence has ever been carried out.

It could be, though.

He spread his hands. We cannot solve the ills of the world. I think it's time we all went to bed.

Clare stood up. Goodnight then, dear Thomas.

He kissed her cheek.

She took Monica's hand. Thank you for having me here, she said. Goodnight.

We will get your Sophie home in one piece, said Thomas.

Ah, breathed Clare, and the fear rushed back in as if he'd opened a door. Thank you, Thomas.

She went to her room and stood with her back against the

wall in the darkness. Outside, night sounds: a clicking, a low screech. She thought of the stories she'd read, first to find out about A'isha and what might happen to her, and then the accounts about those who had been stoned. She undressed in the darkness, went into the bathroom, and put on the light.

But it followed her, the story of the thirteen-year-old Somalian girl. Clare came out of the bathroom, got into bed. Kismayo, southern Somalia. The girl was imprisoned after her family went to the authorities, told them how she'd been raped by three men. She was taken to a stadium.

Clare lay still, breathing in, breathing out. She turned over. Finally, she felt herself slipping into drowsiness.

They stood in a ring, all men, except for the nurses, who had been brought under pain of death to watch the stoning. Fifty men, maybe more, many of them armed. Even if some of them had wanted to help the girl, they wouldn't have been able to; so many of the men had guns. The girl was brought in struggling against her captors. Don't kill me, don't kill me, she cried. She was placed in a hole, buried up to her shoulders, crying. A white head covering, face of anguish.

Don't kill me.

They buried her, packed the earth up to her shoulders. The men with the shovels stepped back. Her body, gone into the earth. A man raised his hands to the sky, chanting. Her feet, never to walk. Chanting. Her hands, her arms. Chanting, then silence. The first rock against the back of her head, the second flying against her temple. Then more rocks, so many they were like hail. Thrown hard. Around her, white rocks in a pattern on the ground.

The nurses were forced to check, after a few minutes, to see if she was dead or alive. They took her out of the hole, rolled her onto the ground, checked for a pulse. Still alive. And so back into the hole she went.

Shouting, pounding feet. A boy tried to do something, tried to save her. He was shot.

Clare yelped, and the yelp woke her. She sat up, her right hand over her chest, over the thin material of her nightgown. No one had been stoned. Clare had bunched up the sheet in her left hand, clutching it. She released it. Nothing had happened; she'd been dreaming. She was in a bed in a guest room in Thomas's house, but her breath came hard and fast, because her heart was crazily scrambled, and she willed herself to slow it down. Someone's daughter died like that.

She sat up and fumbled for her phone, and sat with it in her hand, waiting for her heart to slow down. Whatever she said to her daughter would have to be calm and collected. No, she wouldn't call again.

It would be fine, she told herself. It would be fine.

12

IT WAS NOT A CHOICE SHE'D BEEN GIVEN, as if she was given a choice in anything now. She'd been told that it was for Safiya's sake.

A'isha bent to go through the doorway with her wash basin, soap, and towel, setting them down to tie up the curtain and let the air inside the hut; she wondered whether she'd find her mother dead when she knelt beside her, but no, Nafisa was still alive, her belly more distended than ever. A'isha was almost used to the smell now, and it was always better once she'd taken away the contents of the bedpan. She greeted her mother, and Nafisa's eyes focused on her; in their gleam A'isha could see her dear mother, clinging to life. A'isha set down the wash basin and the soap on its wadding of cloth but kept the towel over her shoulders.

She lifted her mother's legs without retching, and slid out the pan, taking it out of the hut to toss just beyond the cashew tree. It was a putrid mix of fluids. She turfed some dirt over it and spat at the goats trotting toward her eagerly.

The goats waited. Stupid animals.

She yelled to make them scatter and watched to make sure they wouldn't return as she wiped the pan with the rag she kept for this purpose, glancing across the compound to the basket where Safiya lay sleeping in the shade. Little Talata bent down over her, loving nothing in the world more than being asked to watch over Safiya. Soon Talata would be called away to do one task or another, but Safiya would sleep for a while yet.

Standing with the pan in one hand and the rag in the other, A'isha was desolate. Usually she shrugged it off, this sense that nothing would ever be right again, but not this morning. She took the pan back inside, eyes burning, and the smell caught her off guard at the threshold; she stood for a moment to compose herself.

Would it be today?

She knelt down and lifted her mother's legs tenderly and slid the clean pan under her. All her life Nafisa had worked so hard without complaining. Never enough time to be still, until now, and now she was dying. Today, tomorrow.

A'isha put the cloth in the warm water of the wash basin and squeezed it. She soaped the cloth and then washed her mother's body. There was almost nothing left of her mother's buttocks, and the skin of her thighs was slack, but her abdomen was swollen. There must be such pain; Nafisa winced as A'isha washed her. A'isha wished there was some way she could take the pain from her. Maybe it was the last time A'isha would do this, and she was determined to do it well. Nafisa's eyes bored into A'isha as she worked. She couldn't meet her mother's gaze, her mother who knew everything.

The cloth, soft as it was, wasn't soft enough, and might scrape against her mother's skin. A'isha finished bathing one leg, then the other. The thighs, the knees, the calves, the ankles, and the feet. The feet that would not bear Nafisa's weight again. A'isha blinked, rinsed out the cloth in the basin. It was different than washing Safiya, with her tiny hands, clutching and opening, and her cries when she was doused with water from the bucket. Her feet were pale pink and the skin was still so new, without any calluses, but Nafisa's feet were hardened and cracked. A'isha took special care with her mother's feet.

Now the swollen belly, but this pained her mother and A'isha paused, turning instead to the loose pockets of her mother's breasts, which lay against her chest. Then she bathed her mother's neck and under her arms. A'isha concentrated on each arm, the way a fold of skin hung down as she raised the arm up, to be sure to wash the whole of it. When she came to Nafisa's left hand, her mother's fingers worked their way into A'isha's fingers and stopped them. A'isha bowed her head.

I must go away, said A'isha. With Safiya. They told me I have to leave.

A'isha couldn't tell her mother what might happen if she stayed. The compound, everyone in it, and Safiya too, might be killed. Maybe what they were saying was true: that A'isha was to blame.

She felt her mother's fingers, birds in a nest. Finally, A'isha lifted her head. Her mother's eyes, bleary with pain.

I'm sorry, A'isha said. She couldn't say all that she felt, that she couldn't bear to leave.

Nafisa made an effort. She was trying to say something, but it sounded like dry leaves rattling in her throat. She strained forward.

What? A'isha murmured, coaxing her.

Know your strength.

A'isha's eyes stung. She was not strong, not the least bit. Her mother was the one who was strong. She wiped her face with her arm and towelled her mother's body dry. Nafisa's eyes were closed now; it had taken something away from her to speak and be heard, a bit of the life that remained in her.

A'isha finished, and put a clean wrapper around her mother's body, turning her gently to the left and then the right, though this movement must hurt Nafisa. A'isha knotted the cotton material so it would stay. She wanted her mother to be clean and tidy, and she knew it was because she didn't want anyone to find Nafisa disgusting. She didn't want them to back away because of the reek. But who wouldn't back away? The clean fabric she'd brought for a wrapper had been given to A'isha for her wedding: it was a length of green and pink and white material. Flowers on branches. It was better if she wrapped her mother in it, and she knew it was because it reminded her of that wedding. Nafisa hadn't wanted the marriage, but A'isha's second father had decided things, and he had decided that A'isha must marry the old man. He wasn't a bad man, as husbands go, but now he was dead and so was her second father. A flutter, unbidden. A'siha didn't miss either of them. It was better that they were both dead, even if it was wrong of her to think such things.

But she couldn't make herself get up.

Outside, there was a car in the compound: the jumped-up sound of the driver braking was followed by the offended cry of a guinea hen, and the greetings between the driver and A'isha's auntie. A'isha had already gathered her belongings into a bundle and left them with her auntie, and besides, the driver would have to be fed something. He would have to talk to everyone, take a gift from A'isha's auntie for the head man, Alhaji Hassan, and put it into the car, since A'isha and Safiya would be staying with him for the time being, and A'isha's uncle was grateful for that; they wouldn't be his problem. Finally, A'isha and Safiya would get into the car, and they would leave, and A'isha would show nothing in her expression.

She felt her mother's hand, the thin fingers. She leaned down again to hear the halting words.

Don't be afraid.

She held her mother's hand. She stayed where she was, and then it was time.

Be well, murmured Nafisa.

And you, said A'isha.

It was as if A'isha were outside her body as she stood up, gazing down at her mother on the mat on the floor, outside her body as she moved to the door, the light, the car parked in the middle of the compound, outside her body as she walked toward Safiya being dandled in the shade by Talata. Don't be afraid. Be well.

The driver had been given a plate of rice and beans and he was eating it out of an enamel dish on the edge of the porch where there was shade from the roof. She watched his hand go to his mouth, scooping the rice into it. She couldn't watch as he opened his mouth, put the rice into it greedily. He was intent, and soon he would be finished.

She'd forgotten the soap and towel, but she couldn't make herself retrace her steps and go back to her mother. Instead, she took Safiya, sound asleep, from Talata. A'isha was exhausted after a night of quickly shifting dreams – the compound in flames, Safiya nowhere to be found, her mother gone from her hut – but to make herself go away was worse than any nightmare.

A'isha touched Talata's shoulder.

Her uncle came out and greeted the driver. It was her uncle who had told her the head man thought she should leave, and her uncle was pleased about it, A'isha could see. So that she wouldn't have to listen to the men talking, she left them and walked with Safiya to the neem tree, though the sun burned, and even under the green light of the tree, A'isha felt exposed.

Here she had spoken with the woman who had come from Lagos, the one who reported for the newspaper. Sophie. A'isha had been intimidated by her foreignness, her clothes, her way of speaking English, her good-looking boyfriend, but most of all, by her hair, curly and thick, that she flung over her shoulder as if it were a nuisance. What would it have been like to have hair like that, hair that could be flung over the shoulder? A'isha's own hair was cropped close to her head and covered by a hijab. It was partly because of Sophie that A'isha had to leave now, but A'isha didn't regret talking to her. No. She had wanted to speak, and Sophie had listened.

TALATA PULLED AT HER HAND, and A'isha looked down at her. Talata had been sent to bring A'isha back to the small group that had collected around the car: A'isha's uncle and auntie, several nephews, and some friends were talking to the driver, a cousin of the head man. Two smaller boys were kicking a deflated soccer ball, turned yellowish with age.

A'isha moved out of the pale-green and dark-green lights of the tree that had protected her all the time she had stayed in this place and walked across the compound. Her sandals kicked up small whorls of dust as she went, Talata at her side, and her arm, crooked, holding Safiya, who was waking now, and would soon want to be fed. Out of the corner of her eye A'isha could see her mother's hut, with its drooping curtain.

Still with Safiya in her arms, A'isha retrieved her belongings, the bundle that she had knotted in a sheet and put inside a plastic basin. Talata took the basin and put it in the car. Surprisingly, A'isha's auntie gave her a baby wrapper, and said goodbye to her, but her uncle said nothing. A'isha leaned against the car door, not wanting to sit inside until the driver was ready to go. It would be too hot. There, he'd opened the driver's door, put on his sunglasses. Someone offered him a bottle of water for the journey.

A'isha got into the car when Safiya started crying and she covered her daughter lightly with the baby wrapper as she suckled. A'isha's milk, coming down, was a relief, though the car was a furnace. Talata crouched by the open passenger door, telling A'isha she would look after her mother, and A'isha, hearing this, had to gather herself, defend herself against the kindness. Under the cloth, she felt the small tugs of Safiya's mouth on her nipple.

Know your strength. Be strong, A'isha murmured to Talata. It was what A'isha's mother had said to her minutes ago, her mother who was alone with her own pain just across the compound.

Someone told Talata to get out of the way and closed the passenger door. The driver got in and started the car, turning up the air conditioning to full blast and sipping from his bottle of water.

You are ready?

Yes, she said, though she was not sure she was ready. She was certainly not ready for her mother to die and leave her. She was not sure she could bear it by herself.

The driver put down the drink and they drove away, turning out of the compound, and going too fast along on the highway. A'isha glimpsed a girl washing clothes in a bucket outside a hut and yearned to be that girl, with nothing to do but wash clothes in a bucket, but she disappeared, a flash of red and green, a girl who knew nothing, who might live her entire life knowing nothing. It wasn't fair to think of her this way, but A'isha couldn't help herself.

13

IT RAINED HARD AFTER THEY LEFT ABEOKUTA, large drops pelting against the windshield and reducing visibility so that the road in front of them was curtained with grey. It was the tail end of the wet season, but today seemed as though the rains would go on and on. After the news about the fatwa, Sophie was jittery. Felix had woken her early and asked if she wanted to try to cross the border to Benin. They would go to Imeko that day and if all went well at the border crossing, she could continue to Cotonou in Benin and from there she could fly to Germany. He thought she should get out of the country without letting anyone know.

What about my mother? asked Sophie.

It's better to do this quickly and quietly. Anyway, let's see how things go.

My mother thinks we're staying in Abeokuta, but I don't want her to make the trip to Abeokuta if I'm not there.

Your mother will understand, he said. Wait until we get to Imeko and use my mobile. You can call her from there.

A few cars curved around the potholes, slipping into view and disappearing into the rain. And the checkpoint, too, arose out of nowhere: just a couple of policemen wearing ponchos. Two chairs. Two oil drums, a two-by-four from drum to drum, blocking the way. Behind them, a derelict shed with an old tin roof.

Not again, Sophie said.

Felix slowed down, sighing, took the papers from the side pocket of the car, and unrolled the window. Hello, he said politely.

The policeman was laughing with his friend, slapping his palm with a high five. Under his plastic poncho was a gun, a rifle, probably an AK-47.

Sophie hoped it wasn't loaded. It looked like the two of them were playing a game of some kind.

Now the policeman turned to peer into the car, the rim of his baseball cap dripping. End of play. You are coming from where? he said to Felix.

From Abeokuta.

Where are you living?

Lagos.

And you are going where now?

To Imeko.

Come, come, now, good man, said the policeman. No one is going to Imeko.

That's where we're headed.

You and this beautiful woman? He looked at Sophie appraisingly. I think you are not going to spend a sexy, sexy night in Imeko. Not with this very beautiful woman. Leave her now, I will care for her. He laughed. Oh, no, I see what you are thinking. You are not going simply to Imeko, no. You are hopping the border? Yes, this is what I am thinking. He switched into Yoruba and spoke only to Felix.

Felix undid his seat belt and got out of the car. Don't worry, he said to Sophie.

But how could she not worry when she watched the soldier study Felix's papers, made him stand against the car, legs apart, while he was frisked. And then the policeman came around to

Sophie's side of the car. She rolled down her window. It was still something of a game, she thought, and she knew most of the rules. What to say, what not to say. But it didn't matter; this kid with the rifle would see how she was a frightened rabbit, trying to leave the country after all that had happened, trying to scurry down a hole.

Very nice, he said. Beautiful woman, come out of the car now.

She got out of the car. It was raining, but not pelting.

You are slow slow, he said.

He frisked her gently, firmly. Then he bent down and slid his hand along her bare ankle, up, up. He stopped. He gave her a playful little pat, as she stood, splay-legged against the car.

Mmmm, no dancing? No pleasure for me. He laughed as his friend came around the car. Not for Mr. Adejole, uh-huh?

Sophie didn't move. A sudden spray of rain drenched them all. Now her hair was wet, her face, her shoulders and arms.

Ah, now, said the policeman who had frisked her. Too much rain spoils the pleasure. It is sad for us that you have to go away, he said. To Imeko. He laughed, a long, ringing laugh. His face was broad and happy. I mean no harm, beautiful woman. Your man will give us dash.

They went around the car, leaving her. She reached into the car and got her raincoat, pulling it on; it wasn't warm, but she felt a little more protected, looking out from under the hood. If she weren't allowed to cross the border, what would she do?

You can get in the car, Sophie, said Felix, coming around to her side. It's all right.

He opened the door and she got in. Everything she wore was damp. She fastened the seat belt, breathing in and out, waiting for Felix to leave, but he was busy chatting to the policemen.

She sat fingering the ring her mother had given her, a silver ring with a band of heart-shaped leaves and fruits that might have been grapes. She twisted it on her finger as if it would help her, as if there were some power in it.

The rain stopped and the sun shone through a band of cloud. What were they doing? Negotiating? They were talking, talking. One of the policemen threw off his poncho and put it on the chair. A slash of yellow. The road was a rich red-brown colour after the rain, and water glimmered on the drums; the trees at the edge of the road were dripping.

Felix switched to English. And so, there is no place in Imeko to stay the night? No guesthouse?

Five, six, seven checkpoints before you reach it. Nobody there when you arrive, said the grinning policeman. They are all waiting to nab you at the checkpoints.

That place is worse than the hind end of a cow, said the other. All three broke into laughter.

They flipped back into Yoruba. Felix could have been talking to his friends on a street in Lagos, in no hurry to get moving.

A large bird settled on the roof of the shed, dark feathered, its neck thrust forward like an old man's. A buzzard? No, a vulture. Another two birds flew down and landed beside it.

One of the policemen shrugged his rifle off his shoulder and pointed it at the birds.

Baaa, he shouted and blasted a shot.

Sophie jumped. The three birds took to the air, ungainly, even in flight.

No good omen! he yelled.

Now, finally, Felix got in the car and turned the key in the ignition. He waved to the men; they motioned him on and said something in farewell that made him laugh.

What did they say? said Sophie.

They were all right. They could have made me pay a bribe, but I talked them out of it.

Sophie leaned back, closed her eyes. Fear was something she could feel moving lightly over her skin. It was worse when she couldn't sleep. They had stayed with Felix's sister, Serena, in Abeokuta. Felix hoped the whole business would calm down, but it didn't. There were rumours on the news that Sophie was a spy, that she worked for the CIA, and that the fatwa, first issued by Deputy Governor Alhaji Nuhu Mohammed in Niger State, was supported by other states, like Kaduna, Sokoto, and Zamfara.

Felix's sister's place was no refuge. Just after they arrived, Sophie overheard Felix and Serena while the evening meal was prepared in the kitchen. Serena's voice rose, Felix's voice remained low. Sophie, stalling for time in the bathroom, stared at the leaves of the banana tree, their rippled edges, and the spatterings of rain running down those leaves, rain that began and ended, began and ended. In the bathroom, she was safe. She was safe from the newspapers, safe from the police, safe from the reports of violence in Kaduna.

She put the toilet lid down so she could sit on it to phone her mother. There was no answer. She phoned Uncle Thomas, told him she was in Abeokuta, and that she and Felix were hoping to stay put for a while. Uncle Thomas was at work, and she could tell she'd interrupted him. She was about to say goodbye when he stopped her.

Are you well, Sophie? he asked. Will you be all right?

The banana leaves were a blear of green shapes outside the window. Yes, she said.

I'm hoping that is the case, he said, in his quiet, formal way. I'll tell your mother that we spoke.

She turned off Felix's phone. She could still hear Felix and Serena talking, and plugged her ears with her fingers.

We weren't talking about you, Felix told her later. We were talking about what to do, talking about options.

But Sophie knew she was a bag of laundry they'd all be glad to be rid of. Serena and Anthony had a small guest bed, too small for two. What they'd talked about, Serena and Felix, had to do with Sophie. It had everything to do with her, but it would be worse if she argued.

Now, heading north from Abeokuta, Felix and Sophie passed lush trees, their branches and leaves jewelled. It seemed that they kept moving through veils of mist into another world as she dozed fitfully at the edge of sleep. She slipped over the placid estuary at home, where the surface of the water was puckered silk, and under the surface, the eel grass pulled, as if it were the long hair of some undersea creature, strands drifting against the hull of the boat. On and on she'd paddled in the old kayak, threading a different route through the islands from that of her parents in their kayaks, until finally she was alone, drifting under the railway bridge, frightening the water birds, the ducks and cormorants, hidden in the grassy islands just beyond. She stopped to drift under the shadows of the bridge on the current, and stared, mesmerized, at the vista opening up in front of her. It was a place she'd known all her life, but she'd never found this secret part of it. Past the bridge, the water narrowed into a river that branched into two forks, and she decided on the right fork, paddling toward a small cove with rock walls of white gypsum: she was inside a Greek temple, floating through the mist that rose from the water's surface.

And then she realized the light was fading, and it would take time to get back to the railway bridge, back to Williams Point, and across the harbour. Above the rock walls of the hidden cove, the sun was rosy orange, run through with a soft arrow of grey cloud. Soon the great orb of the setting sun would disappear altogether. She'd have to paddle quickly all the way back to get home before dark. Left, right, left, right: it became a rhythm of hard work, but if she kept at it, she would get there in time. Here was the bridge; she glided under it as a yellow-eyed eagle watched her from the highest branch of a dead tree. She was part of two worlds at once: the murky water, sometimes deep, marked by the ripples of a fast current, sometimes shallow, tangled with eel grass and clams along the silted bottom, and the evening air that brushed her face, her bare shoulders, her hair. She was conscious of urgency as she paddled, scooping the water on one side, scooping it on the other, and always, she had the sense of moving between the mystery of what was below and what was above, a portal into the world of water and the world of air; she'd entered both worlds at once. Yet she was leaving it behind, paddling hard, hard, hard.

No, she wasn't in a kayak. She was in a car. She was fleeing the country, that's what she was doing. What had happened to the kayak, the evening air, the water spread out like a blue tablecloth?

You okay? said Felix.

I'm fine. What about you?

He stretched his neck. All right.

They slowed down again; this was what had woken her. Another checkpoint. Then another, and another. Felix was always polite, coolly expert in negotiating their way through. Finally, they stopped to eat at a roadside stall. There was a roof over one section, crude benches, where they ate chicken from tin plates without speaking. From the dark of the roadside stall, the freshly washed world seemed to sparkle. Hens and a rooster pecked in the dirt beyond: heads jerking up, down, up. A child laughed, ran past. She wore nothing more than a long T-shirt. A gaggle of others pursued her, and after a moment, there was shrieking – they'd caught her.

It'll be all right once we get you to the border, said Felix.

They hadn't talked about what would happen once they crossed it.

The chicken was well roasted, delicious. He licked his fingers, drank his beer thirstily. It was time to go, but neither of them made a move.

The light turned to gold, gleaming on their car, parked at the side of the road, glinting on the wrench that a teenaged boy was using to fix a generator. He leaned against the base of a dead tree, one foot out, one foot tucked under him. The rooster waddled past them, comically thrusting its red comb forward. The afternoon was passing, and she hoped they would get to Imeko in the daylight. Felix finished his beer, set it down. Now a vulture flew down and landed on one of the broken branches of the dead tree.

What is this bird of evil omen? she murmured.

What?

The cops back there, the police. They said that when they saw the vultures.

Felix stared at the vulture in the dead tree.

My dad used to tell stories when I was little, said Sophie. Sometimes he made up the stories, and sometimes he read them to me. Or I'd get him to sing. She smiled. He loved to sing. There was one story about a bird, but it wasn't an evil bird. A hunter was after him. My dad would make the sound of the bird: *Tat, ta-tat. Tat, ta-tat.* Like that. It must have been a woodpecker. He'd make shadows with his hand on the wall. He could make any kind of animal or bird.

She opened her purse, but when she found some cash he waved it away.

Let me pay, he said.

She wanted to say something about how grateful she was that he was taking her to Imeko. Even if he drove her to the border, there would come a time, soon, when they'd have to say goodbye.

My grandmother used to tell me stories, said Felix. My mother's mother.

About what?

One was about the creation of the world, about a length of rope leading from heaven to earth, and a man who was given the task of going down the rope to make the world. His servant went with him, carrying a chicken and a calabash, but the man got distracted by palm wine, so he stayed behind, and the servant went down the rope with a chicken and a calabash and left the man behind drinking. And so it's the servant who winds up creating the world, with the help of the chicken.

He leaned over and kissed the tip of her nose.

Moral of the story: stay away from palm wine. Or maybe never underestimate your chicken? He held up a bone from his plate.

She leaned her head against his shoulder. I'm sorry, she said.

About what?

All of this. She lifted her hands.

He got up, pulled his wallet from his pocket, glancing at the boy, kneeling now, head bent over the generator. He looked down at her and grinned.

Don't be sorry, beautiful woman, he said.

AT THE BORDER, there were two buildings, both of which looked as though they'd been thrown up in haste. On one side, a sort of shed, and on the other, a flat-topped garage of a building. A line of cars between them. A queue, Felix called it.

They shouldn't give us a problem, he said. Not the kind of problems we might have run into if we'd gone another way. This is kind of an outpost, and they might let you through more easily.

Sophie got out her passport.

You have your yellow fever certificate?

She nodded, producing it.

Anyway, Felix said, you'll be with me. As if being with him would solve everything.

The border guard scrutinized her passport, paying great attention to the page with her photograph, and then he asked her to get out of the car and accompany him. She had to take her luggage, which Felix wasn't allowed to carry. Since Felix was Nigerian, he was told to wait in line, with the car, while Sophie, a foreigner, dutifully followed the border guard, who abandoned her inside the flat-topped building that looked like a garage. She waited in the office, with its counter, single window, and great ceiling fan that made squealing noises as it wheeled around and around. It was missing one of its blades. Two women, sitting in desk chairs and fanning themselves with pieces of folded paper, sat under it. They told her someone would come.

Take seat, said one of the women.

Is this Immigration? I don't think I need to go through Immigration.

Take seat.

There was no place to sit. Sophie sat on her suitcase, pulled out her dog-eared novel and tried to read. Insects whirred around the single light bulb that hung over the counter. Dusk had fallen, and with it, the electricity chugged and went off. One of the women got up and closed the wooden shutters of the window. Sophie dozed, but couldn't sleep, balancing as she was on the suitcase.

One of the women peered over the counter at Sophie. Now we go home, she said.

But isn't someone coming?

The woman made a graceful gesture with her hand, as if she were winding wool. Come tomorrow.

Sophie couldn't find Felix; he had been allowed through the border and he was parked on the Benin side. She had to ask someone to tell him she was waiting. She stayed by the Customs shed, jury-rigged with a light from a generator, and watched as Felix walked toward it, talked to the border guards. It took time; she waited, and finally they let him take the car back across the border into Nigeria.

Felix put her luggage in the car and he and Sophie slept there with the seats tilted back, or at least they tried to sleep. Felix took Sophie's hand in his, but after a while he lost hold of it and began snoring. She couldn't sleep. It was hot inside the car. She was thinking of that time, kayaking, when she raced back as the light was fading. At first, she hadn't noticed her parents because they weren't moving, but then she made out her mother at the water's edge. Her blue shirt. After a while another figure clarified itself. She steered her kayak onto the thin, pebbly strip of beach, where it crunched on stones, and her father stepped close, pulled the rubber handle at the bow, and tugged the bow up onto the shingle of the beach, edged in slick eel grass.

I didn't notice the time, said Sophie, getting out of the boat. Her feet sank into thick ooze. It was later than I thought.

You need to pay attention, Sophie-girl, said her father, gently.

It could have gotten complicated, said her mother. With the wind changing.

I won't do it again.

I know you won't, said her mother. You almost got yourself in a fix.

SHE WOKE BEFORE DAWN, her neck aching. Felix woke too, wiping his face with his hand.

There's a woman on the Benin side who makes sausage rolls and biscuits and things. Do you want something?

Sure, Sophie said, but she wasn't hungry. She didn't want him to go, but she got out of the car so he could go without her.

He went. Then, groggily, she remembered he had her luggage. She had her purse, her passport and some money, but he had everything else. Well, he would come back.

Now she could see him at a distance, outside the car. They must have gone through it, found her luggage. Her red suitcase was on the ground outside the car, and she could see Felix opening his hands, gesturing, explaining. It took a long time. She walked closer. They were angry because he'd driven across with luggage that had not been checked on the Nigerian side. He explained what had happened; Sophie was close enough to hear him.

One of the Nigerians grabbed his shirt, shouted at him.

What was Felix saying to him? It was a mistake.

The officer didn't think it was a mistake. He was throwing his weight around. He wanted Felix to open the suitcase, but Felix needed the key, which Sophie had.

Where is the key to this baggage? cried the Customs officer.

Sophie produced it, and went toward them to hand it over, but the officer had already asked for metal clippers, with which he cut off the offending lock. He yanked at the zipper. Sophie watched, mute, as he threw things out on the damp ground. What had he expected to find? There was nothing inside except her sandals, tank tops, sundresses, a long navy dress, underwear. Her black underwire bra. He tossed things out in disgust. Occasionally he would speak loudly to Felix, as if Felix couldn't hear. It was a performance: the officer had a role and Felix had a role. Felix's role was to remain silent.

Finally, the officer stopped, motioned to Felix to pick up everything. It was over. But no, not quite; he took up Sophie's briefcase, nodded to an underling to take it. Her laptop. Sophie tried to recall its contents, what she'd left on it. Were there any files she'd forgotten about? She'd transferred everything to a flash drive before leaving Lagos, and put the flash drive – where had she put it? In a side pocket of the red suitcase. She could see the suitcase, an open-mouthed animal lying in the road where the guard had left it. Felix was returning things to their proper places inside it: her blue-backed hairbrush, her plastic bag of miniature lotions, shampoo, and shower gel. He shook her lacy nightgown, folded it, lay it in the suitcase. He did this with each item, taking his time.

Stop, she wanted to call to Felix. He was allowing them to humiliate him.

Someone took her by the arm. Sophie was taken into a curtained room inside the shed where she'd waited earlier. It was not really a room, not even a cell: it was simply enclosed by dirty beige curtains strung around a space the size of a shower. The woman told Sophie to take off all her clothes except her underwear and she complied. The woman frisked her, carefully, not roughly, told her to come out when she'd put her clothes on again. It was an inferno inside the little room with the beige curtains; there was no electricity and the fan wasn't working. Sophie dressed and came out.

Pah, the system is down. The woman slapped the side of her computer.

Sophie's laptop lay on the counter.

Passport, said the woman.

Sophie gave her the passport.

What is your mission in Nigeria?

She tried to think of her mission in Nigeria. She answered, slowly, as a man in dungarees entered. I had no mission. I simply wanted to learn about the country, because my mother was born here.

The woman waved her hand. The man opened the shutters on the window and went out. Maybe someone would find out what Sophie had done, that she had worked for a newspaper, been fired from her job, that what she'd written had started a furor. The man came back in with a short broom and began work in the corner of the shed. Dust flew into the air.

The woman turned and berated him, wheeled back to Sophie.

Did you work for your home country? asked the woman. Did you gather information?

Sophie looked at the woman blankly. No, I did not work for my home country.

Are you working for your home country at present?

No.

Are you carrying information back to your home country?

No.

Everything had been wiped from the laptop, but if they made her show them what she had on her flash drive they would accuse her of carrying information back to her home country.

The woman opened Sophie's laptop.

You will boot it, she said, indicating Sophie should turn it on. She did. On the desktop was a photo of her family: her mother, her dead father, her grandmother, and Cuba the dog. Her grandmother was squinting.

My family, said Sophie, reassured by the sight of them smiling at her.

But the woman was not interested in Sophie's family. She flipped through Sophie's photographs with irritation.

Did you take photographs of government buildings while in Nigeria?

No.

Airports, train stations? Industrial facilities?

No.

Border crossings?

No.

The woman changed tack. Did you carry contraband into Nigeria?

No.

Are you carrying contraband out of Nigeria?

No.

Another guard appeared, spoke to the woman, and slapped the top of the laptop down. They were going to take it from her.

But the woman stamped Sophie's papers and handed them to her, along with her passport and purse.

Go now, said the woman, nodding at the man.

Thank you, said Sophie.

Sophie left the shed, walking behind the man who carried the laptop as if it were a tray. It was still morning, but Sophie's skin was slippery and her clothes damp. The sky was stretched taut and it seemed as though the blue was an elastic band, pulled, pulled, pulled; soon it would snap apart.

They arrived at the border crossing, where the man turned and gave Sophie the laptop. A guard lounged against the shed, but not the one who had harangued Felix, and Felix himself was nearby, with the car and the red suitcase, wearing his old orange cap with a leaping dolphin above the brim.

Sophie sighed with relief. Now they could leave.

Felix moved the suitcase toward her, neatly sidestepping a puddle.

What? she said.

I dashed them. I wanted you to have your things back.

Felix, you didn't. How much?

It doesn't matter. I couldn't let you go without your things.

What do you mean?

They won't let me through. It's their way of pissing with me. They'll let you through, though, and you have to go. You'll be able to get a minivan to –

Not without you.

Yes.

The guard who leaned against the shed with one knee bent, stork-like, against it, seemed to have his eyes closed, but he was taking it all in. He was watching, of course he was watching. The Customs officer, the one who'd given Felix so much trouble, had disappeared.

You'll be fine, Felix said.

His eyes, his hands, his arms, the way he stood, his weight on his right leg, not his left leg. The stain on his cap, the cap with the happy, leaping dolphin, the scars on his knees that couldn't be seen.

What about you? she said.

I'll go home. No, I mean I'll go to Simon's. He smiled his old smile. We'll see each other again, never fear. I'll come to you.

He took a step toward her, gave her the handle of the suitcase. He put his hand over hers.

I booked that room at the Hotel du Port, but don't stay there if it doesn't look good, if you feel worried, he said.

She couldn't say goodbye. She hugged him, quickly, though she knew people didn't do that here, they didn't make public displays, certainly not in Imeko. She felt his arms around her briefly. Then she broke away, taking the suitcase, its wheels dragging, though she could feel him behind her, waiting as she had her papers checked, yet again. She was about to walk through the gate, when the man who had looked at her papers put up his hand to stop her. She could hear two people speaking rapidly in French on the other side of the gate, a kind of dialect, as if the French had softened in their mouths as they spoke, as if it had melted.

What is it? she said.

Problem, said the man. He gave her passport to another man with greying hair, probably the first man's superior, and they leaned over it together.

What is Halifax? asked the man with the greying hair.

That is in Nova Scotia. In Canada.

We are checking the passport number, said the man. It will take time. Step aside.

She stepped to one side. She almost had her foot in Benin, and they had brought her back; the tightness in her head exploded.

Please, she said. Everything is in order. My passport is in order.

We are checking the number.

The man with the greying hair disappeared and left the younger man at his post. He shrugged his shoulders.

Felix was standing where she'd left him. His hand held his sunglasses and when he raised his arm and waved, the loose arm of the sunglasses flapped open, shut. He knew something wasn't right because they were delaying it. They were holding her back. She rubbed her temple, trying to ease the headache. They hadn't told her to wait in the shade and the sun was harsh. She pulled her hat out of her bag and put it on, but there were many small hammers at work under her skull.

At last the man with the greying hair returned. This is a bad number. He jabbed at her passport.

No, she said. It is perfectly good. It was issued only to me by my government. Even as Sophie spoke, she understood that she would not be allowed to cross into Benin. It didn't matter what she said.

She looked away, swallowed, and turned to him renewed, about to plead her case. She could tell by his obdurate expression that it wouldn't be tolerated yet she didn't want to admit defeat.

The man gave her back her passport and she took it without speaking.

She rolled the suitcase over the uneven ground away from him, away from the gate, away from Benin and her chance to leave the country. She paused, collected herself, continued. The suitcase didn't cooperate with her, and its wheels kept catching on stones so she had to yank it, and finally she picked it up by the handle. Her anger at the officials hardened within her, as if she were constructing something she would need later. Felix was clear as she walked toward him: his hands, the shape of his sunglasses, his cap. Walking away from him, she had been one person. As she walked toward him, she was another person. They had taken something away from her, but what could they do to her now?

14

CLARE COULD SEE PART OF Thomas's driver's face in the mirror, and it made her curious about the marks on his cheeks: three straight lines, which might mean he was from Oyo. Jacob drove swiftly, with easy movements, and the rosary dangling from the mirror swung only a little. A few people along the road stood watching as the silver-grey car passed, and a boy clapped his hands at the sight of it, a Mercedes, sleek and shining, washed the day before and polished by Jacob himself, as if it belonged to him, as if it were part of his own body.

Thomas nodded sleepily in the passenger seat, but Clare was wide awake. At the stalls edging the road the umbrellas were tilted sunflowers, and two boys walked lazily, hand in hand, while an old man teetered on a bicycle. Midday. They could have been on the surface of the moon, and even the fields, once they were outside Makurdi, were chalk coloured. Over the refuse in the ditch grew trumpet flowers, pale winged, with vines curling over the garbage.

They had been to church. Clare went first into the pew as the guest of honour, then Hortensia and Andrew, followed by Monica, a hand smoothing the pleated skirt of her dress, the colour of a pinkish-scarlet amaryllis.

Thomas and Jonathan sat on the other side of the church. Andrew had protested, before church, about sitting with his mother, but Monica countered that he was still too young to sit with the men. Now he took one of Hortensia's satin hair ribbons and she clutched him around the waist, pinning him down on the seat of the pew. He was convulsed with silent laughter.

Monica inclined her head, giving Andrew and Hortensia a look, just as Clare had given Sophie when she misbehaved.

Monica hissed at Hortensia.

Hortensia let her brother go, and he dropped to the floor, one hand across his stomach, laughing uncontrollably, though he had the sense not to make a sound. His sister's hand flashed down, into his pocket and out again, quick as a fish. A flicker of hair ribbon, a triumphant grin at Clare as Hortensia released him.

Monica hissed again, and Andrew got up. Hortensia rearranged herself, smiling smugly, already planning her next move.

Clare bent her head over her phone. Why couldn't they have started out that morning, early, in the cool of the day? Abeokuta was a long way to go; but no, they'd had to wait.

The blue-garbed members of the choir sang and swayed.

The priest was at the altar. Oh, Clare thought impatiently, get on with it. But he did not get on with it. He lifted up the chalice and put it down, kneeling, rising. It was interminable.

Get on with it, get on with it.

THEY PASSED A BURNT-OUT HULK of a bus by the road, blackened and buckled in two pieces, an animal with an open jaw, teeth protruding. Onitsha, gateway to Anambra State. Clare must have dozed, yet they were only at Onitsha, still so far from Abeokuta and going the long way around. Jacob glided under the arch of the sign.

We'll be driving in the dark, Thomas, she said, worriedly.

Do you want to stop here? It would be easy enough to find a hotel.

Well, I – that's a good idea, said Clare.

Clare wanted to find Sophie. She wanted to hold her.

I will drop the envelope and we can proceed to the Hilton, he said. Thomas had been doing some work for a firm in Onitsha and planned to drop off the papers personally.

She didn't want to proceed to the Hilton. She wanted to find Sophie and hold her in her arms.

By the time Thomas had delivered his envelope, another hour and a half had passed. It had taken time to find the person who could take the papers and then Thomas had wanted to call Monica, so that took more time. Clare felt the minutes ticking inside her skin.

And so – the Hilton? said Thomas, settling himself in the car.

I'd like to get to Abeokuta today, said Clare. But it's such a long way.

We can get there. We can keep driving: we have extra gas. Jacob has done it before. Is that what you prefer to do?

Yes.

Then that is what we will do.

It was late, nearly evening, the sky a haze of soft colour, as they crossed the bridge over the Niger River, the water a tarnished silver platter seen through the v-shaped trusses. It was not wise to keep going. On the walkway at one side of the bridge, a woman carried a plastic canister on her head, one arm supporting it, but she could have been treading a shelf of cloud out into the river, far off, to the place where sky and water met. The infinity of the river, a mirror for the changing sky, touched Clare. Close to the riverbank on the near side were a few boats, like beads strung together, and one had the alligator snout of a dugout canoe: Clare and Gavin had once crossed the Niger at Lokoja in a boat exactly like it.

A cluster of motorcycles and vans blocked Clare's view, and she couldn't see the dugout until the traffic passed and then she saw the whole of the western sky blazing; the river, too, caught the liquid flame, and there was the dugout, slipping across it. A solitary boat in the midst of that glory. She caught her breath. The sunset was already fading as Jacob drove away from the bridge, and darkness had fallen well before they'd reached the outskirts of Onitsha.

Thomas spoke with Jacob.

We'll get something to eat, he explained to Clare. There's a place Jacob knows about, though it's nothing very extravagant.

Jacob parked the Mercedes by the side of the road, and Thomas and Clare were hustled off to the best table at a roadside restaurant, a wobbling table with a broken umbrella, where they were given hot plates of chicken and rice. A woman presided over the tables, shouting at the serving girls, making sure all of her patrons had what they needed.

Two men were at the table behind Thomas. There was a girl with them, but she sat apart kicking one foot back and forth, as if she were cross. Clare couldn't say what it was that bothered her about the two men, one of them with a lime-green muscle shirt and sunglasses propped on his head. Thomas drank his beer, set it down. Now that they were out of the car, she knew he was in no great hurry to get back into it. He couldn't see the men, as Clare could, and so he couldn't watch the way their eyes slid to the Mercedes, over its smooth lines.

Should we leave? Maybe take the food with us, do you think? she asked.

If you want to go, we'll go. Thomas got up, wrapping a piece of chicken in a paper napkin and nodding to Jacob, who picked up his soft drink to take to the car. Thomas drank the last of his beer as he stood.

They got back into the car, and though the men didn't appear to look at them, Clare could feel their eyes. Was she dreaming? Once she was safely in the back seat, she felt for her passport and credit card in the pocket she'd made for them, attached by a band of Velcro to her underwear, but she was worrying needlessly. She was a master of the art of worrying, Gavin had told her. It was simply that it was evening, and she was tired; she'd have much preferred turning down the clean sheets of a bed in a hotel, so why hadn't she said so to Thomas?

On the road, the headlights of other cars coming from the opposite direction appeared out of nowhere, as if they were about to collide with the Mercedes before they veered off. The darkness was complete, except for a few lights along the road, which must have been kept going by generators, and now and then the fleeting shapes of people standing next to fires loomed up and vanished. Thomas and Jacob had decided to take the road to Benin City, since they both knew the way and the roads were better, but they still had to skirt holes and pits in the road and sometimes Jacob couldn't avoid them. He slowed down. Fewer people walked along the side of the road here, but once they nearly hit a goat that had strayed; Jacob muttered to himself, drinking his cola to stay alert.

A motorcycle zipped in front of the car, snaking from side to side, just ahead, and Clare noticed the skillful way the driver manoeuvred around the road's obstacles. She could hardly see the driver, only the red Cyclops eye of his tail light. After a while it made her sleepy, watching the bobbing of the light. She shut her eyes.

The bump on the back fender was a light touch, accidental. Clare's eyes fluttered open, closed again. Jacob sped up.

What is it? she said, awake now.

An idiot, said Thomas. Behind us.

She glanced back; she couldn't see anything except headlights. Jacob went faster, and she found herself gripping the seat in front.

Another bump, harder this time, and the Mercedes shot forward.

Jacob yelled and snapped the steering wheel, tossing Clare and Thomas to the right, so Clare banged her head against the window. The car leapt ahead, dropping into a pothole, careening out of it.

Undo your seat belt, said Thomas to Clare tersely.

Why?

Just do it.

The Mercedes shot to the left, off the highway, back onto it, but the vehicle behind them bumped them again, harder this time, and Clare, with her seat belt unfastened, found herself on the other side of the car.

Jacob yanked the wheel to the right, and Clare fell against the seat in front. Jacob braked sharply and stopped.

Sir, they are ahead and behind – I cannot –

Stay where you are, Thomas said. He got out and shut the door.

Voices, one louder than the other, a thud against the car, another thud. Clare could see Thomas's shirt wrinkled and flattened against the window.

The driver's door opened. Loud voices. Jacob started speaking very fast and Clare realized he was praying. He was hauled out of the car and the keys were taken out of the ignition. The door slammed shut.

Did they have guns? Yes, they must have guns. Her knapsack – did she have cash to give them? Yes, but maybe they only wanted the car.

Now the trunk was opened, the sound of someone shifting things. It banged shut. Voices speaking Yoruba, then laughter, high pitched, like a woman's laughter, but not a woman, then a low voice: there were two of them, maybe three.

And then the back door opened. Clare didn't move, her face tucked into her arm, and she was dragged out, but her foot caught and twisted, and she cried out. Her foot was freed; she was set upright. A burly man shoved her against the car, pushed her legs apart, frisked her quickly up and down her legs inexpertly, as if he didn't quite know what he was looking for. He'd been drinking and his breath was rank. He took her knapsack, and the phone inside her knapsack, but didn't find her passport and credit card. He tossed the knapsack back in the car, kept the phone. He turned her around so she faced him.

What are you doing? she said.

What am I doing? He laughed. He had thick arm muscles, huge ropes of flesh. A neon-bright muscle shirt in lime green. It glowed even in the dark. Sunglasses, something bright around his neck.

Let me think of what I am doing. Binta, Danjuma, what are we doing?

Danjuma put his gun to Thomas's head.

We are jacking the car, Bartholomew, said Danjuma.

It's not jacking, you idiot, said the burly man. We are not jacking off. Do you understand me when I say jacking off?

I know jacking off.

That is because you do it every night, Danjuma. We are not jacking off. And I said to call me B.B., not Bartholomew.

Binta calls me B.B., but you always forget.

If we are not jacking, what is it to be called?

It's called carjacking.

Okay, okay, said Danjuma, grinning. Honourable Mr. B.B, we are carjacking off.

Honourable Mr. B.B. That's very nice – catchee, catchee. B.B. smiled and when he did, his lips pulled back to reveal his teeth. He was not much older than the other one, but more powerfully built.

Danjuma took the gun away from Thomas's head and shot it into the air.

Clare jumped at the sudden, jolting blast. How loud it was – so close.

Idiot, said the burly man. Idi-*ot*. You make drivers see you now.

They were off the road, but not far off it, beside a shack with a corrugated roof, a tanker with a Shell logo painted on the side, no lights. A sweetish smell. A teenager was holding a gun to her brother's head. He'd shot the gun; he could shoot her brother.

Look down, look down, Clare told herself. She looked down, studying the teenager's high-top sneakers. They were new, or at least newish. They were still quite white. Trainers, they were called here.

All right, what's next? came a voice, a younger voice. A world-weary girl's voice. Or are you two going to stand here all night jacktalking?

The girl must be on the other side of the car. Jacob, too, must have been on the other side of the car. So, three of them. Danjuma, B.B., and the girl. They spoke very fast in Yoruba and Clare couldn't follow what they were saying, except that they said a few words in English now and then. Debating, thought Clare.

Okay, now now, said B.B, switching back to English. Her Highness wants us to get moving, so we move.

Her Highness, laughed Danjuma. Little Binta, Her Highness. It was the high, wild laugh that Clare had heard before. Little Miss Babygirl Binta Highness!

B.B. spoke to the man in charge of the service station, though it wasn't much of a station. It seemed to Clare that he was leaving the motorcycle in the man's keeping. Binta, the girl, was instructed to take the car that had bumped them from behind. Three people involved, and then this man at the service station. Yet all of this happened quickly, in the sudden glare of vehicles from the road, the intermittent flashing.

B.B. grabbed Clare's arm with one hand. With the other, he prodded Thomas. He wanted Thomas in the back seat with Danjuma.

Get in, he said. Am I the only one who is doing the work here?

He pulled Clare into the front seat with him, and she hit her head on the frame of the door. She could feel B.B.'s thighs under her. He was no more than twenty-four, twenty-five. She had to sit curled up, almost facing him, smelling his breath. Jacob was in the driver's seat. Clare turned her head sideways, eyes closed so she didn't have to look at B.B., about the age of her son, if she'd had a son, on whose lap she was sitting. Danjuma handed Jacob the keys from the back, told him to drive. Clare shifted her eyes, watched Jacob's hand move to the ignition, fumbling.

Start the car, Danjuma said. He sounded bored.

Clare fixed on Jacob's thumb and finger about to turn the key, not turning the key.

Stupid fucker, said Danjuma. Give no problem.

Jacob started the car.

Windows down now, said B.B. Fresh air is wanted.

Jacob rolled down the windows.

Thomas must be directly behind her in the back seat, thought Clare. She thought of Thomas, but she could see flashes of Monica in church that morning, the priest, gorgeous in his vestments, Hortensia, the hair ribbon. Her mind skipped to Sophie at the airport, her wild hair, before it skipped again, to Gavin, holding Sophie just after she was born.

B.B. began to move his hands. What did he want? She felt one hand at her waist, one on her hip. The hand on her waist began moving up to her breasts.

What are you doing? she said, astonished at the sound of her own voice, strong and clear.

He wore sunglasses though it was dark and she couldn't see anything more than his broad face, a chain at his neck and a cross hanging from the chain, his glowing lime-green shirt. He was a thug.

Ṣe o maa ba mi jo? he said, laughing.

Don't do that, she said. Look at you.

Is that? He snorted. Ho ho, he cried, clutching the cross on the chain around his neck. Listen to Mama Shame Shame.

Clare shifted her weight. His hands stopped climbing around her body.

B.B. directed Jacob to turn off the highway onto a poorly maintained back road, more of a path than a road. Jacob slowed down as the car lurched into the bush and the warm night air streamed through the open windows.

She wondered what it would feel like to die. And yet, though she was trembling and her mouth was dry with fear, she also wanted to shift her cramped posture.

Stop here, said B.B. Now, now.

Jacob braked hard. It thrust everyone in the car this way and that. Danjuma laughed hysterically.

You are playing around, said B.B. You must leave keys here. Come now! He slapped the dashboard.

Jacob turned off the car and placed the keys on the dashboard.

Now, get out. Hands on head.

Clare disengaged herself from him and got out of the car carefully, putting her hands up to her head. Jacob and Thomas were shadowy forms beside her, but she could tell that they, too, had their hands on their heads. Danjuma trained a flashlight on them, but it didn't illuminate much, except a termite mound beside the road, and the two cars, one behind the other.

The girl, Binta, had followed in the other car. She got out and leaned against the door, tucking the car keys under her bra strap, where they dangled. She sauntered over to the Mercedes, opened the door and leaned in. She shut the door. Hands on head, she said. That is foolishness, because you watch movies. Why do they need hands on head?

Kneel down, hands on head, said Danjuma.

Yes, kneel down, that is good, agreed B.B.

Why is that? said Binta.

Hands on head only, you think, Highness? said B.B.

Danjuma laughed.

Kneel down, said B.B.

Clare knelt. Her body was shaking and she tried to will it to stop. She remembered kneeling earlier in the day, kneeling to pray. Jacob knelt next to her, and beside him, Thomas.

No moving.

They were very still. A mosquito landed on Clare's cheek and she wanted to slap it away. A quilt from the car was thrown over their heads: it smelled old and dusty, and it covered their heads and shoulders like a shawl. She turned her cheek a little to get rid of the mosquito. It would be easier to shoot them if they were covered with a quilt. She could see the shapes on the material in front of her because of the headlights: perhaps the dancing teddy bears would be the last thing she saw. Sophie. The teddy bears had ribbons around their necks. They had bells. Dangling from the ribbons were bells. Oh, Sophie. When she breathed in, the material of the quilt was sucked closer, and when she breathed out, it loosened. Her own flesh and blood, her beloved one. In, out.

Someone took off Clare's sandals. Her feet were exposed, vulnerable. Perhaps they would shoot each of them so they fell over, front first, but then why take off their shoes? They were not going to run anywhere. No, they would not run. It was possible they might not get up again. Clare coughed, choking.

They must be taking off Thomas and Jacob's shoes.

You think they will run somewhere, came Binta's voice. It is foolishness to take off their shoes. First you say, hands on heads, then you say kneel, kneel, then you throw the blanket over their heads. What are you doing? Next thing you will say is for each one to take off clothes.

Hnnn, said B.B. Foolishness, you are saying?

Yes. Let them go. They are doing no harm.

And let them run to the police?

Why would they run to the police?

Ah-ha, cried Danjuma. I have it! Let two go and keep one.

You are a fool, said B.B. This girl here, your sister, she is worth two of you. And you have been drinking and carousing.

You also, drinking and carousing and womanizing and Satan-making –

Satan-making? Who are you saying? Not B.B., named after B.B. the Golden King of Blues-Making?

Ah-ha, said Danjuma. No, no, no.

Say again? Say No, no, no, Honourable Mr. B.B. Sir.

No, no, no, Honourable Mr. B.B. Sir.

Now, you, Sir Danjuma Idi-*ot*, remember your manners.

The Lord is my shepherd, Jacob murmured. I shall not want. He maketh me to lie down in green pastures. He leadeth me beside the still waters.

Clare saw the heels of her father's new shoes, the dingy, plum-coloured carpeting on a stairway, coming loose at the edges. His new shoes, made of black leather; she was following him, and Thomas was following her. They were going up the stairs to look at a flat in Glasgow, an unfurnished flat, where the light poured in without the obstruction of furniture, a soft bronzed daylight that was new to her. The rooms smelled foreign, especially the closets, which she and Thomas opened and closed. They opened the drawers in the kitchen too and slid the breadboard back and forth. It came out like a shelf, slid back in above the drawers. There was a small refrigerator and it was working, though there was no food inside except ice in the ice cube tray in the freezer. She and Thomas bent the tray until it made a cracking sound and were able to work two cubes free before their father found them sucking the ice, moving the freezing chunks around in their mouths. He laughed when he saw their faces.

Someone took Clare by the arm, helped her to stand up.

He restoreth my soul. He leadeth me in the paths of righteousness for his name's sake.

Come.

Yea, though I walk through the valley –

No more holification from that one, said B.B.

Danjuma hooted. Bibblebabble, ho ho!

Jacob stopped praying. Clare was taken to the car, to the open trunk.

No, she said.

It was one thing to kneel and wait to be shot, another to be put in the trunk of a car.

Get into the boot, said the voice behind her and she realized it was B.B.

No.

A shot was fired into the ground beside her foot and she leapt in surprise as dirt sprayed against her feet, ankles, legs.

He laughed, fired again. Again she leapt; it was involuntary. The sound of the gun was like a whip.

She yelped.

He yelped in a high voice, mimicking her. He walked around her. He'd put on a cap, taken off the sunglasses. He was drunk, but he was enjoying firing the gun.

It made her angry. You should have respect, she said, knowing she should keep quiet. I am your sister; you're my brother. You should have respect for me.

He turned surly. He motioned for her to get in, as if his hand were an extension of the gun.

She scrambled into the trunk. He closed it, dropping it down so it clunked shut. There was hardly room for her, even though she had made her body as small as possible.

She must have shouted without knowing it, because the trunk lid was opened.

It would be a big problem for you, she said. Big problem. To have a dead person in the boot of the car. She saw herself as she must look, curled up, barefoot, in the trunk of a car.

He laughed, slammed the trunk.

She could hear him telling the other two. Big problem, she heard. Hoots of laughter. Big problem for you.

It was hot inside the trunk. A coffin. She willed herself to stay calm.

Now they were talking, no, Thomas was talking to them in a reasonable voice. He was steady; he just kept talking and so long as he talked, she knew he was all right. She shivered, she needed to pee, but she focused on his voice. Now the others were talking to him, back and forth, back and forth, an interminable argument. But whenever Thomas spoke she knew the men must be listening to him, because they didn't stop him.

Silence. She could smell the leather of Thomas's suitcase. Something was jammed into the back of her head, maybe a handle. She waited for Thomas to start speaking again.

A popping – *poppity-pop-pop-pop* – like popcorn against the side of a covered pot. Shooting.

It stopped.

There was nothing at all. No sound.

Clare thought of Sophie, of what she used to say to her at night, when the light had been turned out. I love you so much. How she took Sophie in her arms, her warm, chubby child body.

The trunk was opened. *Wallai,* big problem, here she is. Come now, big problem, said Danjuma. Get out.

15

WHEN FELIX CALLED, he told Simon they hadn't had success at the border.

Sorry-o, said Simon. You can certainly stay with me when you get to Lagos.

If you're at all worried about safety we'll go somewhere else.

What? No, it's not a problem. There are a few people coming over here anyway. You can join us.

Well, the deputy governor of Niger State was on the news. He said it gave anyone the right –

That whole business has been nixed by the president, Simon told him. Obasanjo. That's the end of it, end of the fatwa.

I don't know if that's the end, but, yes, it's better for Sophie.

Sophie could hear the exhaustion in Felix's voice. How weary he sounded.

When they finally got to Lagos it was dark and by then Felix was making small mistakes, mistiming things so that a man on a motorbike almost clipped them in an intersection. They hadn't really slept the night before, and they'd been in the car for hours at the border during the full glare of the day. They arrived at Simon's to the thrum and din of music that had been turned up so the bass whumped inside Sophie's head. Nothing was as she remembered. It didn't seem like the same place, that spacious condo, painted yellow gold. Simon was having a party; he hadn't just invited a few people over. Standing at the entrance, wobbly with fatigue, Sophie saw her own dazed self in the sunburst of a mirror, couldn't figure out why she was wearing a potato sack of a dress and a scarf over her hair. She shivered. The air conditioning had turned the hallway into Austria in January.

Someone floated into the hall.

Hi, she said to them, Simon said you'd be coming. She put her hands up on either side of Felix's face, and her chiffon sleeves slid down her slim dark arms. She kissed him on both cheeks, and did the same to Sophie, and Sophie felt grimy, unwashed, but somehow welcome, perfumed by her. The woman was a butterfly gliding out to the balcony through the French doors.

Who was that? murmured Sophie.

Aurora, said Felix. She's with Simon.

He went to find Simon, but Sophie stayed where she was.

A man was speaking German or Dutch to a woman in the kitchen, and he leaned toward her under the pot rack that hung from the ceiling, with its gleaming copper pots. He was trying to make himself heard over the music. The bubble of his glass, with the garnet-dark wine tipped inside it, went up to his lips and back down to the counter. Sophie could smell a whiff of something good in the pot on the stove, maybe red wine sauce. The woman turned from the man and gave the pot a languid stir; he came from behind and kissed her bare shoulder.

A screech of traffic in the street, horns, someone shouting: the people on the balcony came inside and closed the French doors. The couple in the kitchen didn't notice. The woman's face was half-hidden, but she appeared to be smiling as the man kissed her neck. Sophie felt far from them, and close at the same time, as if the man were kissing her own neck. How easy and how strange it was to drift off from herself, from the woman reflected in the broad, round face of the hall mirror that would have made anyone happy, rimmed as it was by golden rays. But what was Sophie doing here? The odd part, the mystery, was that she was still in Nigeria, when she was supposed to be somewhere else. She was supposed to be in Cotonou in Benin, soon to fly to Frankfurt on her way home to Halifax, but she hadn't gone anywhere, except around in a circle that went out of Lagos to Abeokuta and Imeko, and back to Lagos.

Then the man in the kitchen turned, saw Sophie. Maybe he was trying to place her.

Sophie stepped back, out of sight.

Soph, you're here, said Simon, when he came into the hall. He wrapped her in his arms. I'm sorry about everything.

At least that's what Sophie thought he said, but she couldn't be entirely sure because of the music.

Oh, look what I've done, he said.

It's all right, she said. I'm just tired. She wiped her eyes. It's good to see you, Simon.

It was hardly what you'd call a border crossing, said Felix. It was a hole in the wall, but we thought she'd get through.

Those guys are from the bush, said Simon. Imeko bush. They were messing with you.

They said the number on my passport was a bad number, said Sophie.

They throw their weight around in places like that, thinking they can get away with it. He strode down the hall and opened a door. There, you can unpack, freshen up. Take your time.

The guest room had its own bathroom. Sophie kicked off her sandals and dropped on the bed. You go first, she said to Felix, waving a hand.

She drowsed for a few minutes, opened her eyes when Felix came out after showering. He put on his trousers.

She roused herself and sat up. You must be dead tired, she said.

I'm all right. You?

Everything seems strange, sort of unreal.

She rose and went into the bathroom, showering in a glassy cube under a warm-hot spray of water. When she came out, Felix had fallen on the bed without having put on a shirt. Sophie was still damp; she hadn't dried her hair; she unwrapped the towel and left it on the floor, a swirled cream puff, and nestled next to him. He turned, pulled her close, not minding her wet hair. The music had stopped, and they basked in the silence.

Sophie relaxed in Felix's arms. They'd pointed to the number in her passport, telling her something was wrong. No, nothing was wrong with that number. Her government had issued it to her. There was nothing wrong with her passport. Did they see? No, they didn't, the number was wrong. Now somebody put the music on again; it woke Sophie. It was a tune she recognized, but couldn't name; it was under her ribs, inside her head, reverberating. A woman was singing, *Oh, you, electric eel, my electric eel,* but that couldn't be right. It wasn't the right number. It was wrong. Sophie dozed against Felix's body, his arm around her. She wanted only to be here, lying here, even though the song drilled through their heads.

They half-slept, half-woke, half-slept. Sometime later, Felix got up, put on a shirt, and padded down the hall, leaving the door a little ajar. Quiet. It was finally quiet. Sophie got up, hair still coiled and wet, leaving a dampness on the pillow. Cold from the air conditioning, she put on the fluffy, thick bathrobe that hung on a hook in the bathroom, though it was odd to put on such a thing in a tropical country.

When she appeared in the living room, it was just Aurora and Simon and Felix there, talking quietly. Aurora was on the brown leather couch with one foot in Simon's lap. He was leaning over, talking seriously to Felix, one hand having paused in the stroking of Aurora's foot. They were drinking brandy in belled glasses, except for Aurora, whose eyes were half-closed. Felix ran his hand down his face. I don't know, he was saying. They didn't notice Sophie until she came and sat in a chair next to the couch.

Soph, said Simon. Would you like something? Cointreau? Scotch? Brandy?

She hadn't wanted anything, but now she asked for Scotch.

Simon drew Aurora's foot away from his lap and got up. Neat or on the rocks? Or maybe a little water?

I don't know – I never have Scotch, she said. Neat, I guess.

Neat it will be, said Simon. You have to catch the moment as it flies, wouldn't you say, Soph?

Sophie looked at him, but he was hunting in a cupboard for the Scotch.

Felix said, Sophie doesn't have any idea about your project.

It's a hare-brained scheme, said Aurora unexpectedly. It was hard to imagine such a floaty butterfly having such a strong, willful voice.

What scheme? said Sophie.

I've been talking to Felix about my idea of going to Minna, said Simon, having located the Scotch. He put the tube-shaped box on the counter and pulled out the bottle. Don't jump to conclusions.

Minna! exclaimed Sophie. That's where the rioting is.

Simon handed her a very small tumbler of Scotch. She looked down at the liquid in the glass, the amber-dark colour of guilt. How could she drink it? It made her think of Charles Oluwasegun. Thank you, she said. She put the glass down on the coffee table made of a carved plank of teak, put it down carefully, firmly, to put Charles Oluwasegun out of her mind.

Simon's doing a documentary, said Felix quietly.

It has the potential for people to take us seriously, Simon said.

No one would go to Minna, not right now, said Aurora.

Sophie was awake, fully awake, her heart tat-tat-tatting its assault. Aurora's right. It's crazy. Simon, it's crazy.

Not entirely, said Simon calmly, reasonably. We'll take precautions. We won't go into the areas where they're fighting.

We? said Sophie.

I need Felix's help. I've been wanting to do a really good piece, something that is politically significant. This is it. This is the moment to do it.

Sophie looked at Felix. But you won't go, Felix.

Felix didn't answer, and for the second time that day she felt a jolt of anger. Her entire body was alight, incandescent.

I've got another mobile lying around, said Simon. You'll have that, Soph, and we'll be in touch with you. We'll put Felix's car in my parking place, in case you need it. You're safe as houses in this place. Security cameras, the whole nine yards.

The way Simon said the whole nine yards made his proposal seem perfectly acceptable. As with the fatwa, he believed it was just a minor inconvenience, like having a fly in the room. It could be managed. She was in Lagos, after all, not Kaduna. He had a satin-smooth face, and a smile that set anyone at ease. Felix, on the other hand, could be inscrutable, his expression almost fierce at times, as it was now, so that he didn't seem gentle even though he was the gentler, quieter of the two of them. They were so close they could have been brothers, and of course Felix had to accompany Simon on the trip into the madness. Of course.

Felix knows the code for the condo, Simon said. But I'll be sure to show you before we leave – and we'll just be gone for the day.

I won't be going out, said Sophie.

BY EIGHT O'CLOCK the next morning they were gone. Felix and Simon to Minna, Aurora to her own condo. She was the last to leave; she slung a huge orange purse over her shoulder and kissed Sophie. Come with me, she said. I've got room at my place.

Sophie shook her head.

Try not to think about them, Aurora said.

We had an argument.

It's all right. You two will be all right. Felix adores you. Aurora kissed her again and went out the door, holding it open with her knee. Call me if – call me anytime. My number's on that mobile Simon gave you.

It was impossible not to think about them. Sophie put away the dishes from the night before; she ran the dishwasher.

It's stupid, she'd said to Felix. Goddamn it, it's stupid to do this. She lay in bed, at two in the morning, raging at him quietly, in a non-screaming screaming voice. Nothing he said could placate her.

How can you go there? she said.

Simon needs me. He sighed. It won't be for long, he added. You'll be okay here.

This isn't about me. I'll be fine, she said. But I won't be fine thinking of you there. *You* might not be fine.

She was too proud to say she was also worried about being left alone.

So it went on, and they grew more unkind with each other, until Felix said she was the one who – and bit off the rest of what he was about to say. Sophie gripped his arm. She turned on the light and leaned over him.

The one who what? Started all this?

Felix didn't speak and rolled over to sleep, and after that he left with Simon, though first he gave her his car keys and told her he'd let her know when they got there, speaking to her as if she were across a river, somewhere in the distance.

He'd kissed her, Simon had kissed her, Aurora had kissed her. Twice. Told her not to think about them. But how could she not? Simon, Felix, Simon, Felix. Couldn't they just let her know they were fine? But no. And Sophie would not, no, she would not call either one of them. She took out the phone Simon had lent her and called her mother instead. No answer – she left a voice mail. Call me. She paced the hall into the kitchen, around the blocky leather furniture of the living room past the French doors to the balcony. Call me – I'm not where you think I am. The large abstract painting in the living room was too brazen. And what was it, really? A vortex of yellow, orange, red, with a large indigo-purple smudge just off to the side. She began to detest it as she circled through the hall, kitchen, living room, hall. The painting in the living room, the clock on the microwave in the kitchen. Felix adores you. Painting, clock. Simon, Felix, Simon, Felix. Where was her mother? There was something in the painting. The smudge was not just a smudge; it was an animal, a shadowy creature deep in the yellows and reds of the canvas. She returned to the kitchen, opened the fridge; the light inside went off; she closed the fridge. No power. Off went the breezy air conditioning with a clunk, and the clock on the microwave began blinking in agitation. Do something, it shrieked. Do something, do something.

Too much had happened all at once, and now, nothing. Nothing except the small sounds her body made, her stomach growling because she hadn't eaten. When had she last talked to her mother? In Abeokuta. And when was that? She sat down in the kitchen on the pale, honey-blond of the flooring, maybe bamboo, and drew up her knees, wrapping her arms around them. She wanted her mother beside her, explaining what to do next. Her mother was sitting next to her for an instant, stroking her hair, and then she wasn't. And because her mother vanished, she wanted Felix's arms around her, or just his hand on her shoulder. And where was Felix now? Simon's phone would not ring no matter how she willed it to ring. She called Felix, but he didn't answer. She was alone, alone, alone.

She called her mother again.

If she couldn't talk to her mother, she could talk to her uncle, and her uncle would do something to put her in touch with her mother. She knew her Uncle Thomas's number, didn't she? She tried, but it was wrong. No, it was the three before the five – she tried again.

Hello?

Is that Aunt Monica?

Sophie?

I'm wondering about Mom –

Sophie, is that you? Where are you?

I'm in Lagos.

But we thought you were in Abeokuta.

I was, but –

Monica raced on. Your mother and Thomas have gone to meet you. You said you'd be with Felix's sister, and we all thought you'd be better off with us.

I was with Felix's sister, Sophie recalled. It seemed so long ago they'd discussed this. The truth was that she'd forgotten about her mother and uncle. At the border, she hadn't remembered to get in touch with her mother as Felix suggested, and later it slipped her mind when they returned to Lagos. Now she felt sick.

– they left yesterday morning after church, Monica was saying. Thomas called last evening from Onitsha to say they would stop there for the night, but since then I haven't heard from him.

And I can't get hold of Mom to tell her I'm in Lagos, Sophie said. She doesn't pick up, and she almost always picks up when I call.

No, and Thomas – the same. I've rung and rung him and still no answer.

Monica's voice rose, quavering like a little girl's.

You're worried, said Sophie.

I'm sure it'll be all right, Monica said, but her words sounded like a question.

Sophie wanted to tell her aunt about Felix and Simon in Minna, but what good would it do? Her mother would have comforted Sophie, gently drawing her back to an optimistic view, from darkness to light.

Yes, it'll be all right, said Sophie, surprising herself. Her voice was firm, solid as a bench on which they could rest. They'll be all right. You'll let me know if you hear anything?

NOW SHE HAD TO HOLD Felix and Simon on one side and her mother and uncle on the other as if her shoulders were braced by a yoke with two buckets hanging down, left and right. She paced again: hall, kitchen, living room, hall. The painting in the living room, the furious stabs of green from the stuck microwave clock in the kitchen. Even though the electricity had come back on, she needed to reset the clock. Painting, clock. The indigo-purple smudge in the painting had grown from an animal into a monster and her pace quickened when she passed it, even though she was carrying the yoke with the buckets and they were both full of water, and the water could spill. She had to be careful. She carried the phone with her; she hadn't eaten; she felt as though she might fall over. Fear was in her mouth now, and even when she drank water she couldn't get rid of it. The afternoon gradually dissolved into evening, and evening gradually dissolved into the water she spat into the sink. She ate a small container of peach yogurt from the fridge while sitting with her back against the wall, licked the inside of the container for bits of peach that were stuck there. Her legs would come apart, then her arms. Her ears had already separated from her head. She got up, made another round of the condo.

As a child, she'd run inside the house to give her grandmother some pansies she'd picked. Purple and yellow pansies. Grandma, Grandma. She bumped into her grandmother and fell over, grazing her knee on the edge of the little table with its glass top and its curving legs. Oh, honey, cried her grandmother, and Clare came and disinfected the cut and bandaged Sophie's knee. Her grandmother, smelling of talcum powder; her mother smelling of the garden. Sophie dozed on the kitchen floor, dozed on the leather couch, dozed on the guest bed, but fear was in her mouth. Now it was 1:04 when she clicked on the phone, 1:04 in the morning, and still Felix hadn't called. The pansies were scattered on the floor, across the linoleum, purple, yellow, purple, yellow. Everyone she loved had gone away from her, purple, yellow, purple. It's stupid, she'd said to Felix, but he and Simon had gone away without thinking of her. They'd simply gone away.

16

CLARE CUT HER LEFT HAND on an edge of exposed metal as she climbed out of the trunk of the car. When she pressed her fingers against it some warm blood spilled over – Binta offered her a rag – and so it took Clare a moment to focus on Thomas and Jacob. But there they were, just a short distance away. Thomas was unbuttoning his shirt, slowly and methodically; he undid the cuffs, took the shirt off, let it fall, as if the shirt had a life now abandoned. It was nothing, there on the dirt, just a pale skin. In the same, careful way, he undid his trousers, unbuttoning them, unzipping his fly, letting down the trousers one leg at a time and stepping out of them. It was too intimate, almost unbearable, for Clare to see her brother undressing, however dim it was in the clearing, yet she couldn't look away.

Jacob was quicker, and now he stood, resolutely, in his red and yellow boxer shorts. Yellow lions on a red background. The lions floated in the darkness: they could have been anything. His legs were thin, shaped like table legs, and his chest was not firm and manly, but somehow hollowed out in the centre, perhaps because he was hunching his shoulders. Thomas finished undressing and stood in his white boxer shorts beside Jacob, who was shivering. He stood close, as if to protect him, but as far as Clare could tell, his eyes were on the ground, as if examining his shoes, Jacob's shoes, and Clare's sandals, placed before him.

The pump and pull of Clare's heart was loud in her ears. She couldn't bring herself to think what would happen next. She stared at the collection of shoes, just as Thomas himself was doing.

B.B. began to laugh. He couldn't seem to stop.

Danjuma laughed too, uproariously, slapping his thighs. Dance now, he said.

Yes, dance for us, cried B.B. Come now.

Thomas and Jacob were stiff puppets; they moved their feet, but it was not dancing.

Take each other's arms and go round, instructed B.B.

They jigged in a circle. Clare couldn't watch.

Look happy, called Danjuma.

Happy, happy, cawed B.B.

Pffaaahh, cried Danjuma. He himself was turning in a circle, mimicking them, roaring and flapping his arms. We will show you, he laughed, and caught B.B.'s arm, wheeling and cavorting, hardly noticing Thomas and Jacob, who had slowed to watch them.

You must leap, Danjuma instructed.

Danjuma leapt energetically, spreading his arms to show B.B how easy it was. Clare watched the flight of his white trainers through the air.

B.B. couldn't leap and he tumbled to the ground, sprawled out. He raised his arm and Danjuma helped him up.

Always extend courtesy, Danjuma shouted. Women desire you to extend courtesy.

Always extend – B.B. repeated, chortling with laughter.

Extend yourself, so! squealed Danjuma, and he pumped his fist up and down in front of his crotch.

Ha, Mr. Longnose, cried B.B.

B.B. fell over himself, doubled up with agony as Danjuma circled around him. He put his hands out to B.B. who took them, if only to support himself, whereupon Danjuma began to glide forward.

Thomas and Jacob moved slowly at first, then more quickly. They walked along the track past the two cars and Clare edged away from where she'd been standing by Thomas's car, determined to follow.

Ha, *Wahala*, they are all leaving us, cried Danjuma. Look, now.

We cannot have this, can we? B.B. boomed. A woman should not run from us, hey Danjuma?

Quite right, agreed Danjuma. He moved quickly, slipped his arm around Clare, and pulled her back with him as he retrieved his gun. A woman, a car – we will keep them.

Clare tried to wrestle away from Danjuma, but he gripped her tight, while B.B. trained a flashlight on the departing figures. White and red and yellow. Even without the flashlight, Clare would have been able to see them. B.B. gave the flashlight to Binta to hold, but she allowed the light to play over the deep tire tracks in the ground, the castle of earth made by the termites, the shadows of the trees. Jacob glanced over his shoulder.

B.B. shot the ground, and so did Danjuma. Thomas and Jacob jumped wildly at the sound of gunfire, and now they ran along the track, heels kicking up dust.

Ha, off they run now, going fast fast, cried Danjuma, letting go of Clare.

The flashlight strayed into the trees, back to the two men, away, flickering, so they vanished and reappeared in its small cone of light, until they were gone.

We have sent them packing without clothing to cover their backsides! B.B. put his gun aside and flopped himself down on the quilt with the teddy bears and bells. He put his hands behind his head.

Have no thought of running now, Danjuma told Clare as he sat down on the quilt to roll a joint, gun between his legs.

Clare didn't know how angry she was until she saw Danjuma's hands deftly packing the joint. She went forward, thinking how Thomas and Jacob had been humiliated, had been afraid, and neither B.B. nor Danjuma stopped her from picking up the clothing that Thomas and Jacob had taken off, their shirts and trousers, one sock, another sock. Jacob's shoes. Thomas had been wearing a suit jacket, of all things. She gathered everything up and took it toward the car, where she stood with her back to Danjuma and B.B. She shook out each article of clothing, folded it. She did this calmly, or with the appearance of calm, and she found that doing it soothed her, quieted her heart.

When she came to Thomas's shirt, she checked the pocket, where she found his money clip. She hadn't expected to find such a thing, and, hurriedly, she slipped it down her bra and went on with her task, concentrating on putting socks together, buttoning up the shirts and folding them. Now Thomas and Jacob would be close to the service station with the Shell sign, she thought. One of the buttons on Thomas's shirt was missing. Now they would be near the road. She didn't know how they would manage once they got to the road, two men without their clothes in the middle of nowhere.

She held his shoes, Thomas's shoes, in one hand, and her own sandals in the other. She would not cry over his shoes, she told herself, simply because they were polished brogues.

No, she would not. She placed them in a corner of the trunk, slipped his socks inside. Putting her sandals on her feet, she put the trunk down and leaned against the car, closing her eyes. They were not dead.

SHE OPENED HER EYES. Binta, standing near her, might have nudged her, or maybe she had only imagined it. B.B. and Danjuma were together on the quilt: Danjuma lay with his legs spread like a boy, with his back to them, and B.B. sitting up, guns and phones beside him. They were sharing the joint that Danjuma had rolled, and the smell of it, the pungent smoke, was almost sweet. It was as if they'd done a good night's work, thought Clare, since they had the car, and, for extra insurance, they had her. Now they could rest. She put her left hand to her lips and licked the blood, which had congealed along the seam of the cut. She tasted salt and metal in her blood.

Clare felt a touch. She hadn't imagined it. Binta opened her hand, and there, in her palm, were the car keys, the keys Clare had seen Jacob turn in the ignition of the Mercedes. A medallion with St. Christopher hung from the key chain, which made sense to her, a crude image on a metal disc. She knew what the medallion looked like, since Jacob had put it on the table at dinner. St. Christopher seemed to be wading through a river with a sack. No, not a sack, a baby with a halo.

Yes, now she remembered how Binta had tucked the keys to the other car under her bra strap, and somehow she had also managed to snatch the keys to the Mercedes from the dashboard without anyone noticing.

Clare didn't move; she watched as Binta's fingers closed over the keys. She clasped Clare's wrist, telling her to wait, they had to wait. They simply stayed where they were, brushing away a mosquito now and then, careful not to make any noise. The two of them leaned against the car, half-awake. Clare thought of plush curtains, and gave her head a little shake, remembering where she'd seen the plush curtains. It was in the funeral home in Glasgow. Her father had died, someone was offering tea in a gold-edged cup and saucer. Thomas was with her. He had not accepted tea in a gold-edged cup from the funeral home director, but Clare had. The plush curtains had been pulled across a fake window with frosted glass that looked out on nothing but gave the impression of a living room. The tea in her cup was cold; their father was dead; that was the end of it.

BINTA'S TOUCH AGAIN, the firmness of her hand. How many minutes had passed? Or had it been hours? She pointed. Both B.B. and Danjuma were sleeping on the quilt. Clare moved around the car on one side, Binta on the other, and then Clare quietly opened the passenger door, got in. There was no movement from the two men. Binta opened the driver's door, jammed the key in the ignition, and turned it.

The car jumped forward with a jerk, but Binta had inadvertently turned on the spray for the washing fluid and windshield wipers as well as the headlights, and Clare saw filmy, elongated versions of B.B. and Danjuma rise clownishly out of their sleep. B.B., a blur of lime-green, seemed to be pawing at the air as he lunged forward, but Binta was undaunted, sweeping the car around and nearly hitting them both, driving straight over the quilt and swinging to the right in a sharp curve before straightening the Mercedes to roar away. The bear-like figure of B.B. lurched out of the way, as did the taller, thinner figure of Danjuma, but they were shadowy caricatures of themselves, half-awake, half-asleep, straining to catch, and stop, what could not be caught.

Binta drove the Mercedes with a mixture of wild cowboy bravado, and deeply serious intent. There was no stopping her. Already she was racing along the track, bumping in and out of the ruts, and the men, who must have been bumbling to get into the other car, were far behind them. The windshield wipers were still flailing back and forth against the glass: *clack-a, clack-a, clack*. It was comical, even ridiculous, thought Clare, that a mite of a girl should be driving the car with such ease. She was no more than sixteen.

Where are we going? asked Clare.

We are running away, replied Binta calmly.

Clare said nothing more. She waited for the lights to appear behind them.

Binta laughed lightly. I took the keys to their car. They will not catch us, they will be looking. She rolled down the window and tossed the keys – a good, strong throw.

Well done, said Clare.

When they came to the service station, Binta didn't slow down; she simply charged straight through it, turning the wheel hard to avoid a motorcycle. A man in the shack beneath the Shell sign bounded to his feet and galloped after them.

I will not stop for him, said Binta. He is a friend to my brother Danjuma.

She turned the car onto the highway, and the Mercedes immediately collided with someone on a bicycle: there was a *clunk*, a weight dropped on the hood of the car. It was a man, a man with his face squashed sideways against the windshield, his body having stopped the wipers. The car was still moving, but the man pushed himself up with both hands, as if he were doing pushups, an expression of utter bewilderment on his face. The wipers, freed, batted against his hands. Binta swerved the car to the left, then violently to the right, and the man rolled off.

Clare turned to see him getting up in the road, where he spat abuse at them.

Binta didn't stop. The wipers clacked.

You might get us killed, Clare said. Not to mention people on bicycles.

Binta turned off the wipers and turn signal. We should not take the Onitsha Road.

Could we look for Thomas and Jacob? said Clare.

We must not delay, said Binta. Even with the keys out of my brothers' hands, we must go.

A woman loomed out of the darkness on the side of the road. She was slowly jogging, balancing a load tied up in a sheet on her head.

Don't hit this one, said Clare. Which way are you taking us?

Into the bush.

Is that a good idea?

The way ahead was ink black and there were few cars or motorbikes. It was just as well, since Binta's driving consisted of short bursts of furious speed, then a brief lull in which she encountered an obstacle in the road, and wild speed again. When she came upon three goats in the road, she missed them by inches, careening onto the shoulder and veering into the opposite lane.

You are afraid of me as to the driving? Binta sang out as she swung back into the right lane. I will go slow slow, she said.

Clare closed her eyes, but she was being jarred and jostled

too much to rest. She thought of Thomas. The light of occasional motorbikes flickered in and out, in and out. Her head bobbled, the car raced.

She was in Nova Scotia, on the road to the beach. Gavin was singing "O Canada," because she'd bet him that he didn't know the words. When he forgot the words to the second verse, he slipped into a Scottish folk song. Give me a boat that can carry two, he sang, lustily. The windows were open in the car and the dust blew in on all of them as they bumped along.

Dad, yelled Sophie. A heron.

Gavin slammed on the brakes and backed up so they could see the heron, apparently one-legged, tranced, immobile. Then it flew off.

CLARE WAS STARING AT raggedy pieces of cloud, white against blue. The raggedy pieces came together, broke apart, as if someone were pulling them. She lay in the back seat of a car, and the car was not moving. A breeze came through the open windows. The edge of cloud curled, spread out, fanned across the blue, and, tissue-like, slipped away from the large, soft cloud. Tree branches fingered the cloud; they branched and branched into fine filigree, a net of branches that would catch the cloud. It was an acacia tree. She was in Nigeria.

It came back to her, flashing, how they had put her in the trunk of this very car, made Thomas and Jacob dance, shot the ground under them. She sat up, her stomach knotted and tense, and saw a broad, flat river spread out far below the car, parked under an acacia tree where it was shady. A hill, a river. But no Thomas or Jacob. A shiver went through her. Yea, though I walk through the valley, Jacob had chanted. Yea, though I walk through the valley of the shadow.

Binta returned to the car with two paper plates of food, put them on top of the car and opened Clare's door.

I have plantain, she announced.

Where are we? asked Clare. Her throat was coated with what felt like sandpaper.

It is Lokoja.

Clare could feel stubble and dust under her sandals when she got out of the car, taking the paper plate. Early morning sun, already warm. She ate a piece of the fried plantain, and it turned out to be delicious. A woman on a bicycle wobbled along the shoulder of the road, one arm balancing the load on her head with such difficulty that it seemed she would fall off, but she righted herself and continued. The world was new and shining. It was a miracle to Clare that she was alive in it.

She walked around the car and opened one of the doors to hide behind as she squatted. Her urine smelled sharp and sour. For some reason, her sandals were decorated with rhinestones in a flower pattern. How silly. And someone had painted her toenails a dark satiny pink, and each toenail was the deep colour of a gemstone. One or two were chipped. She had done that, she recalled, several days before setting out on this journey from Canada, but it was ludicrous, it made her want to laugh. She was clad in the same clothes she had been wearing the night before, a flowered cotton dress, dirty now, like her feet. There was a bloody cut on her hand, and the congealed blood was smeared with dirt. But there was her knapsack in the back seat of the car, and inside, a packet of wet wipes. She wiped her face, her hands, her feet.

Binta was stuffing pieces of fried plantain into her mouth. Her face was greasy around her mouth: high cheekbones, wide grin. Greasy mouth, lovely girl. Like Sophie.

Eat all, laughed Binta. You will become very fat. She handed Clare a bottle of water.

Thank you.

There is plenty. Binta waved toward an old woman sitting on a stool down the road. Back and forth, the bent woman passed a frying pan over the heat of a little kerosene stove.

I was here once, said Clare. With my husband.

You have a husband?

Not anymore, she said, opening the water bottle.

You are divorced?

Clare drank some water. He died a few years ago.

Uh, uh! Binta clucked. I am sorry for you.

I came here because of my daughter, Sophie. But I can't call her – one of those men took my phone last night and I can't even call my sister-in-law to tell her all of this, that my brother has vanished, that the car was taken, that I am alive, that I don't know where he is or what has become of him, and I can't call Sophie. Clare couldn't stop the rush of words. There, you see. I've failed everyone.

I am sorry-o that we cannot go back to look for your brothers.

Clare drank more water. She looked at Binta. Your family, where do they live?

My mother is dead. My father, she shrugged her shoulders. I lived with my cousin and his junior wife. She told me what to do. Sweep now, Binta! Get me green leaf from the market, Binta! She had juju over my cousin. I wanted to run from there, but there was her daughter, Fari, my sister. I cared for Fari. But Danjuma was the brother of my cousin's junior wife, and he made me go with him and help to steal cars. Binta stood up, wiping her hands. Her face was heart shaped. I hated him for it, she said.

A breeze took up the loose collar of her yellow blouse and a flap of her cotton wrapper, so it rippled like a flag around her body. She took off her headscarf and shook it, a length of bright pink, and then wound it around her head. Except for that flash of rose-pink, the landscape was sand coloured: the banks of the river, the almond-shaped island that divided the river into two broad strands, the flats where the egrets landed and flew up, as if out of a magician's hat, and the rim of land beyond the river, where shapes slipped into other shapes. Clare wanted to rest in it because she was so tired, and because its tranquility lulled her, the way the river seemed to have no colour at all, except for a glimmer across its surface, pale gold, and beyond that gleaming band it dissolved, again, into a wavering line.

Husband, thought Clare. Binta had asked about her husband. The word hollowed her out. She had been a wife. Gavin had been her husband. Partners who were no longer partnered, a right shoe missing the left. She must not be lulled, must not rest. She finished the plantain and folded up her paper plate.

A-a! said Binta. My mobile.

You have a phone? With you?

Yes, but it is not working. It has died-o. Come, we can take tea.

They walked past a tanker-trailer to a picnic table, covered in old newspapers, where an energetic young man was serving hot drinks, helped by a small girl. The man scanned Binta's yellow blouse, Clare's dirty flowered dress, and his eyes went back to Binta, travelling over her frayed wrapper.

Bournvita, please, said Clare sharply, to make him stop looking.

Orisa, called the man, and a sprite of a girl appeared and tried to hoist the kettle off the kerosene stove, but it was heavy:

he took it from her. She ran and got two plastic mugs, spooning out Bournvita from a big can. As the man poured hot water into the mugs, the girl stirred one mug, then the other.

It would be a sultry, heavy day, but now the air was almost cool. On the water, leaping light. Sophie – where was she now? When Clare closed her eyes, the glitter was still there. Thomas, undressing. She opened them. Binta stood on one foot, the other foot resting on her ankle. How like Sophie, that posture. Standing in line at the visitation, greeting people one by one. Sorry for your loss, they had said to Clare, and she listened to each one, conscious of Margaret, Gavin's mother, frozen in place beside her. And here was the woman who'd invited Clare to join the choir, the woman with the name that sounded like poplar leaves in the wind. Small round body, shiny hair cut in a fringe across her forehead.

He was a good man, Tressa said. I can't think of him gone.

I know, Clare said. Then it caught her, what she'd said – a good man – and the lights sparkled. Tressa blurred, until her husband put his firm mitt into Clare's hand.

Sorry for your loss, he said, shaking his head. He was the same size as Tressa, but bulkier. His name was Philip, but he went by Phil.

Thank you for coming, murmured Clare.

I went to school with Gavin, said Phil. I won a penknife off him once, you know, with a fancy handle and a silver crest on it. I still have it.

Clare nodded. She smiled.

But there was more, and he struggled on. Gavin was true and good, like Tressa said. So I want you to have it.

The penknife?

He put it in her hand.

Clare didn't mean for her eyes to fill. She dabbed at them with the balled-up tissue in her free hand; the other hand clutched the penknife.

BESIDE THEM, two men finished their drinks, slapped down money on the table, got in a blue car, and drove down the hill to join the haphazard queue. They left their newspaper behind, and one page flipped over. Clare took the newspaper and set it in front of her on the table, turning it back absently to the first page, her gaze drawn to a small ferry that was moving so slowly around the island as to barely move at all.

See now, said Binta, pointing.

Some cattle herders were standing in a dugout canoe with long poles, prodding long-horned cattle across the river. The dugout, a long half-moon, black against the water, rose up at stern and bow. The herders were calling, singing, driving the cattle forward.

Hey-wah-awk, they cried. *Hey-wah-awk*.

Their long poles slapped the water; the animals thrashed to swim away from them. They struggled to keep their heads above the surface: their long heads, curved horns, and humps on their backs were like floating debris. And this line of ungainly creatures, not made for swimming, but swimming crazily anyway, wild eyed, hooves cycling around and around beneath the surface was like a tripwire for the ferry as it came around the island. The boat made a wide arc to avoid canoe and cattle, though by this time the cattle were strung out across the river.

Heeywah-awk, cried the herders.

The little girl, Orisa, set down hot drinks in front of Clare and Binta. Some of the liquid sloshed onto the table, and Clare set her mug on top of the newspaper, with its headline, *Blood*

Spills in Niger State. The dampness from the mug seeped into the photograph of a Nollywood actress. Clare waited for her drink to cool. Orisa grabbed a toddler and lifted him away from the kerosene stove, though he was almost as big as she was. She carried him away with her.

And below, on the river, the ferry had finally made a sweeping detour around the cattle. It advanced, low in the water, and after a long interval in which nothing seemed to be happening, nothing at all, it arrived at the wharf. Several men hopped out and moored it, and then an ancient ramp descended.

Clare picked up her drink and sipped. Some of the cattle reached the shore close to the wharf at the same time; a few herders were waiting there, and the exhausted animals were jostled and jabbed up the slope as they came ashore, flanks wet and heaving, water streaming from their bony sides. It was a dream, and it made her think of the way Thomas's shirt had detached itself from his hand, dropped to the ground.

Simultaneously, a line of cars was disgorged from the ferry, each moving slowly down the ramp, bumping onto the pavement, and dividing into two streams that passed around an old minivan resting on blocks, an ancient dinosaur of rust. The ferry was also packed tightly with an array of people, all shapes and sizes, who disembarked onto the wharf, carrying loads on their heads, plastic bags in their hands: a crowd spilling forward, accompanied by yelling, hawking, honking.

Egrets circled. *Hey-wah-awk.*

One driver stopped his car close to where all the vehicles were disembarking from the ferry. Because of the obstacles of a rusted minivan on one side and a parked vehicle on the other, there was now a tangled knot of traffic, around which only one or two small cars threaded their way. The driver of the parked car got out and used a rag to raise the bonnet, propping it up. He jumped back, went close, drew back. A few people clustered around the car, and the man began flapping his arms. From the top of the hill, the group around the car seemed small, almost doll-like, but the sound of their voices carried.

And the herders. *Hey-wah-awk*. And the snorts and grunts and moans of the cattle.

A few people in the queue for the ferry now circled around and drove back up the hill, and others followed, driving too fast: here, at the crest, they were stopped by a line of cattle, still wet from the river, crossing the road in single file. More honking. Drivers leaned out of their windows to yell at the herders.

Clare had almost finished her sweet, milky drink. She was waking up. Orisa returned with the squalling toddler still in her arms, set him down on unsteady feet, where he dropped to all fours and began crawling under the table. Binta drank the rest of her Bournvita and plopped her empty mug into a bucket of soapy water.

I am coming, she said, and walked away.

The people who had gathered around the car jumped away from it. Clare rose, still clutching her plastic mug. Was the radiator on fire?

Binta, she called. Where are you going?

The driver of the car with the open hood was beside himself now, even as a boy came rushing with a half bucket of water and splashed it over the smoking engine. Most of the water missed its target, and off went the boy for more water.

Tails of smoke wavered, drifted away from the car.

Clare couldn't watch; she sat down abruptly. She spread out her hands on the table and scanned the newspaper, its dampened print.

Blood Spills in Niger State

She stared at it, held it closer.

Published one week ago today in *The Daily Leader*, the controversial article "Who Will Cast the First Stone?" has sparked —

Here the words slipped together soggily. Clare skipped down, began reading again.

— the Muslim North, where shariah law was recently instituted in a number of states, Niger State among —

Clare stared at the newspaper. Sophie's name.

Pointing her finger at an unknown male culprit, American journalist Sophia MacNeil has done no one a service, least of all the young woman sentenced to death by stoning, A'isha Nasir. Miss MacNeil asked who should be considered the guilty party —

Clare tried to stand up, tried to get free of the picnic table. She was holding the sodden newspaper. Get the car – she must. Leave as soon as possible.

Muslims in Niger State, home of A'isha Nasir, took immediate offense to the article, which they claimed had been written by an American spy.

Binta – where was Binta?

Before Miss MacNeil made a swift departure from the country, the Kaduna and Lagos offices of *The Daily Leader* were sacked. No injuries or loss of life resulted —

The people down below had set up a bucket brigade, passing one bucket along, another, another. They passed the buckets, and when each one reached the car, they doused it. When they finished with one of them, a child flew with it down to the water. Another bucket, another child, but there were not enough buckets.

However, a fatwa issued by the deputy governor of Niger State, thereby putting a price on her head, has been deemed illegal by the president of Nigeria himself, Olusegun —

The smoke from the car shrouded the other vehicles, filling the air over the wharf, over the river. At least there was no sign of fire. The buckets continued to be poured over the engine: one, two, three, four.

Indeed, it has gone well beyond the case of A'isha Nasir. street fighting remains fierce in Minna, Kaduna, and Zaria, since the fires of sectarian violence have been fanned by this incident. Christians and Muslims are killing one another indiscriminately, with upwards of forty people dead.

The herders' canoe had disappeared behind the curtain of smoke, but the sounds of their voices could still be heard. Their poles thwacked the water. *Hey-wah-awk*, they sang. The cows bellowed. *Hey-wah-awk*. The second herd to cross was being kept on the riverbank, huddled together. A price on her head. The herders stayed with them, striking any cows that strayed. But the first herd had gone up the slope.

Something exploded in the car like popcorn in a pan; the line of people passing buckets scattered. One collided with another and they both fell down: a comical collapse. They regrouped in a haphazard line, and the buckets were passed hand to hand to hand.

As for the vehicles that had disembarked from the ferry, the traffic was now gridlocked on the hill: a confused mass of cars, motorbikes, and frightened cattle together with their herders. Incessant honking. People were getting out of their cars, and one man threw up his arms as if to say that nothing could be done, while the honking continued, in intermittent blasts. One driver swung up on the cab of his lorry to see whatever it was that had caused the obstruction. A cow. One of the herders, easy to spot because of his deep blue tunic and conical hat, attempted to move the creature from the middle of the road.

Go, whispered Clare. Get out of there.

But the herder wouldn't leave without the cow, and the cow refused to budge. He had a long stick and he whipped her flank. She would not move. The herder became frantic; the cow held her ground, stoically.

Go, go, go!

A man walked up to the herder and pushed him in the chest. The herder fell back.

Then a flash of rose pink. Binta. She stood in front of the herder, in front of the cow, hands on her hips, speaking rapidly and angrily to the man who had pushed the herder. She raised her arms, making a wide gesture, and everyone watched her, even the man on the cab of the lorry. The herder swatted the cow again, but it simply waggled its head.

Binta's low, resonant voice.

Another herder came and together two of them slapped the cow, and, startled, it stepped forward, stopped. The man who had been sitting on the cab of a lorry jumped down and came toward the herders, surprising the one in the deep blue tunic by wresting the stick from his grasp. The herder ducked as the lorry driver swung the stick; it broke on the cow's withers, making the animal shudder.

Binta leaned into the face of the man who had struck it. What do you do? she cried.

Clare could hear her clearly. Oh, don't, she murmured.

The man moved back, gripping the broken stick.

What you think you do, now? Binta mocked. Big-big man-o?

She advanced on him. She wasn't finished. Yes, look at this man, who takes a big stick because he has no big stick of his own! He lays that stick on the cow to make it dance!

There was a roar from the crowd.

Such a grand stick-o!

They were laughing. And it was because of Binta, who was beginning to enjoy making them laugh. The man melted into the crowd.

Clare ran forward. She threaded her way between people at the edge of the road, through the motorbikes and cars. Binta! *Binta!*

It seemed to take Clare so long to get to her, to reach out for her hand and pull her away. Come. We have to go.

It was as if they were both moving through water and the water was keeping them from going faster, but this was part of the dream Clare was dreaming, and in this dream there was no time to lose, they had to hurry.

17

A'ISHA WASN'T HAPPY ABOUT staying with the head man, Alhaji Hassan, though his place was much more comfortable than any hut at her uncle's compound. She had been offered a guest room in a house that seemed to be entirely white. The room she shared with Safiya gleamed, and the bathroom, which was for her use, and Safiya's, exclusively, could have been the inside of an eggshell, though there was the faintest rime of red dust that had worked its way between the clean tiles. Why would anyone have such a house? In harmattan, when the dust from the Sahara settled everywhere, it was bound to get dirty, though A'isha supposed there was someone to clean the bathrooms, just as there was someone to cook the meals. She wondered what Alhaji Hassan's wife, Alhaja Tani, did with her time.

Yet the taps in the bathroom were a miracle, even when there was no running water, which was much of the time.

Look, Safiya, she cried.

At the sink, A'isha turned on the cold water tap, shut it off, turned on the hot water tap, shut it off. She turned them both on together and the water gurgled and spurted. She laughed, dipping Safiya down so her toes could be bathed in the rush of lukewarm water. Safiya babbled in delight.

When Safiya napped, A'isha could have a shower and step out, through a glass door, onto a bath mat where she could see her blurred body darkly in the steamed-up mirror. This became a pleasure to which she looked forward. But when it was time to eat, A'isha was overcome with embarrassment, since she had to go out and be with Alhaji Hassan and his wife, Tani, who seemed as different from him as night from day.

A'isha took up Safiya, and, without waking her, put her in a wrapper on her back, and went down the hall into the room that was called a living room – a strange name for it, because didn't they live in all the rooms? – across the white rug that seemed as big as the whole of the Sahara, past the white leather couch to a room that was not a room at all, simply part of the living room, where the Alhaji and his wife, and their daughter, Salima, and sometimes a few of her five children, ate their meals at a table. Salima's husband was working in Ghana.

A'isha had rarely eaten at a table; she usually sat on a bench outside, or the low stool from which she cooked over the kerosene stove; she picked food out of a bowl with her fingers. Here she had to be cautious, sliding into her chair so that she didn't hurt Safiya. She dared not put her hands on the table, at the place setting that was provided for her, with the knives and forks and spoons. The knife blade glittered and she moved it. A bowl of groundnut stew was put before her, to be eaten with pounded yam, but this was another puzzle because she didn't know how a person could eat pounded yam with a spoon. Salima's eldest girls were at the table; she tried to disregard them, even though they knew better than she how to get the food into their mouths. They were picking up the pounded yam in their hands, kneading it into shape, and dipping it into their stew, as A'isha longed to do. Rasheed, the youngest, who was about five or six, had climbed into Salima's lap, where he stared at A'isha with large brown eyes to see what she would do. Should A'isha pick up some pounded yam and dip it into the stew? Should she take bits of meat from the groundnut stew with her fingers and pop them into her mouth? The food looked so good, especially the rich, steaming groundnut stew, but she was perplexed by it. Rasheed made a face at A'isha, stretching his mouth high on one side and down on the other. A'isha had to lower her head so she didn't laugh; he was doing his best to make her laugh.

Tani used a spoon, but why? She didn't look like she was enjoying herself. She made A'isha think of a desert woman, a Tuareg, because of her eyes and her polished skin, though she was not at all a woman of the desert. She was a slim column. When she sat down, A'isha wondered how she managed to bend herself so gracefully. A'isha shivered because of the air conditioning; she had put an extra wrapper over her shoulders so she wouldn't shudder. Tani, though, seemed to thrive in the chill.

The alhaji took some pounded yam and dipped it in the stew. He saw her watching him.

Eat, he commanded, not unkindly.

She followed his example, but how would she get through the lake of groundnut stew before her? But, oh, it tasted spicy and hot. It was wonderful. She ate more.

Both of them, the alhaji and his wife, had put themselves in danger by inviting her into their home. It had probably taken some doing, since A'isha was under her uncle's protection until the appeal, and then –

There is someone who wants to talk to you, A'isha, said Alhaji Hassan. He is with the BBC, the World Service. He held up a hand, though A'isha had not spoken. I know you'll wonder why I think you should speak to a reporter, given that things are still chaotic in Kaduna and Minna, particularly.

Tani made a little sound of protest.

I think that if the international community knew about your circumstance, Hassan continued, more could be achieved for your benefit. They do not know. They accuse Sophie MacNeil of every sort of offense, but my own feeling is that she was trying her best for you, trying to do the right thing.

A'isha had trouble comprehending most of what he said, even though he spoke in Hausa, but she understood the last part about Sophie MacNeil. She scooped the stew with more pounded yam, intent on her food now. She tried not to devour it.

His name is Fabian Beck, said Hassan. He'll be here tomorrow afternoon. And don't worry; I will be with you.

A'ISHA FELT SHE HAD SEEN Fabian Beck somewhere before, but she hadn't encountered many white men. Didn't they all look the same? She decided that they were odd, especially their noses, and their eyes, which frightened her: Fabian Beck's eyes seemed to flare, the bluest part of a flame, deep under his brows, and there was the smell of him, too, entirely different from any other smell, maybe because of his pale skin. She tried not to look at him when he asked her a question.

Hassan told me that a date has been set for an appeal for you, A'isha, he began. This is good news.

Fabian Beck seemed to be asking a question without asking a question.

She looked at Alhaji Hassan, who waited for her to speak. Yes, she said.

Has it been difficult for you? asked Fabian.

Yes, said A'isha. I had to leave my mother.

The riots – began Fabian.

She does not know much about the fighting, explained Hassan.

People died, I know, said A'isha. She could hear Safiya beginning to waken in the guest room, the soft grizzling, and knew that soon the cries would be full blown. I must go, she said, with a dip of her head to Fabian.

In the guest room, as she sat on the edge of the bed with Safiya tugging at her breast, A'isha wished she did not have to go back to sit with the men. She had never sat together with two men before without other women being present. But when Safiya had finished suckling, A'isha returned, carrying her.

This is your child? said Fabian.

Yes, this is Safiya.

He surprised A'isha by leaning over and tickling Safiya's foot. It seemed altogether strange and unwelcome, as if he had tried to touch A'isha's body. She sat, her eyes on Fabian's sandals, which he had not taken off at the door, aware of the skin of his feet and ankles and toes, especially his toes, pink and curled. She shifted her gaze to Safiya.

The father of the child, Fabian said, has been named by you, but he himself did not acknowledge to the authorities that Safiya was his child?

No, said A'isha. She felt a sudden heat in her chest.

So it will continue to be a case of your word against his word, said Fabian.

You are right, this remains a problem, interrupted Alhaji Hassan. But there were several aspects about the trial that can be contested.

People were shouting some distance away.

I have asked a lawyer based in Lagos to help with the appeal, he continued. Her name is Farih.

The shouting swelled and receded and swelled. A'isha stood up, dropping the thin cloth that had been around her shoulders, so it made a puddled shape of deep red and dark blue on the rug. Salima ran into the room.

Father, she cried. People are coming! Where shall I go with the children?

A'isha pressed Safiya close to her. She went to the guest room, where she hardly knew what to do with herself, with Safiya. Sit in the corner? Lock herself in the bathroom? Between the flowered curtain and the screen of the window, she saw men arriving with machetes, a length of broken pipe, a spade. They were calling her name, chanting it.

A – isha Na – sir, A – isha Na – sir.

It would end as it had so many months before, when they had dragged her off to the police station.

Alhaji Hassan had gone out of the house. He spoke in a calm, reassuring voice. What do you want?

We have come for A'isha Nasir, said one. The whore. And we have heard that a spy has come.

A whore and a spy! At my house, said Hassan. You are mistaken.

The men roared. They cried out her name in parts, breaking it. A – isha Na – sir.

You are holding spies in your house. You are keeping a whore in your house!

I am doing nothing of the kind.

They were getting the better of him, A'isha could tell. Soon they would strike him down; they might beat him to death.

She wondered where Tani and Salima were hiding with the children.

You are not thinking of what this will cost your families, cried Hassan. All of you, before you do violence, you must think of them. How will they survive when you are packed off to jail?

A – isha Na – sir.

She should go out there, get it over with. Maybe if she went, they would spare Alhaji Hassan and his family. She swaddled Safiya tightly, put her on the floor under the bed to hide her, and went swiftly out of the room without looking back. When she reached the door of the house and tried to open it, Fabian Beck put his hand on hers to stop her; a pale hand on her own dark one, sharp white stones of his knuckles.

No.

But I am the one, she said.

She let go of the door abruptly and so did he. It was her trick to get him to release her, and, once free of him, she opened the door. Something streaked past her – little Rasheed. She could not yank him back, because he'd gone straight for his grandfather outside.

Fabian closed the door and hauled A'isha away. They'll kill you. He kept pulling until she sank down behind the white leather couch.

They could hear the high, sweet sound of Rasheed's voice.

Grandfather, what are they doing?

Go inside, Rasheed, came Hassan's voice. Go.

No, I want to see! There is my friend, Hirsi. Hirsi! You're here.

A laugh from someone.

Ha – he is crawling up your leg, Hirsi! Watch yourself.

Rasheed, cried Hassan.

I am in the arms of my friend, Hirsi! I can't come, sang Rasheed. He giggled. It was the sound of bubbles.

There was a roar from the crowd, but not the same as before.

He will turn me upside down, Grandfather. You see how he does it? Do it, Hirsi! Please turn me upside down!

Wild squealing of a boy's laughter. A ripple, then a bright burst from the crowd as people laughed.

Rasheed. We have business here.

No, Hirsi, cried Rasheed. Please, again! I like being upside down!

Another roar.

Rasheed, Rasheed. It was Hassan. Come, my boy.

I am with Hirsi now. He will take me to his house and feed me goat meat.

The crowd whooped and hooted. Goat meat, someone cried. Hirsi, give us all goat meat!

When they quieted, Hassan said, Go now, to your homes. There is no need of trouble. Go to your wives and children. You are good men.

I am a good man, yelled Rasheed. I am a good man too.

Rasheed, you are wild, said Hassan. Come to me now. Thank you, Hirsi.

But I am a good man, Grandfather, said Rasheed. Aren't I?

Your soul is good, Rasheed, said Hassan, as they entered the house. Let me look to see – Yes, they are going.

A'isha rose out of the shadows behind the leather couch, wanting to disappear through the floor into the ground below.

A'isha, said Hassan. You must not think –

Does that mean I am good, Grandfather?

Fabian Beck plunked himself down on the couch, taking

a small notebook from his shirt pocket and scratching in it rapidly with a pen.

Oh, Rasheed, Salima cried, one hand on her chest. Anything could have happened to you.

Hassan put up his hand to stop Salima. He got down and put his hands on either side of Rasheed's face. You are good, Rasheed.

Then I am the same as my soul? Rasheed persisted.

Yes, the same as your soul.

But where is it? My soul?

Hassan picked him up.

A'ISHA LAY IN BED BREATHING, listening to a distant motorcycle. She'd been awake for hours; she needed her heart to grow quiet, but it would not, so she breathed in and out, in and out, trying not to think of what could have happened to Alhaji Hassan, to Rasheed. What could have happened to her, if Fabian Beck had not gripped her hand and pulled her away.

The far-off motorcycle came closer, closer, and light swept A'isha's room before it vanished, and the sound cut off abruptly. The motorcyclist banged the door of his house as he went inside, a man who had stayed out late. She couldn't stay out late; she couldn't escape. She could go nowhere. She had to be still. She had to do nothing and be still.

Over and over, Alhaji Hassan's words to Rasheed came to her. The way he bent down, kindly, and took Rasheed's small face in his hands. Rasheed had a soul. Why didn't A'isha feel her soul inside her? Why didn't it help her?

It was one thing to think of the goodness of souls, their sweet purity, which she knew was true of a small being like Safiya, next to her. But it couldn't be true of A'isha. Could it?

If she had a soul, she would like it to accompany her, a bird that could be inside her or outside her. A bird that she could look at sometimes, a wood dove maybe, a bird she could look at when it left her, when it returned, one that she could think about whenever she liked.

My head.

My body.

18

AROUND DAWN THE PHONE RANG. Sophie couldn't find it at first because it had slipped down between the cushions of the couch where she'd fallen asleep. It was Felix, finally, it was Felix. No, it was Simon.

Soph, I need you to come – he said.

What's wrong?

– to Minna. There's been –

Sophie couldn't make out what Simon was saying because dirt was being shovelled over what he was saying.

What is it? She was sharply awake. What happened? Where's Felix?

He's – all right, it's just –

His voice was wobbly, but she needed him to speak clearly. Simon, she said.

My brother is coming to get you. His car is a Toyota, a silver one. His name is Franklin.

Who? Franklin? she repeated, trying to figure it out. Simon, tell me about Felix.

He lost a lot of blood. He's hurt. They hurt him. Simon's voice went up and down. But he's alive, he's talking.

I'll come, she said. I'll wait for your brother. Franklin.

He'll call you on this same mobile – the one I gave you. He's going to come for you with Aurora.

Through the French doors came a spill of clear, early morning light. The world was still cool, still unmade. Sophie stared at the elongated shadows of the furniture on the floor. She was clear, almost steely. Franklin knows how to find you in Minna?

Yes.

We'll be there as soon as we can, she said.

SHE MET AURORA in the foyer, tears sliding down Aurora's face, and together they went to where Franklin had parked the car.

I shouldn't have let him go, said Aurora. I *did* say that it wasn't a good idea, you heard me say that, didn't you, Sophie, but if there's something really wrong – Did he say whether he was all right? Simon? – and Felix, I feel terrible – for him – for Felix. But I don't know if I've ever – you, how are you? – you seem so calm.

Franklin was a larger, squarer version of Simon. He opened the passenger door for Aurora, the back door for Sophie, impatient to be off, because it would take so long to get out of Lagos. Sophie noticed how the traffic stopped, started, stalled, how on every side there were cars and motorbikes worming between other cars and motorbikes and lorries, and people threading across the lanes of vehicles with basins and boxes on their heads, someone selling candies in silver wrappers who knocked on the window; she took all of this in, but it was distant, remote. Felix had lost a lot of blood. Simon called, not Felix. Sophie might have seemed composed to Aurora, she might have seemed calm, but her hands moved together, apart, together. Yet Simon was the one who was crying, not Sophie.

Ahead of them, a man was seated rigidly on a bicycle, his shirt crisply white, as he slipped between a tanker truck and a yellow minivan. The cars lurched ahead. Left on Bajulaye Road, then the Iyana Igbobi bus stop, and a right turn onto Isaac John Road. Light slathered Sophie's eyes as Franklin steered around a woman in a gorgeous turquoise dress. Felix could die before they got there. One hawker, chasing a car, dropped his plastic basket of drinks, which were crushed under a taxi. He picked up a few bottles as the driver honked at him to get out of the way. The man surfaced, screeching, his mouth turned into a wide O.

What had happened to Felix? Did he have a head injury? Would he be able to walk or had they attacked him from behind, mutilating his spine? The traffic slid one way, then the other, with cars melting into one lane, back to the next, and the hawker with the anguished face was left behind. They negotiated Oyebanjo Street and Latude Labinjo Avenue, passing the church before merging into the flow of cars onto the ramp for the highway. Ikeja, where Felix's mother lived, was close by. She'd laughed with him about her trip to Los Angeles. The back of Sophie's neck felt frigid, as if someone had put ice cubes there. Hello, it's Sophie, she might have to say. I'm calling about Felix. All that she felt for him drifted behind her out the window, a pale flutter trailing from the car as they sped along the highway. Oh, Felix, Felix, Felix.

They went north, through Ibadan, Ilorin, and then Bida, before arriving in Minna. It took hours, most of the day, before they arrived at the hospital. They got out, Franklin locked the car, and Sophie and Franklin followed Aurora's gold sandals, *takk takk*, across the asphalt to the entrance. The parking area was being resurfaced, but only a portion of it had been completed, and the road roller stood to one side. A driveway passed under an arch with the barely visible name of Blessed Saint Margaret Hospital with Blessed Saint Margaret crossed out. It was terrible to walk under the arch. The driveway became a gravel track that circled a garden where a tangle of overgrown roses grew, and a dust-covered sign over the entrance read Minna-Bida Specialist Hsptl. It was as if, up to this point, the day had been scratches on a surface, but now they'd arrived, now they'd have to face it.

Simon met them, and Aurora embraced him. He greeted Franklin, and put his hands around Sophie's, but one of his hands had been bandaged so it was a white paw.

He's sleeping, said Simon. But he was asking about you.

Felix lay on a cot with tubes going into him, immobilized, in a ward with six beds, with a person, or what might have been a heap resembling a person, lying in much the same way on each one. A sheet had been folded across Felix's midsection, and there was a bandage on his chest, with a tube snaking under his skin. His arm was held up and bound to the side rail of the bed. The other hand was not leashed to the rail.

Ahh-uhh, said Aurora.

They went closer. Felix's head had been bandaged with gauze, but rusty reddish brown showed through the white. A thin, livid gash knifed across the bridge of his nose, but this was the least of it. On a pole hung a clear bag of fluids and a bag of blood – dark, burgundy, shaped like a lunch sack – with tubes feeding into Felix's body. A machine was beeping.

Franklin and Simon were talking behind Sophie. She wished they wouldn't talk; she couldn't concentrate. A *beep,* and her mind went soft grey as if with obscured with fog, another *beep.*

Felix, said Aurora, leaning close.

Simon stood beside Sophie now, and spoke quietly to her. It happened so fast. It was in the market. The main market. I lost sight of him and the next thing I knew he was –

Beep.

Sophie was trying to figure it out. It was Felix. He was a bundle on a bed. His eyes were closed; he was in another realm. She could see there were other injuries. His legs stuck out of the sheet that covered his midsection and had been propped up on pillows. The machine beeped and beeped.

A nurse came in.

Is he doing all right? Aurora asked her. Will he be all right?

He was brought in before I began my shift.

There are machete wounds –

The doctor is coming, said the nurse, when she was finished. She went on quickly to the next bed. Everyone in the ward was a trauma patient; the place was filled with an overflow of suffering.

Sophie brushed past Simon, past Franklin, scanning his mobile, and went out into the hall to get her bearings. The dividing line between the white and grey paint of the wall skewed up and down drunkenly. She breathed in and out to steady herself, a hand on her chest, but the florescent light was too bright. The floor was not clean. How tired she was. Bits of a psalm, a framed psalm on the wall in her grandmother's kitchen, came to her. Lest thou dash thy foot against a stone. It was not clean. There was a great roar from the generator that powered the hospital and it made the wall vibrate against her back. Because he hath set his love upon me, therefore – Felix looked like a person who had been tossed up on a beach, a half sheet across his waist. She walked down the hall, one hand up to the white-grey wall so she could lean on it if needed.

Then she was beside Felix's bed again.

Felix, she said, or at least she thought she said it. She didn't know where to put her hand on him, or whether she should even put her hand on him. His shoulder. She touched him. It was Felix, whom she loved. The largeness of it was too much, and she couldn't keep it inside her body. It went out of her in heaving breaths, and she let it go, trying not to make noise, only the smallest of garbled sounds.

Felix's mother came with his sister Serena. Both of them looked weary. Serena didn't speak to Sophie, except to greet her, but Grace held Sophie's hand loosely in her own. She put her hand on Felix's chest. She bowed her head; she wept.

Sophie sat on the floor with her back against the wall, her knees drawn up and her head propped on her folded arms. Simon and Franklin went out to get something to eat and Aurora offered some fried puffs to Sophie, who drank a can of orange soda instead. Sophie was thinking of how one thing had followed another. How she'd wanted to hit Musa, send him sprawling, but had saved her anger for her article, the very article Felix had warned her about, the one he'd helped her with, and the same anger had fanned out into the world. It was her doing. Sophie's doing. She got up and left the ward to find a toilet, a stinking latrine with balled-up pink toilet paper and shit in the floor drain. It should have been clean. The stench filled her nostrils, made her vomit into the blocked floor drain, a thin yellow stream from the orange soda. She retched again and again.

IN THE MORNING, Sophie left Felix's side, left the ward, and walked down the hall with her hand held up to her forehead to shield her eyes from the light. She was cloudy, thirsty. She wasn't hungry. It was Felix's newly arrived brother who stopped her before she went outside to get cold drinks from the vendor. He said his name was Clifford.

Sophie was about to introduce herself, but he said, You are Sophie MacNeil.

Yes.

You wrote the article, the one in *The Daily Leader.* I read that.

He would say that Felix was fighting for his life because of her. She waited, reminded of the indistinct figures on the television carrying posters. Go Home American Whore. The effigy in the shape of a woman, a white cut-out with a bull's eye painted in red.

He said, I'm sorry for you.

She tried to think of words to answer him.

How this thing got started, he said. It wasn't because of you. Anyway, it's turned into something else. It's Christians against Muslims, Muslims against Christians, always the same battle.

She must have said something to get away from him, to go out into the explosion of light at the hospital entrance. She had slept on the floor near Felix's bed after Simon got her a sleeping mat. He and Aurora and Franklin had gone somewhere, saying they would come back in the morning. It was morning now. She was confused about morning, confused about night. A boy was selling sunglasses listlessly, a child wandered with her tray of groundnuts, a man in hospital whites fanned himself in the shade. No one should pity her. It was Felix they should pity. She felt feverish, but it was only because of the tarry heat and the smell of the newly poured asphalt being rolled in the parking lot. Between the scorch of sun and the shade of the entryway, there was a line.

The thing working its way up from deep inside came to her now. Her mother. It was her mother she'd forgotten because of Felix, and now she remembered that the last time she called her mother was in Simon's condo in Lagos.

One of the taxi drivers got out of his vehicle and beckoned to her.

Madam, he called. Come now.

She turned away and bought a cold lemonade, drinking half of it without stopping, so it filled her insides with sweet coolness, and took out the phone that didn't belong to her, Simon's mobile, and called her Aunt Monica.

Sophie, said Monica. I left voice mails for you. You're still in Lagos?

No, I'm not there, I'm – Have you heard anything about Mom?

Ah-uh, cried Monica. It's been over forty-eight hours, but no word from your uncle, your mother. I am worrying. They were in Onitsha – yes, I told you this, I said to you that Thomas called me. You remember? I thought they would stay the night in a hotel, at the Hilton, that's where Thomas has stayed before, but I don't know, I simply do not know. I have been up in the night, walking the hall. My heart-*ooo*.

Sophie tried to absorb what Aunt Monica was saying. She said words like Onitsha, Hilton. Her mother couldn't be found. Uncle Thomas. Her voice went on without pause.

Sophie heard herself say, You've called the police?

The police – *uuh!* – they will do nothing.

Sophie watched a family emerge from a taxi. A woman helping an older woman, two girls, and finally a man who began bickering over the fare with the driver.

You will be all right by yourself? said Aunt Monica.

I'm at a hospital in Minna. It's my – my boyfriend. He's here. Is he all right?

Sophie's hand was clutching the can of lemonade. She looked at it. She was expected to say something.

Take care of yourself, Sophie, said Monica, finally. Perhaps she had worn herself out with talking. This is the mobile you'll be using?

Yes, said Sophie.

I will call if I hear anything.

Sophie sat on the hospital steps against a pillar. Nothing could be put right. She leaned against the pillar with her eyes closed.

What is it? said her mother. Tell me.

I'm so scared, said Sophie.

Everyone has moments like that.

Sophie reached out and twisted off a few dead leaves on the geranium in the pot on top of the old pine trunk, fingered them, held them to her nose. Home. Above her head, through the window, a swim of gold green, pale green, dark green, the birds of late summer flicking to the feeder, flicking away.

Her mother put a hand on Sophie's shoulder.

It wasn't her mother's hand, it was Aurora's.

Sophie stood up and went back into the dim hallway, walking slowly with Aurora, Simon, and Franklin, the sunlight still roaring in her ears.

Sophie sat with Grace and Serena by Felix's bed. Aurora and Simon came and went; Franklin was out in the hall. There was someone else – who was it? Felix's brother, yes, that was it. Sophie noticed urine in a pan under the bed on the curled plastic of the flooring. A fly whirled, buzzed, batted itself against the screen of the window. It wasn't clean, this place.

Felix's brother, Clifford. There were others in the ward, some slumped in the beds, which were like cots, and family members near them. One woman came and went, wrapping and rewrapping her skirt, orange and brown. *Neaaaaah*, groaned a man in another bed. His wife put her hand on his arm.

She gazed at Felix, at the length of him, too long for the bed. His eyes were half closed but he didn't seem to be sleeping. Grace bent over him, hands clasped. Her head almost touched his body. There was no fan in the room, which was stifling, and there was only the frantic sound of the fly that couldn't get out. The smell of food that family members had brought in enamel dishes. Rice and beans. Felix opened his eyes.

Sophie leaned over. Felix?

He turned his head.

How are you?

There's pain here. He put his hand on his chest and fingered the edge of the bandage. Like a weight pressing down. I don't feel right – I feel like I have the flu.

Pain all over?

He shook his head. My chest.

Grace touched his forehead. You're a little feverish.

Serena said, That bandage needs to be changed.

It was Serena who got the nurse.

He hasn't been urinating, Serena said to the nurse as she changed the bandage. Not enough, anyway. She put her hand on the nurse's arm. Could we get a new saline drip for him? She squeezed the empty bag hanging from the IV pole.

I will bring it, said the nurse.

He needs attention, said Serena when the nurse had gone.

Sophie heard Serena, but she was fixed on Felix. She was on the side of the bed next to his hand that was fastened to the side rail. She touched his fingers. She shut her eyes, still feeling his fingers. His thumb, his index finger. Blue, green, red, yellow. She could see the blooms of colour against her closed eyelids as she listened to his breathing. His sleep was not a calm sleep. The hospital wasn't clean, the nurses were overworked, and where were the doctors? Serena was saying that he should be moved to another hospital, but the thought drifted away from Sophie. It was too humid, too hot. The paramedic was shocking her father again. Second time. If they tried to shock him three times – three times was usually the limit. After that, she didn't know what could be done. This was the time in between. Sophie was in the time between. She was moving along MacKenzie Mountain, the tabletop of the highlands. They were going to Cheticamp and she was driving her grandmother. They were behind the ambulance that carried her mother, her stricken father. It was just a little clinic, not the hospital at Sydney, but Sydney was on the other side of Cape Breton. There was no siren, Sophie realized. No siren. If there was no siren, there was no emergency, and if there was no emergency there was no one who needed help. Wetness on her cheeks. She tasted salt. Jewels came and went in front of her eyes.

She could see the winding loop of the road as it travelled down French Mountain, behind the ambulance that followed a lumbering trailer, and a motorcycle, and a small blue truck all making a slow descent. Beyond the great hill to the west was a gleaming pan on which beads jumped and sparkled and dropped and jumped, in grey and silver and silver white and white gold. It was the ocean with the morning sun on it, but for Sophie the world had split open and something shone through it that she'd never seen before. Was it time that shone through?

Her father must be dead. She tried to keep her eyes on the road, on the ambulance that carried her father through the skittering light.

Soph, said Felix.

Sophie returned from the dazzled ocean. I'm here, she said. Right here.

Felix, said Grace. What is it?

It doesn't smell right.

What doesn't smell right?

He didn't answer.

You just had a bad dream, Felix, said Serena.

No, it's not – something's not right –

He slipped back into himself. He opened his eyes when Serena spoke to him.

Soph, he whispered.

She took his hand. Yes.

He's worse, said Serena. He's getting worse.

Ahhh, breathed Sophie. What can we do?

But Serena didn't say or didn't hear. Sophie wasn't part of it. Serena got up and talked to Simon and Aurora and Clifford in the hall. Grace went after her. They conferred: Serena, Grace, Clifford, Simon, Aurora. They spoke in Yoruba; they switched to English. They came back to Felix's bed.

He's got to be moved, said Serena.

Abuja, said Simon.

Not Lagos? asked Grace.

I know a very good hospital in Abuja, said Simon.

Grace and Serena spoke in Yoruba, arguing back and forth without appearing to come to a resolution.

You can see for yourselves, said Sophie, and they broke off. Perhaps they'd forgotten her. We have to do something.

19

AT THE MAIN MARKET IN MINNA, Clare and Binta got out of the car, struck by the quiet, the calm, broken only by the snuffling of a goat with a knotted cord around its neck. An overturned wheelbarrow, a blue bucket, a yellow one. The smell of burning rubber.

Above, tatters of cloud. Heat was a stick, earth a drum.

Where were the women? Where were the women talking to each other, without looking around as they walked? They should have been walking two abreast, or three abreast, a long, meandering river of women flowing out of the market, carrying calabashes of beans, of yams, of cassavas, calabashes all much less full than when they had arrived in the morning. Green-skinned oranges and plump mangoes and papayas and peppers and tomatoes and onions.

Clare said, We should leave.

I can't, said Binta. I must find my auntie.

But it wasn't right: there was a mechanic's shop, but no mechanic. A tire iron had been thrown on the ground together with a tire. Someone had been prying a tire off the hub of a car, and there was the hubcap, as if it had rolled away and no one cared. Above the mechanic's shop was a tree with its pods hanging brown and dry, some on the roofs of the stalls, some on the ground.

I'll go with you, said Clare.

Binta grabbed Clare's wrist.

Just beyond the shop, two bodies lay sprawled on the ground. A stove on its side, fried bean cakes, a red sandal, and not far away, a taxi, burning.

It's not wise to go on, whispered Clare. It isn't safe.

Wait for me, said Binta. Wait.

No, Binta.

But Binta couldn't be called back. She vanished.

Clare went back and took refuge in the mechanic's shop, where she sank into a chair. From this vantage point, she could see the Mercedes, the dust that covered it – Thomas's car, untouched, without a mark on it. She couldn't see the two bodies, but there was a boot, fallen, and because of it she got up from her chair and inspected the heel coming away from the sole. She went around the mechanic's shop to the place where Binta had left her and leaned against the wall with her eyes closed. Then she forced herself to look. Yes, there they were, the two of them. One must have been the mechanic, legs outstretched, stopped in the act of running across the ground to an old market woman, her fingers not quite touching a small, upended kerosene stove just out of reach.

The smell, the sweetish smell of fried bean cakes, pooled oil. She gazed at the small glass case in which vendors put their food after it was cooked. The case lay on its side, with the door open, and the bean cakes were scattered across the ground.

Clare's arms and legs were jelly, her breath raggedy.

They were asleep, one fallen here and another there.

A rack of mirrors toppled at that moment, and she jumped. The mirrors fell into the dirt, bright faces up, bright faces down. A person would have to step over the hundreds of mirrors, step over the mops, step over headscarves spread like injured birds.

Belongings were strewn this way and that. An old straw basket, smoked rounds of blackened fish, tossed. White beans that could have been marbles poured out. Green-skinned oranges, a calabash. A piece of corrugated tin, part of a roof beside an overturned table, slabs of freshly cut meat curled over, covered with sand and flies. Nearby, a young brown goat, the one she'd seen before with the cord around its neck, searched for smoked fish; soon it would come upon the slabs of meat.

The mechanic's boot. The other boot was still on his foot.

Clare felt she had been slicked with hot butter. She put a hand up to her forehead, because something was swinging against her skull, something hard and slow. She couldn't refuse to see.

CLARE FELT FOR A PULSE in the woman's neck. She tried a wrist, tried the neck again, but her hands were not working the way they were supposed to. Anyway, there would be no pulse. Why was she hunting for one? The woman's headscarf had come off, her hair, cropped short, was sparse and greying. A gold earring was hooked in her ear; the back of the earring, with its loop of wire, showed in the velvet of the lobe, and it was this, the woman's earlobe, so intimate and hidden and vulnerable, that made Clare sit back on her heels.

When she got up, she saw another body further away, and a young woman, or a girl, legs spread, a rumpled length of cloth beside her, blue flowers on yellow cloth. It could have been Binta. Clare knew, just as she had known about the woman with the fried cakes, that this one, too, was dead, but because it could have been Binta, she went to check. It wasn't Binta; it was a girl of about eighteen or nineteen, with a smooth, childish face, with eyebrows that were lovely arches. Her dark eyes were open. Around her neck was a cheap necklace. Someone had hacked at her chest, and it was slashed with dark red, and the blood itself formed a pool underneath her body.

Clare reached out her hand, paused, and nearly touched the girl's eyelids, but she could not close them, could not make herself.

She was dizzy when she stood up; she turned, startling the goat, which made it scuttle away, wailing its dismal *Baaaaa*. A pretty girl, eighteen or nineteen. Clare raised her eyes above the lopsided roofs of the stalls because she couldn't look at what lay in front of her. It was the tag end of day, but grey-blue smoke marred the softness, the baby's blanket of evening. Nothing moved except the goat, fish bones crunching in its mouth.

She went forward into the market, stepping carefully, slowly.

Someone was moaning in a seamstress's shop. A woman, rocking back and forth under a table on which several black sewing machines stood. Coloured zippers on a stand. Hundreds of buttons in jars.

Madam, said Clare.

The woman's leg was cut, sliced through on the shin, but she made no attempt to stop the bleeding, as if she didn't know anything was the matter. Clare went to her, lifted the woman's leg in her hands, but still she moaned. Taking some material from the table, Clare ripped it into lengths, and bound the leg; she had nothing to disinfect it, but maybe the flow of blood would stop.

I'm a nurse, she said, taking the woman's hand. It shouldn't bleed so much now, she added.

The woman didn't see her. Kanya, she moaned.

Who is Kanya? asked Clare.

Kanya.

Your daughter?

THE WORDS SHE'D READ in the newspaper when she'd been only half-awake looking down at the river. Street fighting remains fierce in Minna, Kaduna, Zaria. Sectarian violence.

Street fighting.

CLARE LEFT THE WOMAN.

When she was a little girl, she had been angry with Thomas. He'd taken her doll, the one her parents had brought back from Edinburgh. They'd gone to see a specialist, but the specialist couldn't have been very special, because afterwards, back at home in Nigeria, Clare and Thomas's mother took to her bed.

The doll's hair was golden and hung in curls, pinned back with two small blue ribbons. She had lace petticoats, something Clare had never heard of before: petticoats turned out to be long white cotton trousers edged with lace, which is what people wore in Scotland because they were always cold. Underneath, her doll body was pink and shiny, and that, too, was because she was like the people who hadn't been warmed up by the sun. People in Scotland looked like this.

Over the doll's white lace-trimmed trousers was her plaid skirt, with lace collar and puffed sleeves, her green velvet bodice, and her plaid shawl, fastened by an imitation silver brooch with the design of a Scottish thistle. She had silky white socks and black patent-leather shoes, each buttoned with a pearl. Her parents had brought her from Scotland in a blue cardboard box; she had rested in white tissue paper that rustled when Clare had opened it. She lifted the doll out and fell in love with her. Her name was Elsbeth, because that was a perfect name. Each night, before Clare went to sleep, she kissed Elsbeth on her curved lips. She knew Elsbeth would be homesick in Nigeria until she got used to it.

Thomas had not received a doll. He had received a new suit. After a week of watching Clare, he took Elsbeth and strung her up by one leg to the tree in the garden. It was awful, seeing Elsbeth's skirt fallen over her face, her lace trousers showing, her shoes missing. Hanging from the tree. She found Thomas, slapped him. He ran away to tell on her, and even before Clare could get Elsbeth down from the tree, she was called inside.

Clare held her right hand, the slapping hand, inside her left hand when she was called in to see her mother, who lay with her head nestled into several pillows. Her face was sallow, an unhealthy white, and it seemed that her eyes were glossy.

Clare, said her mother.

Thomas shouldn't have done it, said Clare.

But two wrongs don't make a right, do they? The eyes of the mother of someone else bored into Clare.

Clare lowered her head so as not to look.

He's younger than you are, but you slapped him, someone younger and weaker.

He's not weaker. He's adopted.

We love him as we love you. And you are the oldest. Remember that. You should never hit someone, anyone, no matter what the circumstances.

Circumstances, thought Clare. She knew that word. Circumvention was another one she knew. She could set one word against another; she could circumvent her brother.

I want you both to take care of each other.

Clare kept her head lowered.

Clare.

Yes.

I'm tired now, so you'll have to go. But you are my strong and beautiful daughter. And I love you. Now, you must go and say you are sorry to Thomas. I shouldn't have to tell you to do this. Do you understand?

Clare went outside and sat in the full glare of sunlight, wishing with all her wishing strength that she had a sister instead of a brother.

THOMAS, Thomas, Thomas.

IN THE RUINED MARKET, pieces of corrugated tin had fallen where the stalls were trashed, cars had been torched, and a few of them, like the taxi, still burned, yet the quiet was unearthly, a silence only to be found at the end of things. Clare had come to the edge of the market and there was no sign of Binta, only a fence, sagging, and a road, and beyond it, a church, in which the windows on either side of the entrance were smashed, so that glass teeth hung down from the broken frames. And as before, that insistent, pervasive smell of burning rubber.

There was no traffic, though in the blue distance, blue from the smoke, with its strange chemical smell, she could see a few policemen getting out of a lorry. She went across the road, stood beneath a bleached Christ on a white cross, placed on the overhang above the entrance. Someone must have climbed up and hacked at the statue's feet, so they were partly gone, but otherwise it was intact. The sculptor had raised the figure's arms off the cross, instead of keeping them fixed against it, and its arms appeared to embrace air, even now.

The lower part of the church, painted a dirty pink, was covered with a scrawl of letters, signs, cartoon faces. The doors had been battered, but they were solid wooden doors, and they still hung resolutely in place, ajar, opening to the tumble of chairs inside. Clare was drawn to it, even though she imagined finding Binta there, arms outstretched like the statue.

On the threshold, she closed her eyes, waited with one hand braced against the door for the rush of blood in her head to subside. She stayed where she was; she had walked into a black cloak. Gradually, the blackness turned into edges of chairs, backs of chairs, legs of chairs, upside-down chairs – evidence of panic, as if people in them had all jumped up at the same time. The platform from which the choir sang had been tipped up, so it lay on a seasick tilt. The offering box had been toppled; coins poured out of it. Above, the blades of the fans turned lazily, because the electricity was on. The pulpit still stood, and so did the lectern, the altar.

Her eyes travelled from the high windows of the gallery, to the breeze blocks, to the altar and back to the banners that fell over the railing of the gallery; one of these, with large blue letters on gold cloth, had come down on one side. But some words were still visible. For I the Lord thy – She approached the chancel, went up the steps, and walked in front of the altar. There was no one here, either. The door to the sacristy was open, the light was on, and she could see fabric spread out on a cabinet. A chasuble. And by the cabinet, neatly set on the carpeted floor, stood a pair of shoes with nobody in them, black men's shoes polished to a high gloss.

She turned around and gazed out at all that lay below, a litter of white chairs, bones on the bare floor. And through the broken glass in the windows, through the open doors at the entrance, she saw that dusk had fallen. It would be night soon, but she stood where she was, without moving, and a drooping banner came loose, rod and brackets breaking away and crashing to the floor. There it lay, in a great heap of gold fabric. It galvanized her, and down the stairs she went, frantically, missing one of the steps, sandals clapping against the floor as she hurried through the door below the statue on the overhang with its arms reaching out. She could not get away quickly enough. Everyone had run away before her.

How had she gotten so far from where Binta thought she would be waiting?

Dusk slipped into evening, indigo dark, ocean dark, and the deep blue seeped across the sky. She looked wildly in both directions along the road, but there were no lights, no traffic. She ran across the road, around the sagging fence, back into the market, where the fire, from the taxi she'd seen earlier, was burning out. Her sandals crunched over glass she couldn't see.

WHAT CLARE COULD NOT TELL her mother was how it made her feel to think of the doll, hanging by one leg from the branch of the tree throughout the night with the moon coming down through the blades of the leaves that cut it into slivers. Bats climbing into her doll's dress and folding their wings.

Clare's dolls had lives that they lived mutely. Thomas would never understand, she was sure. And afterwards, after the string was cut and the doll restored to her, the image remained of the way Elsbeth had looked, legs wheeling apart clownishly, one strung up. Her dress and petticoats were dirty. And there was an oily smudge on her face that couldn't be removed. She was not as she was before. She was utterly different.

Clare was outside, on the step, trying to clean the doll's face with rubbing alcohol and a ball of cotton when Thomas came to her. She would not speak to him, would not, would not.

I'm sorry, he said, in a voice so small it hardly belonged to him.

She looked at his white T-shirt that needed a good cleaning, his big eyes. His glasses always slipped down his nose, as they did now.

She's going to die. Clare could feel the words, red hot, going out of her as she spoke them.

His mouth wobbled a bit. She wondered what it would do next, but he took a breath, stood straight.

I know that, he said. He gave her the ribbon that had fallen out of the doll's hair. He gave her the shoes with the pearl buttons. Anyway, I'm sorry.

Clare cradled the doll, and finally Thomas went away. The doll wasn't Elsbeth anymore.

CLARE WALKED INTO A PILE OF TIRES without seeing them, falling forward against them, before picking herself up, dusting off her hands. Surely she had walked past those tires earlier? Or had she? She swayed, hand on her heart. Staccato bursts. What a fool she'd been. She swiped at her face with the back of her hand.

Oh, Thomas. Where was he now? It would not do to cry. Her mother, in all the time she'd been sick, had not cried. She'd curled up in agony, she'd rocked back and forth because of the pain, but she had not cried.

A small sound, like a soft animal.

She wheeled around, but all she saw was someone's forgotten purchases from the market, a left-behind bundle, except that the bundle moved. Clare stooped and bent over it, unfolding the top layer of cloth, half-knowing what she would find. A child. Even in the dark, the child's eyes gleamed. Gold in her earlobes, just like the old woman Clare had found with her stove and glass case and cakes strewn around her: the detritus of her life. So – a girl, a surviving girl. She peeled back the cloth to find a lacy dress and beribboned socks on small feet. The tiny girl kicked, began to flail her arms. Clare picked up the bundle, could feel the child begin to tense up all over.

Shhh, she murmured.

The child worked herself up, began wailing.

No, no, hushed Clare. You'll be all right.

But the child's mouth was wide, her eyes pressed shut. She hollered.

Shhhh. Clare held her, rocking her back and forth, back and forth, as she had with her own baby girl, and went forward in the dark.

THE WOMAN SWOOPED OUT OF NOWHERE, grabbed the bundle, the child in the bundle, and raced across to the other side of the market, a crooked stick of a woman who took the child that was not Clare's to begin with, and even though Clare had not held the baby for more than a few minutes, long enough to get her to stop crying and suck on her finger, she felt bereft. She sat down on her haunches, huddled over.

Someone took her arm and helped her up. She let herself be helped, let herself lean against another human being.

Come, said Binta. She glanced around, breathless, sweating.

Binta's auntie had left the market early, at the first sign of trouble. Binta had raced through the market to her auntie's abandoned stall and kept on going, running to the slum where her auntie lived. Everyone had closed and bolted the doors.

Is she all right? asked Clare. Your auntie?

Yes. She's scared. She has a little boy. She gripped Clare's hand, pulled her along.

Clare was bewildered. But why didn't you stay with her?

I said I would come. I told my auntie you helped me.

The car was exactly where they'd left it. The goat had disappeared. But they were abandoning the mechanic and the market woman and the young girl lying in the dirt. It wasn't right.

We have to go, said Binta, firmly.

It was not the case that Clare had helped Binta. It was the other way around.

CLARE AND BINTA LAY TOGETHER on one large bed in a room at the St. Christopher Good Traveller Guesthouse on the outskirts of Minna on Abuja Road. They'd chosen it because the name was that of the saint on the medallion hanging from Jacob's key chain. The electricity was on in the guesthouse, and though the air conditioning wasn't working, the ceiling fan, which looked as though it might fall at any moment, was turning quickly above them, long wings keeping them cool. On the floor was Binta's flip phone, which she was recharging.

Binta slept, her young body stretched out on the bed. Clare thought of Sophie, the way her lip curled a little more on the left side than the right when she smiled, the dimple in one cheek.

Clare got up, went to the windows and lightly knotted each of the lengths of cotton curtains so a breeze would come through. The glass louvres of the window needed adjusting. Beyond, through the bars and the netting, she could see the full, heavy moon, the colour of a ripe mango, reddish yellow and fat and sweet. She stood still, waiting for her heart to slow down, staring at Binta's phone on the floor.

The moon rose higher, and now its light became almost bluish. It was no longer a juicy mango. Sophie had not known.

It was not Sophie's fault that her words were taken up and allowed to enflame people, Christians and Muslims both. It was not Sophie's fault, no. Unless it *was* Sophie's fault.

She picked up Binta's phone. It had recharged, though not completely. She knew the number; she'd have known it in her sleep.

A woman answered.

Monica, said Clare.

Clare, is it? Is it you?

Yes.

And Thomas, where is he? Is he there?

No, said Clare. I have your car, but he and Jacob –

Aaaaaaaiiii, wailed Monica. He is not with you! I don't know where he is or what he is doing or – I don't know. *O-o!* you must call Sophie. She has been waiting.

20

THE DRIVER CAME TO A STOP WITH A FLOURISH, screeching the emergency brake: a chicken having its neck twisted. Safiya, who had been fussing throughout the trip, calmed down as A'isha got out of the car and nearly tripped over little Talata, with her round, upturned face.

Talata, said A'isha.

A'isha could see that two of the huts had been burned. The mud walls were badly damaged, and the palm fronds used to thatch the roofs were blackened. One roof was partly intact, but the other had collapsed inside the hut.

A'isha's mother had died in the night. She might have been aware of shouts of the young thugs who had tried to burn down the whole compound several nights before. There hadn't been many of them, the driver told A'isha, but A'isha's uncle came outside with his ancient rifle, one that had been used years before in the civil war, and fired two shots, and they went off on their motorbikes, afraid to show their faces. Nafisa must have heard the crackle of fire, the shots, the raised voices, the skid of tires.

Her mother had died. And this was the reason A'isha was brought back to her uncle's compound, since her mother's burial would take place before the day was over. A'isha couldn't move from where she stood by the car, as if all that she held inside her chest was ash. Her auntie beckoned her from afar, and she willed herself to go forward, her auntie who would be sorry for her, her uncle who would be sorry, even though they were probably both relieved that Nafisa had died. No, no, that was unkind, A'isha thought.

Know your strength, her mother had said, and the light of her mother filled her. It filled her with bright, undulating waves.

Little Talata glided in front of her and one of the outraged guinea fowl flew up as Talata clapped it out of the way. Two little boys slipped by, legs and arms wheeling, one boy's shirt flying out at the back. It all swam and shifted and slithered, the main house, the kitchen hut, the low shed beyond, and even A'isha's auntie, presiding over it, wearing what seemed to be a blotch of dark green, though A'isha knew it was her very best clothing, and she wobbled into a green smear as if she were rising up when she was sitting still. When A'isha glanced down at Safiya, her face composed now in sleep, with her curled eyelashes nearly touching her smooth cheeks, it seemed she was made of silk and would slip out of her arms.

A'isha blinked. Her auntie motioned for Talata to take Safiya before she greeted A'isha. She was formal in her condolences, more formal than A'isha expected, but everyone had loved Nafisa, even A'isha's auntie, who wasn't given to sentiment, and it was her auntie who took A'isha to the car, where A'isha's cousins had begun packing clean cloths in plastic baskets. One of them, Durah, shook out a freshly laundered sheet and folded it, putting it in the back seat with everything else. The women were going to the mosque to prepare Nafisa's body, which had been taken there.

It is already late, said A'isha's auntie, motioning for her to get into the car. There is much to do.

There was no time to mourn. They went straight to the mosque: A'isha's uncle drove them, and when they collected all their belongings and got out, he turned the car in a circle and sped off. The mosque was newly built, spacious and impressive, with a glittering gold dome and four slender minarets needling the cloudy sky. A'isha moved forward with the rest of them, distracted by the red dirt, how it would cover her best shoes. A hunchbacked man in an ivory riga spoke obsequiously to A'isha's auntie, who was much broader and taller, towering over him as they negotiated over some problem; he glanced at A'isha and back at her auntie, perhaps uncomfortable about letting them in because of A'isha. Everyone knew about A'isha. Or maybe it was because there were professionals who washed the bodies of the deceased and he was saying that the family didn't have to do it. A'isha's auntie seemed to be remonstrating with him in a quiet, dignified way.

It is late, said A'isha's auntie. Let us go in.

A'isha knew she was also saying they would have to work quickly to clean and shroud the body so that the prayers could be said before the sun reached its peak at noon. The hunchbacked man showed them the way to the room where Nafisa was laid out and stood by the door as the four of them entered.

A'isha had to set her jaw partly because of the smell, but also because she dreaded what lay before her. Nafisa had been placed on a counter in the middle of the room; her eyes had been closed. It bothered A'isha that her mother lay on the counter with nothing comfortable under her, except a folded piece of material under her head. It was not her mother; it looked like her mother, though the face was made of dark leather and pleated with age. Her mother was gone. It was this clear fact of her mother's death that released the tangles in A'isha's stomach. Her mouth was dry, but she hardly noticed; she would do what she was here to do and do it swiftly.

The tap wasn't working, but there was a bucket in the sink and water stored in the two large drums outside. Jummai went out and came back with a bucket of water, which she set down gently, the handle clanking against the side of the pail. A'isha's auntie had brought the cloths, a stack of clean ones, and, when Durah unrolled a piece of cloth on the table against the wall, A'isha's auntie set them down on it, everything in order, unpacking the plastic gloves and giving a pair to each of them. All this was done wordlessly, in the muted dimness of the room. A'isha put on the gloves she'd been given, squeezing her eyes shut to stop the tears. How many times had she washed her mother's living body? That was different, because even when her mother had been very sick, her body had still been pliant. Now there was a distinct odour, despite the incense that was burning, smoking upwards in a grey, scrolled line, but A'isha was not going to breathe it; she was not going to wipe the wetness from her cheeks.

THEY GOT TO WORK. Her auntie covered herself with an apron, and her hands, encased in gloves, pressed on her mother's stomach to rid the body of its fluids. It was very warm; it didn't matter that air came through the breeze blocks at the top of the walls on both sides of the room. The blood and shit and gas from the corpse gave off that peculiar smell that A'isha had already noticed, and something else, like rotting meat and tainted eggs. Jummai put her arm up to her face, buried her nose in the crook of her elbow. A'isha and her auntie, who was breathing heavily with the effort, began the first cleansing, and Jummai and Durah joined them. Her auntie said the prayers, wheezing as she explained what she was doing – I am washing the body – so that the soul of Nafisa would understand.

The monotony of the words comforted A'isha. Even though the cloths had been wrung out, some water dribbled across the skin of Nafisa's body, over her ribs, over her swollen belly. It was not her mother, thought A'isha; it was not her mother, and yet they must tell her, must help her to understand.

I am washing the body, intoned A'isha's auntie.

A'isha did not hesitate. It was she, not her auntie, who cleaned between her mother's legs. Then Durah lifted up the legs by the ankles, and A'isha helped her, so Jummai could clean under the body. A'isha stood back from them, rocking slightly on her heels. She felt dizzy. The first cleansing was finished, and Jummai went to get fresh water, while A'isha's auntie handed out new gloves. Durah, who had brought a few sprigs of hyssop, picked off some of the leaves and dropped them in the water when Jummai brought it.

They began again, all of them this time, starting at Nafisa's head, turning the body and working their way down the right side, though the right arm was rigid and resisted any efforts to move it. A minty scent of hyssop was released as they turned the body so they could clean the left side, then each emaciated leg, and finally, the feet, one foot and then the other, with A'isha's auntie leading them.

Once again, the pail of water and the cloths and towels were taken away. A'isha felt dazed. She had been wakened in the dark hours of early morning at Alhaji Hassan's house. Now she couldn't go back to that time before waking; it was over; her mother had vanished. Jummai returned, and there was a final washing of the body, this time with a soft sponge, soap and water, until the body was entirely clean, and a new scent rose up: the smell of camphor. Durah and Jummai towelled the body and A'isha's auntie powdered and padded the underwear, which they struggled to pull on, and finally, when it was in place, they had to cover the flat pockets of Nafisa's breasts with a brassiere. Nothing could have been more difficult than dressing the body with the requisite pieces of clothing, and all the while the air was becoming thickly humid as the morning progressed, yet the camphor overpowered the smell of death.

A'isha's auntie continued chanting as they shrouded the body. The head was covered, and now Nafisa was utterly gone. A white-veiled head: egg sac of a spider. And though A'isha tried to banish the memory, there was her mother's face next to her own when she had been a child, her mother telling her the story of the spider, sent down to earth to fetch something. A'isha could hear her mother's voice, could see her pretty, almond-shaped eyes, her mother's younger face.

To fetch what? asked A'isha.

Oh, what did that spider have to fetch? said Nafisa. He didn't know. That clever spider disguised himself and went back to find out, by spying, that he was supposed to get the sun, the moon, the dark, the light. And so off he went to get them.

But he couldn't do that, A'isha said.

Yes, he could.

Her mother's fingers crawled up A'isha's body, and soon they were both laughing.

NAFISA HAD BEEN FULLY GOWNED in white. Her head was covered; her body was covered. Now A'isha's auntie led them in shrouding her; they bound the shroud with the five ties and then the body was ready for burial, snowy white, a long, wrapped package lying on the counter. They lifted it, put it into a wooden coffin. Finally, they cleaned the room and took away all the cloths and towels. It was done. They had made her mother ready, and within minutes her body would be taken into the mosque for the prayers.

Outside at the tap, A'isha washed her hands with soap along with the others, rinsed them, and took the towel Jummai handed her. Air. She breathed it in. Car exhaust, dust, a smell of rubber, but not the smell of death. She opened her palms under her nose after rubbing them with crushed bits of wilted hyssop that Durah handed her as they went back inside; her mother's clean scent was the fragrance A'isha would carry with her. Now all of them gathered with the women where they could hear the imam beginning the salat al-janazah, the prayers.

THE MEN GATHERED IN THE STREET behind those who carried the coffin. The sky was full of ragtag clouds, not the heavy reddish dust of harmattan. The dry season was upon them, though, and soon there would be sand everywhere. A'isha, her auntie, and her cousins clustered with the other women under an oleander tree where several young women fanned themselves with battery-operated fans taken from purses. A'isha could feel the air spun toward her face.

Look now, said Durah. The police – they are so many.

They are anticipating, said Jummai.

Jummai didn't say the police were anticipating trouble, and A'isha said nothing, knowing that she herself was the trouble. They all knew that she was the trouble. There had been riots in Minna and no one could say whether they had ended.

So many, murmured Durah.

It was strange not to be with Safiya for such a long time, especially now that A'isha's milk was coming down and she could do nothing about the wetness coming through her blouse except try to cover it with her hijab. A mother who couldn't do the job of mothering. She closed her eyes, swaying a little beside her auntie. A'isha dreaded being seen by people, knowing they would turn and whisper to one another, yet it must be done; all that protected her was the knowledge that she was doing it for her mother, for her mother's soul, which she thought of now. It was a clean and pure soul, far cleaner and purer than A'isha's, if indeed she had a soul. How strange it was to think of her mother's soul apart from her body.

Someone nudged her, Durah or Jummai, and she began to move forward with the others. Was it grief, the sense that she was slightly above the ground, shimmering? Why did she feel such peace, as if it were evening and she were holding Safiya, watching the patterns of leaf shadow on her daughter's face? She walked slowly, aware only of other sandals and shoes, other feet slapping gently beside her own, as the women began to walk, behind A'isha's uncle helping to bear the body, behind her other uncles and cousins, behind the men who knew the family. It was quiet outside the mosque, and policemen lined the road on either side under the trees; A'isha didn't look at them, but she knew they were there, a dark, tense presence.

And she knew they were passing the Madame Fine Chop Restaurant, with several rough tables and mismatched chairs, and the electrical supply shop, where Balarabi would be sitting, chewing in that cow-like way of his, so his entire mouth seemed to revolve. A'isha stepped aside to avoid a pothole, and it was about here that, if she glanced up, she'd see a little stall that sold bread and eggs and matches and batteries, and, beside it, the place, painted lime green, that sold mobiles in a glass cabinet, and, nearby, the bicycle shop where Musa worked. On a wall behind the shops was a hand-painted sign: No Urination.

A'isha's best shoes were thinly soled, and she could feel the press of stones underfoot. They passed a cluster of huts where someone was cooking over an open fire, and the smoke and roasting meat reminded A'isha of her hunger; near these huts was the cell tower, and close to it was Laila's sewing shop with its black sewing machines made in China, and beside that, the pump where people got water in the early morning.

They passed ancient Danladi, no more than a skeleton, who possessed only three teeth; A'isha could see the lower part of his wrapper of brown and yellow, his yellow plastic shoes, the staff against which he leaned. One of his eyes, she knew without looking, was a pale, milky blue, but he managed to see out of the other one. Because he wandered in the night, his sister used to leash him, though A'isha's auntie heard she'd given it up and now he did as he pleased.

They passed the huge banyan tree that had stood for generations on generations, a tree that was about as old as Danladi himself, Jummai said. A'isha wanted to reach out and touch it, as she often had as a child, straggling behind her mother after a long day at the market.

Goodness lives in that tree, Nafisa told her.

How do you know that? asked A'isha.

I don't, she said.

Then why did you say it?

I think because a tree like that has weathered many, many years, and it still opens its arms to the sky.

All trees do that, said A'isha, doggedly.

Her mother said nothing in reply, and A'isha thought she had won her point. But whenever she passed the tree, the question rose in her mind, and she wondered if the banyan looked kindly on her.

THE WOMAN MUST HAVE BEEN waiting at the roadside; she seemed to pounce on A'isha. She blocked her path. A'isha's eyes travelled from the woman's shoes, turned in at the arches, all the way up to her face, but she didn't recognize her.

You are nothing but a harlot, a whore, the woman said, leaning close, so A'isha could smell her breath. She spoke fast in low, harsh tones that only A'isha could hear. You're no better than that. I know you, she continued. I know what they've said. It'll be a good thing when they –

A'isha stared at the woman, stunned.

It was Danladi, of all people, who appeared at her side. Danladi with his stick. He beat the ground several times at the woman's feet, narrowly missing one of her shoes.

Go, now, he said. Old baboon.

Danladi might be ancient, but there was strength in his thin arms. And he was taller than the woman. Who had said that Danladi's mind had slipped away from his body? It had not; he was in command.

The woman flapped, or seemed to flap, sputtering.

Danladi waited, stick raised, until she shuffled to the edge of the road, and A'isha remembered only when she watched the woman's lopsided gait, her flat feet, and the way her left hip gave her trouble. It was one of her dead husband's relatives, one of those who'd claimed the house from A'isha after her husband had died. Was there no end to this business?

DURAH LINKED HER ARM in A'isha's. Come, she said.

A'isha would not stop here; no, she would not. She would go on, helped by Durah. They passed a flurry of children, one of them muttering about a ghost, an older boy scaring the younger ones, until someone shushed him. They passed more huts, and a rooster made a noisy cry, so the hens answered – *cluck cluck-cluck* – as they pecked in the dust of a compound. As they neared the cemetery, everyone stopped because of a traffic jam; they waited while the police cleared the road.

A'isha raised her head. A girl was struggling to pull a goat away from the road, a goat whose mouth was lined with white foam. A sick animal. The child tried in a panic to haul it away, tugging the creature by the hind legs, and when the goat didn't budge she tried again, ripping the pale-green dress that hung on her slender body; this time she pulled hard enough to yank the goat to the edge of the road, where it lay on its side between two cars.

There was a gaping hole at the waist of the girl's ugly dress. She looked down at it, picking at threads with her fingers, and A'isha knew she was already devising a way to fix it. But there was no fixing the goat; it would die. Someone might take it upon himself to kill it, and, as if coming to the same conclusion, the girl backed away from the animal, and stood on a narrow plank over a sewer ditch, balancing there, the skirt of her dress drooping where it had been torn. Aware that someone was watching her, she looked up, straight at A'isha, her large eyes all the larger because her face was small; it was a sweet, childish face. A'isha saw Safiya, grown into a girl.

A'isha shifted her gaze to the ground, to her good shoes, faintly scuffed and layered with red, the same red soil that had already been dug in the cemetery so her mother's body could be placed in it. Her feet ached, but she hardly registered this. Was her mother near, close enough to brush A'isha's ear? She closed her eyes, swaying. This was not the end of it. It was not the end. She was lifted, floating on rocking waves of light she'd felt earlier. A mosquito-small thought passed through her: she felt this way because she was thirsty, because she was exhausted, because she had been called a whore, because it had been difficult, preparing her mother's body, because they were standing in the road in the glare of a sun that had come out from behind the clouds.

Why did she sense joy and not sorrow? Why did a glow radiate within and without her? Her whole body was dazzled with it, tingling from the top of her head to her neck and shoulders down to her fingers, from her legs down to her toes. She felt lifted up, lifted out of the world. A'isha opened her eyes, and though she felt very tired, the glow within her didn't diminish as she stared at the velvety red dirt. She would not leave Safiya, no. She would do whatever she could for her daughter. She must live.

A policeman came over to inspect the dying goat, and the girl in the green dress, sensing trouble, vanished as if she were nothing more than a soap bubble, a bright, iridescent, wobbling thing that left no trace.

21

MONICA FELL ON THOMAS, holding him, weeping, standing back from him, weeping. Thomas-*ooooo!* she yelped, and fell on him again. But why? Why did you not tell me? And Jacob, you are here. Are you well? You are living, you are *living-o!* Come into the house, come inside now now. Yes, come. It is the middle of the night! Here is Hortensia to see you!

Jacob smiled broadly, eyes shining.

Hortensia, in her cotton shift, came sleepily down the hall, and Thomas caught her up in his arms. He kissed her and tickled her until she could not stop giggling.

You have no car, went on Monica. She was laughing and crying, crying and laughing; her hands had flown to her face. How did you come? And your clothes – whose clothes are these? You are like tramps.

You have a big hole, said Hortensia.

In my shirt, a big hole! said Thomas, sticking his hand through the hole so she laughed.

Andrew and Jonathan came running.

Oh-ho, two young tramps! said Thomas. Andrew, Jonathan! He swung them in circles so they hooted and hollered.

No car, no money, said Jacob. We footed it some part of the way. He showed Monica how one shoe had come apart. See now! He laughed.

But what happened? she said.

Thieves took us. They took our car.

Carjacking, said Jacob.

But Clare has your car. Doesn't she?

Clare is living? She is well?

Yes, she's very well, but worried about you. She is in Minna.

We must go. To Clare. We must go there.

Monica laughed, swatting the air as if to get rid of flies. Yes, we will go, but now it is not yet morning!

Thomas got down on his knees and hugged Hortensia, tousled her hair.

Daddy, said Hortensia. You're crying.

I am crying-o.

22

FELIX HAD BEEN MOVED FROM MINNA, and now he was in intensive care in the hospital in Abuja. Within one day he'd worsened; he was being given fluids and antibiotics, and nurses were checking on him frequently. There was the possibility he had sepsis. In this new hospital, everything was white and blue tiled, sparkling with light, terrifying. Dr. Osungwe had come immediately after Felix had arrived, and she'd given orders quickly. Faith, one of the nurses, took blood from Felix as Sophie, Grace, and Serena watched. Already she had two vials of burgundy-coloured blood.

When will you know if it's – if he's – said Grace.

Dr. Osungwe said, Rest assured that we will do everything we can for him.

The swift efficiency should have comforted Sophie, but she felt she was at the bottom of a pond with Felix drowning beside her. Rest assured. If it was sepsis, there was a danger of his organs failing, a danger of his body being overwhelmed by infection. Sophie sat with him, his unresponsive hand in her hand. Grace and Serena sat on the other side of the bed. Where had he gone? Sophie left to find a washroom and came back to find Grace sobbing in her daughter's arms. Serena had her arms around Grace, had tucked her mother's head against her chest. It was private; it was between them.

It should be me, said Grace.

No, said Serena soothingly. It should not be you.

But it shouldn't be Felix. Not my Felix.

Felix might not make it. They hadn't noticed Sophie at the door. He might not. When a nurse came, she took Felix's blood pressure, clucked to herself, vanished. Another nurse came in. They talked quietly, not in English, but Sophie could tell something was wrong.

What is it? asked Grace.

The doctor arrived, interrupting the nurses, not Dr. Osungwe, but a young man with square glasses. He assessed the situation, went out of the room and talked briefly on his phone, returned to Grace. We are going to induce a coma so his body can recover, he said.

A *coma*? said Grace. Shouldn't you ask Dr. Osungwe?

We have spoken just now.

But she said –

Will he be all right? asked Serena. I mean, if you induce a coma. It seems like a drastic measure.

We are taking all necessary precautions, he said soothingly.

Grace and Serena gave consent; the doctor induced a coma. Now Felix would not speak to them.

SOPHIE LAY IN DAMP LEAVES. When she finally sat up, she realized hours must have passed, and the day that had begun in warm sunshine was now grey, bitten with chill, and a wind was pulling at the tops of the trees. Felix, did she see him there? And Grace, stooped over a basin of oranges on her low stool – No, nothing but trees.

Sophie woke, rubbed her face. Grace was in the chair next to Felix, her head down, praying. They had put Felix on a ventilator and his breathing sounded gusty. Sophie shifted past the monitor to get close to his bed. The disinfectant smell. They could lose him. His organs could fail. Maybe they had already begun to fail. She wanted just the touch of him, living. She couldn't touch his nose or mouth, but she could run her hand over the fine, very fine curls on his head. If Grace hadn't been there, she would have kissed his head, she would have told him that he couldn't leave her.

When she went out of the hospital to get a breath of air, she had no idea what time of day it was. Day had become night and night had become day. They'd induced a coma, that was all she knew. There was a white sky, heat that drilled into her. She tried to get her bearings, but someone honked at her, and a hand emerged from a car window, gesturing for her to move out of the way. She felt drunk with fatigue as she began walking. There was no sidewalk, but at least the street was lined with trees. Maitama, she remembered. In Abuja. She was in Abuja. She glanced back at the hospital so she would recall it. I'm scared, Felix had said to her. She could find her way back. But she hadn't counted on the way the sun lanced her eyes.

A woman reversed out of a driveway without looking. Sophie leapt out of the way. A woman in sunglasses driving a blue Audi. Sophie didn't see the cabin. And it wasn't the right clearing, with the bench from which she could gaze into the blue-grey distance, the fringe of barrier beaches and the ocean, the Northumberland Strait, unchanged and deeply blue, with the soft blur of hills behind. They sprang into action because no heart should beat that fast. She should have been able to look to the left, to the cabin built on the slope, half-hidden by spruce, but it wasn't there. His heart could fail. She was in the middle of an unknown city with no idea why she was there. Felix explained, We're doing this for Simon. She'd been standing beside Felix on a shining floor, standing on the buckled ribbons of white and pale-green and dark-green marble.

Oyinbo. Someone on a motorbike yelled at her.

She was lost. The world darkened into deep blue and the air cooled around her, so she shivered in her damp clothes. Nothing was where it should have been. If she wasn't near the cabin, where was she? The man on the motorbike swerved around her. Her father had once told her that if she got lost, she should aim for the ridges, not the valleys. She could hear his voice saying it, as if he were beside her. Clouds moved across the sky, pulled by an unseen hand. Soft ribs of white, loosely curved. A spine of cloud. Children played behind a courtyard wall. Was it day or was it night? She was on Cross River Street. The children were laughing on the other side of a wall covered in bougainvillea, sweet waterfalls of sound. But there was no telling which direction was the right one. I'm just trouble for you, she said. Oh, Felix. A smell of damp earth, the sound of her shoes through the piles of leaves, maple leaves mottled with black spots, spider-backed leaves. The next few days will be a make-or-break time for him, Dr. Osungwe had said. His body will have to work very hard to get rid of the infection.

He wasn't out of the woods. He was deep in the woods. Sophie went on, tired now, cross with herself, a snag of pain at each step, through the brokenness of dead trees, the spoked branches overlaid with other spoked branches, climbing over and crouching under, over and under, getting scratched and weary. The cabin was nowhere to be found. If he died – Sophie wasn't going to cross Takara Street because there was too much traffic. The owl, again – what time was it? Farther along was a great old hemlock, with a massive trunk forking into two; it had been struck by lightning on one side, burnt black. Blood pressure too low, heart rate too high. A car alarm panicked and panicked and panicked somewhere. She was in Abuja, that was where she was. And here in the woods, another tree right beside the first one, which must have been hit in the same lightning strike. They could so easily lose him. She drew her hand over the surface of it, a tree like old dead bone. She needed to settle herself before walking any farther. It could take over his body, the sepsis, no matter how hard the white blood cells worked. The car alarm stopped as suddenly as it had started. She'd stay here, rest near the pair of struck, burnt trees. It was too busy; it was too hot; it smelled of exhaust.

Hello, said someone. Are you Sophie?

No, she couldn't stay here. She had to leave, and she roused herself, saw the way the clear water rounded between the stones, foaming as it spilled over a branch. A reddened leaf was caught under the flow. A padding of moss over stones on its banks. Don't be sorry, beautiful woman, said Felix. He was grinning. It was as if it had all been caught and held inside amber: the water and stones, the red leaf, the moss, the sound of the hoot owl, *whuuo-whuuo,* Felix's smile.

Is your name Sophie? A woman's voice, or a girl's.

They had put him on a ventilator. Some of the moss was feathery, different than the moss that covered the larger stones. Maybe the antibiotics were wrong. In places, the moss was emerald green and in other places it was nearly golden. Sophie shivered, shivered, she couldn't stop.

Someone touched her arm. Sophie, she said. It was a young girl.

Yes.

I am Binta, said the girl.

Who –

Your mother is here, and your auntie and uncle. They told us you went out of the hospital, said Binta.

She took Sophie's hand. Her voice was gentle, encouraging, and she kept her hand loosely linked with Sophie's. She squinted at the sky. The sun is too much.

Sophie nodded.

You will come? said Binta.

They walked, hand linked in hand, under the leafy branches of the trees in Maitama. Cross River Street, Jos Street. The shadows of the leaves puzzled the asphalt, but they walked through the dark and the light. Sophie was outside herself, inside herself. She was lost.

They were near the hospital now. Across the road, its many windows shone, glazed with bronze gold.

Your uncle and auntie will let me stay with them, said Binta.

Sophie was trembling. She couldn't make herself go across the road. Would Felix be worse than before?

They tell me I will stay with them in their house, with their children. They are kind.

Yes, said Sophie, but she was looking at the bronzed windows. She had to say yes to whatever came next. Felix would live or he would die. How many windows? They were like openings into another world. She couldn't be afraid of what came next. She had to face it, even though she knew, now, how fiercely she loved him. Someone was hammering nearby. She might have to lose him. She had to be like her mother when her father died. There was a way to walk into it, and she walked into it, holding Binta's hand in her own hand. One foot in front of the other, hammering, even though she was frightened. They went across the road.

Felix was coming through the woods. Yes, he was. She could hear his shoes in the leaves. *Whissht, whissht.* She opened her eyes to a few slaps of cold rain; she watched a fat brown spider hunkered on its web, but it might have been dead. It might have clung there through the winter. A jay cried raucously, not one cry but two. The rain stopped, her heart lurched on. Felix wasn't there. Where had he gone? But she had said yes. She had said yes.

CLARE WAS OUTSIDE THE ICU to greet Sophie. She pulled her close, held her. Uncle Thomas, Aunt Monica. Binta. Felix's sister Joanna. Now Felix's brother Clifford came through the heavy doors with Grace. There were too many people; they had to make way for an orderly. One of them said, Sophie, we didn't know where you'd gone. Someone else said Felix looked better, he was really looking better. The antibiotics were doing the trick. Sophie put her hand against the wall. Trick, she thought. She could feel herself shivering. She wanted only one thing, but there were too many people talking at the same time. Joanna said she was going to take her mother away for a little rest, and she'd bring her back later. Who was Joanna? Where was she taking Grace? Clare asked if Sophie was all right, whether she needed to sit.

I have to go and see him, said Sophie.

Yes, go to him. We'll come back for you, said her mother.

Sophie left them behind as she went through the doors, into the woods. In the shadowy gloom, she saw nothing but trees, then a strewn place, like a basket of sticks, where the fire had gone through and reduced a vertical world to a horizontal one, punctuated with one or two black spruce. Darkness lay under the deadwood, under the bayonet branches; she sensed it as the hoot owl began, and though she realized she had been hearing its call throughout the afternoon, it took on the tone of a warning now. *Whuuoo-hoo-hoo-hoo – whuoo whuoo.* It was the ventilator. Felix was on the bed, and his body was being tricked by the antibiotics. He was no different than before: no better, no worse. Or so it seemed. Serena was at his side and she glanced up.

You don't have to be here, said Serena. I'll stay with him.

Sophie put her hand on Felix's arm, as if for protection. Where was Grace – where had she gone?

A crisply attired nurse came in, and Sophie stood to get out of her way.

Checking vitals, she said, picking up Felix's wrist with the hospital band on it to read his full name.

The nurse inflated the cuff – *whuff, whuff, whuff* – and released the air slowly, a soft rush, listening to the stethoscope and observing the meter at the same time. When she was finished, she took off the cuff, and there was the ripping sound of Velcro. She went out of the room without speaking.

Sophie had the feeling that the spruce and larches wanted her gone. Feathering of panic. Serena's eyes bored into her; surely Serena could see Sophie was in a hummocky, wet spot, bordered by sedges and cattails, where her feet sank into muck. What would Felix have wanted if he'd been able to say? Felix would have wanted Sophie with him. Sophie was sure of it. Something was being trundled along the corridor – a cart or a gurney. Sophie's hands were clutched; she pressed a thumb hard into the palm of her other hand.

You're just one in a long line, said Serena, as if she were talking to herself.

What? said Sophie.

He's had a lot of women in his life. He's never settled. He was with that one who's with Simon now; Angela, I think her name is, no, Aurora. He was with her for a while, but it didn't work out. She was ringing him every minute of the day. Felix, I can't *live* without you. Serena raised her arms, let them fall.

Sophie took a breath, let it out.

I've seen it all, said Serena.

Sophie felt something turn over inside. It was all she could do to study Felix's hand, his limp hand, black against the white sheet. It was dim and chilly in this place, and there was the owl, again – *whuoo, whuooooo.* She made an effort to keep gripping her own hands together, so she wouldn't lean across the bed and give Serena a slap.

You've got some idea that you're different, Serena went on. You're a white girl. You thought you were special. Who said anyone wanted you –

Sophie was too slow; she couldn't formulate her thoughts. It was beginning to rain, and the hard, quick drops were cold enough to be sleet. There was no place to shelter from it.

Who said anyone wanted you to come here and make such a mess? snapped Serena. Did anyone want you? No.

Sophie could only keep her gaze fastened on Felix's hand.

I don't know – you people think you're saviours. But see what you've done. Look at what you've done.

Serena was crying. That sound, that whimpering sound, was Serena. Sophie raised her eyes and saw how she rocked. Serena had held everything in while Grace was with them, and as soon as Grace left, she collapsed.

Goddamn it, said Serena. You people.

The sudden rain eased, but the wind came up and a few wintry leaves rasped noisily on a branch of wild oak. If Sophie could have let her tears come, she would have, but she wasn't family; she didn't belong. She put out her fingers toward Felix's hand. *Had* she thought she was special?

Go, cried Serena. Please.

Sophie went out; she stood in the corridor with her back against the wall. She closed her eyes. There was nothing to be done, or there was nothing Sophie could do, anyway. When she opened her eyes, she saw Clifford, Felix's brother.

She wants someone to blame, Clifford said.

Sophie fixed her eyes on her feet, her sandals. If she looked at him, his deep-set eyes, she would crumple.

We'll go out, maybe get you a cold drink, he said. You have to leave Serena by herself, and then she'll realize what she's said. She's hurting. He sighed, rubbed his face. Felix, Serena – they're close. But don't believe a word of what she said.

They passed the ward clerk reading his newspaper, went outside into the stifling heat, and drove to a place that sold cold drinks and ice cream. *Dreamcake,* the pink-lettered sign announced. Clifford was too large for the doll-sized chair, and sat backwards in it, propping his arms on its wrought-iron scrollwork.

Drink up, he said.

Sophie's frosted glass was frigid to the touch.

When was the last time you slept? You'll make yourself sick, he said.

He'd said the word that made them both quiet. Sick. Sophie concentrated on Felix, and the thoughts were so loud in her head she thought she'd spoken. She watched Clifford's fingers moving on the glass tabletop and they could have been Felix's fingers. Who said anyone wanted you to come here and make such a mess? The tabletop was scratched as if someone had drawn a knife across it several times. Just another in a long line. She sipped her lemon-coloured drink, put it down on the pink cupcake coaster. It was too much of an effort lifting the glass to her lips, setting it down, picking it up again. Felix didn't love her, didn't love her, didn't love her. She had imagined it all. Felix, on his bed of ice. She was a white girl, thinking of herself as special. Serena said so. Yes, now she recognized the place, with the three sinkholes her father had told her about when she was small. Devils' wash basins, he'd called them, pointing to the sour water at the bottom.

Clifford finally drank the lemon drink because she offered it to him; he took her away. He said, I don't care what Serena said, Felix is crazy about you. They pulled into the semicircular drive at the hospital. He said, almost sternly, Don't forget that, and he left.

Sophie was afraid to go back to where Felix was, though time was slipping, time was in the slender thread of water that came out of the tap in the washroom. Time slid into the inky vortex of the drain. She left the washroom, stood outside Felix's room.

Are you family? said one of the nurses. Only family are allowed in the ICU.

Anyone could see that Sophie wasn't family. She went out the doors and along the corridor where it was less busy, though startlingly bright, and saw that dusk would fall soon, abruptly, and the windows would be blue black, reflecting her pale face, one in a long line of faces. Most of the dark water had seeped out of the sinkhole at which she gazed, the deepest, steep-sided, like a vessel, and lined with leaves darkened by winter and glazed by the quick rain that afternoon, as if a child had used glue and scraps of old paper. Sophie was so far from Felix, here in the woods. She just wanted to touch him, talk to him in the language only they knew, but she'd been kidding herself all along. He didn't love her. She was the one who'd set things in motion, and it was because of her that he was in the hospital. Serena was right, had been right all along.

Then Grace came with Joanna, and Grace pulled Sophie into her arms, into her sweet-smelling embrace. Together, the two women drew Sophie toward the ICU, but the light glared, and Sophie didn't know if she wanted to be drawn along. She would have to go into it again. She stopped, closed her eyes, listened to the gurgling creek on the near side of the sinkhole. There might be enough light to make her way back if she started now.

Grace whispered, Come. Soon they will bring him out of the coma.

Sophie shook her head.

Felix needs us, said Grace. Come.

23

FARIH, I AM GRATEFUL TO YOU FOR COMING, said Hassan.

Well, there is a great deal to go over when it comes to this appeal, she said. Time is of the essence. Do you know anyone who might help us, preferably someone who is versed in shariah law?

I will do my best to find someone.

Farih was gorgeously attired in dark blue patterned with yellow flowers, and a head wrap made of satiny material, also dark blue. Sometimes Hassan wondered if women's head wraps were made in the style of architectural wonders. The Gardens of Babylon. Would it be hard to keep such a thing on one's head? But in the case of Farih Hussaini, he could be assured that it would stay on her head, even when she laughed and her head tipped back. His wife Tani would think otherwise, of course, intimidated by such an exotic creature, but Hassan knew Farih's skills as a lawyer.

I have sent for A'isha, said Hassan.

You know that when I represented Halima – I mean, I was part of the team representing Halima – I could do nothing for her. Surely she could have been spared the pain.

But you also represented Lami Abdullah and Fayola Usman and you were successful.

Yes, true, but in this case we have not had luck on our side up to now, as you know. I expect the judge for the appeal will be another country bumpkin. Ah, you must forgive me. I am quick to anger.

Hassan smiled. There is nothing better than a lawyer who must contain her temper.

And what has made this a case for you to take up? she asked. You have worked tirelessly for A'isha.

When an injustice has been committed – Ah, she has come. He stood to acknowledge A'isha, who got out of the car and shut the door. She had not brought Safiya with her.

Alhaji, said A'isha.

A'isha, my condolences on your mother's passing, he said.

She lowered her eyes.

There is much to be discussed before the appeal, he continued. Farih has come to talk to you. I will leave the two of you, but I will return.

Farih rearranged the material over her shoulder, the same lustrous blue as her head wrap. Come and sit down, A'isha. You are well?

Yes, I am well.

A'isha, we have to go back to the beginning. I must ask you some questions, said Farih.

A'isha sat down on the edge of a chair.

These are difficult questions, warned Farih.

I will try.

In the time after your husband died, did any man want you to have sexual relations with him?

A'isha didn't answer.

A'isha, please understand that I would not ask you if it were not of the utmost importance.

No one asked me. I was taken.

You are saying that a man took you without your permission?

A'isha bowed her head.

And you told no one? Farih pressed her hands together.

I wanted Musa dead, she said fiercely.

I can imagine you did.

Afterwards, I could not bear to speak of him. I was thinking of my mother, how she would hear of my shame. Now she is gone, but there is Safiya also, and I must think of her. Shame follows from mother to daughter. And there is Musa himself. I am afraid of what he will do.

But you must speak the truth.

I do not want to speak of Musa.

A'isha, it is your life that we are trying to save. I should tell you that someone has come forward, someone you know.

Rahel, murmured A'isha.

Yes, Rahel told us what happened. She would be willing to speak for you, to be a witness, if that were admissible in court. Farih turned the bangles on her wrist as if trying to command her thoughts.

Rahel must not – A'isha began.

She has given this a great deal of thought. She is willing to speak. If anything were to happen to you, she said she would hold herself responsible. Of course, we might not be allowed to bring forward a witness for this appeal, but we will see. Anyway, perhaps that is enough for the moment, do you think? It is a great deal for you to think about, I know.

She beckoned to Hassan, who came outside. Tani stood in the doorway behind him.

My wife has made sweet tea, he said. There is nothing better. And if we indulge her, we may be given some of her small biscuits.

Tani brought a tray with a teapot and cups, a plate of biscuits, and a small dish of figs, which she set down on the table between them without looking once at Farih. She left quickly. Hassan thought of what Tani would say after Farih had left, how he would have to soothe her.

Farih poured herself tea and stared into her teacup as if mesmerized by it. She roused herself, adding a spoonful of sugar and stirring it thoughtfully.

It is time for me to tend to Safiya at home, said A'isha.

Yes, of course. He is nearby, the driver. Let me call him. Hassan slid his phone out of a trouser pocket under his riga.

I am going to work for you, A'isha, said Farih. I think this appeal can be won. We will have to be very well prepared.

Hassan set down his phone after calling the driver. Indeed, it can be won.

But I have no money to pay, said A'isha.

The Spreading Acacia can't take up every case, but some, yours among them, might be won on appeal if we work hard enough, said Farih. We receive funding. We are receiving more money now than before, because there are reporters who are telling people about you.

About me?

Yes. And the more we can communicate your plight, your predicament, the more we can tell the world, the better for you. We could use a lawyer who is well known, for instance, who could discuss this case with the media.

I do not know very much, A'isha said. What I learned in school was not enough, but I want – Her voice trailed into a whisper.

What do you want, A'isha? asked Hassan gently.

She shook her head.

I FEEL FOR HER, said Farih, who watched as the car reversed, turned, then sped forward out of Hassan's compound. And yet she is not embittered, as one might expect.

Hope is not lost, said Hassan. But it is much too hot under this awning – look, even the lizard is seeking shade. He pointed to the reptile that had found its way atop the railing on one side of the patio, an orange-headed creature, a curiously ancient relic of another age, with dark, charcoal-coloured scales covering its body and a tail that appeared to be nothing more than a stump.

Ehhh! Farih shifted away from the railing.

He has had many fights. See his tail?

No, she said.

Hassan laughed.

The lizard's eye was fixed on Hassan and Farih.

Well, come indoors, Farih, he said. My wife has turned on the air conditioning, and if the power stays on, it will soon feel as though we are in the path of a blizzard. There will not be a single lizard to bother you!

Farih was tired, he could see. Soon her sister would arrive, and they would drive back to Abuja, but there were still some questions to which he needed answers.

Once inside, she settled happily on the white leather couch in the living room.

Would you like anything? A cold drink of lemon squash, perhaps?

No, she said. Thank you. I have taken tea.

So, he said, seating himself in the armchair. Of all the cases you know, has the fact of rape ever been used successfully to appeal a conviction?

In Nigeria, yes, there are a number of such cases, said Farih.

But in several of them, the sentence, like Halima and her sentence of lashes, was carried out before anything could be done, even when the woman had been raped. I must tell you, though, in some cases rape has been turned against the woman, used against her. We do not want that for A'isha.

Mmm, he said. But you think there might be a chance for her?

Yes, a chance. It would be best if you could devise a way for the international media to keep apprised of this case. I don't know what you could do, but they are hungry for information.

Well, that will rouse the hornets from the nest.

Do you recall that famous case – Rahamma Yusuf? She received the same sentence as A'isha, but it was appealed successfully.

I recall the name, but not the details.

It was the same charge of adultery, and, in fact, Rahamma did have a relationship with someone. The man was not charged; you recall that there have to be four morally upright citizens who must actually witness the act of adultery.

They would not be morally upright citizens in that case.

I agree, but so it is. Rahamma gave birth to a child out of wedlock. Now do you remember?

Something about a sleeping embryo?

Yes, said Farih. You are right. Her lawyer studied every detail of the case in order to appeal. She went back to the hadith, and discovered the Mudabbar of Imam Malik, who said an embryo might be "dormant," that it might sleep in the womb of a woman for several years. And you see the relevance, I am sure, because as you might recall, Rahamma had been married three years before, to a man who divorced her.

So, said Hassan slowly. By this line of reasoning Rahamma might have got pregnant by her husband years before.

Yes, and the appeal was won on those grounds. The story of Rahamma's sleeping embryo was not at all credible, of course, but it allowed the court to save face. The appeal succeeded. Unfortunately, that lawyer has gone to work in the United States, so we can't ask for her help. Farih looked at him penetratingly. You said before that it was because of injustice that you took up A'isha's cause.

You do not believe me?

Yes, I believe you, but I wonder if there is more to it.

He looked at the soft, white, very impractical carpet. He was always afraid he would spill something on it.

I knew Nafisa, A'isha's mother. We were the same age.

Ah, she said quietly. A tale of romance?

No. We grew up here, in Paiko. I was sent away to London for university, while she did not have the opportunity. I finished at the LSE and came back here. In the meantime, she was married off to a man who, well, he was not her equal. And then she had A'isha. That first husband died, and Nafisa was urged to marry a second, but he was more useless than the first.

And history repeated itself. A'isha was married off too.

Yes, and so, you see, I was incensed by that. But I never expected, no, I never imagined, that A'isha might find herself in worse circumstances.

And so you feel the guilt of the one who has not experienced such things.

Hassan was conscious of the hum of the air conditioner, and distantly, Tani's music.

There is someone who might be helpful to an appeal, though he is not well versed in shariah law, said Hassan. He knows something of it, though. He is capable and well known. And he could speak to the media.

Ah, my sister has come. Farih stood up and smoothed invisible wrinkles from her elegantly wrapped skirt.

Hassan opened the door for her. She went through, dipping her head with its gorgeous head wrap: she was a bird of paradise. He'd have liked her to stay longer, but it was out of the question. Usually he was surrounded by people with one complaint after another, people wanting him to do the impossible, but Farih's mind challenged him. And he didn't mind that the scent of her, that almost imperceptible fragrance of sandalwood, would linger when she had gone.

And maybe you would contact this person who could be helpful to the appeal? she said.

Yes, I will, Hassan assured her.

They stood on the terrace under the awning, where the lizard had not budged.

Your friend is waiting for you, he said slyly, tilting his head in the direction of the lizard.

A-a! she cried.

He would fight on your behalf. And he would be a natural, I think, on television. Don't you agree he strikes a good pose?

She laughed, then grimaced, and hurried past the lizard to the car, as the creature held its flaming head poised, immobile.

Hassan stood on the terrace after he'd waved to the departing car, after the whirl of sepia-coloured dust had settled, after the lizard had finally jerked into action, swiftly running along the balustrade and down the steps. It was time to go inside, into the chill of the air conditioning, an artificial coolness he'd never much liked. He was more at home outside, with the lizard. But he was unable to get it out of his head: A'isha's contorted face, the things she'd wanted to say.

24

FELIX COULD HEAR THEM as they talked. Kidneys. Blood clots.

He was in a place underground, tunnelling through dirt. He was tangled in the upended roots of a tree, somewhere in the woods, crawling on the mottled ground, mottled with light and shadow. Pine needles, mushrooms the size of giants' ears. He tried to get up.

Where was Sophie?

Felix had gone to see her. He'd gone all the way to where she lived on the other side of the world. He was in the middle of a forest on his way to her.

But it was here, in the woods, that he lost his balance, toppling down and sliding on his side, crashing into an upended spruce that lay across the path, where he lay like a child against it, hands over his head, one boot on and one boot off. There was the lost boot. He could see it; he could almost reach it. Yes, there it was. He put it on his sockless foot. He found the lost sock and stuffed it in his mud-covered pocket. Mud plastered his left side from his shoulder to his knee.

What have they done to him? asked Sophie.

He knew he must look comical, splattered and streaked with what might have been reddish-brown paint, though it was just mud, and, caught in his hair, a stripped, broken branch with a few clinging oak leaves. Sophie was with him now. Was she laughing or crying?

Why didn't she just put her arms around him? Sophie, he tried to say. Something was blocking his tongue; something prevented him. He wanted her arms around him.

Ssssbbb, he said.

The two of them made their way over a roughly made footbridge, three logs, and came out of the woods, draggled, miserable, Felix ahead of Sophie. He was nauseous, cold. The snow, on the cusp of sleet, had turned to rain, and this sheeting rain, as if it weren't rain but corrosive acid, promised to dissolve the road and transform it into a series of badly eroded ditches. There was a long, downward sloping hill, then a road, and the gunmetal water of the harbour that lay beyond it. But the rain had already diffused the harbour into a cloudy nothingness that was neither earth nor water, and Sophie's home, somewhere below, was entirely obscured, turned to mist, and because the world had fallen into itself there was no distance.

There, he's quiet, said one of them. Was it Serena?

He's sleeping.

In this strange otherworld, they descended the slope through the torn, wet snow, the remnants of spoiled corn cobs – blackened kernels, toothless patches – and cropped stalks showing through, then the slimy mud as they continued stolidly down and down, bitter rain in their faces, Felix followed by Sophie, slipping and sliding until they came to the barn and the outbuilding for the cattle and the farmhouse with its long driveway, and so made their way across the highway, streaming with water, and along the lane to the house from which they'd come. But no, it was a dream, and when he looked around, she'd vanished.

He always slept as a baby, said Felix's mother. He did not give me trouble.

I didn't give you trouble, said someone. Clifford. It was Clifford.

No, you didn't.

I did. Serena's voice.

You didn't sleep much. Felix was a sleeper, said his mother.

Her voice comforted him, his mother's voice. She scooped him up, though he was too heavy for her. He was too heavy for her, but she cradled him, and he let himself be rocked back and forth and back and forth. Her voice soothed him. He had never given her any trouble. The rain had been hard pinpricks as they'd made their way down the slope, but now the whole sky was alive with colour, with gold and ruby tints. The water of the harbour, which had been flat and unremarkable as the bottom of a tin pot, became a blinking field of lights, and he could see through the birch and spruce to the spangles.

You were all alone, said someone.

Felix considered what it was to be alone. He didn't mind being alone. But he missed Sophie.

We'll pray, said his mother. Dear Lord God –

The sound of someone crying.

He was lifted into air, his mother lifted him with her words. Over the tips of the spruce he went, the black-tipped or the green-tipped brushes of the spruce, over the old hemlocks, above a logging road curving up a hillside, curving up through the mess of snow on the ground, and above it, mist, parting and re-forming and parting, as if someone were drawing away a lace shawl. He couldn't see the harbour, couldn't see the spangles. Was God here? His mother was calling on God, but there was only mist, and below the mist was the unseen water. The mist shredded and now he could see what lay below.

Take care of Felix –

He went farther, over the lip of a river, over the mess of dagger-sharp pieces of wood, upended roots of trees, dragged there by beavers, over an ink-coloured pond in which the branch of a birch lay upturned. Snow at its edges. Up the hill he went, and down to the boggy place, where the tasselled cattails made a soft, papery sound in the wind, a sound that could hardly be heard, erased by the brazen talk of crows.

Please, Lord, help him.

The crows were tilting the sky, turning it over.

But Sophie wasn't there; Sophie was nowhere to be found. She was lost. He had to find her. He could hear water pouring over stones somewhere, perhaps a waterfall, and he rose up near the clouds. The sky was grey in places, silver in others. He could keep going, but he wanted to find Sophie. Was she beyond the ridge, or the next, or the next? Was she down by the ocean, the ocean he could see from this vantage point, with its edge of white surf beating the strip of beach? Now he could see it all. He could see where the water of the harbour poured out into the ocean. He could see where he'd come from.

Amen.

He could hear Sophie, but he couldn't see her.

She said, I'm here. He felt her touch.

He wanted to tell her how far he'd come, but he couldn't. He wanted to tell her that he'd been looking for her. There was so much he wanted to tell her.

HE FOUGHT THEM. The thing in his mouth – he tried to yank it out. He was angry. What had they done without his permission?

Felix, cried Sophie. *Don't.*

He doesn't want it!

Don't let him –

Yaaaa. We can do this without you, Sophie.

Serena, stop.

It had been soft in the clouds. Everything had been gentle, without edges. Here there were lights and noise and someone yelling. Who was yelling? Someone grabbed his hand, but he was stronger. Whoever it was got the better of him.

Why was he being punished? Why were they holding him down?

HE RELINQUISHED HIMSELF TO IT. He let himself be lifted up, becoming light and airy. They'd tried to hold him down, but he could free himself as he pleased, except for whatever was in his mouth.

On the ground below were the scattered things that had been thrown out of Sophie's suitcase: her blue-backed hairbrush, her plastic bag of miniature lotions, shampoo, and shower gel. Her tank tops and sundresses, long navy dress, flowered underwear, black bra, lacy nightgown.

All these things needed to be put back carefully. He could do that for her. He knew he could do it.

Felix, said Sophie. Her voice was full of feathers.

He could hear her. She was crying, and he didn't want her to cry, but he was being pulled away into mist. There was no resisting it, and he wanted to tell her that it was such a small thing. If only she could see for herself, but he was too far away to tell her.

25

SERENA YELLED AT SOPHIE.

Serena, said Grace. Stop.

Sophie stood up; Grace stood up. Stay with us, said Grace.

Sophie shook her head. She bent down so she could whisper into Felix's ear. Then she straightened, embraced Grace, and went out the doors of the ICU.

Clare was waiting. She held her daughter as Sophie cried. It'll be all right, Soph, she said.

People had said the same words to Clare after Gavin had died, but it was a useless thing to say. Felix wasn't dead. She should have known better than to say it to Sophie.

Sophie didn't notice. She wiped her face.

In the hall was a woman was dunking a mop into a bucket, then pressing the mop against the bucket's side to get rid of the excess water. Clare watched as she put it on the floor, pulled the ropy strands, the grey snakes, around and around. Slippery, glistening. He could die, but Sophie wouldn't be there. The mop made a slopping sound against the cement floor, the sound of something half-dead that wanted to be alive. The woman wore a soft orange-pink wrapper, and over it she had a white smock, untied in the back. Or Felix could wake, but Sophie wouldn't be there. What if he called for her? The woman's sandals were worn and old, and her feet turned a little outward as they bore the weight of her body. Clare knew that she would not be able to get it out of her mind: the woman's untied smock, its dangling ends, her feet in the sandals. They passed the woman, who smiled, almost apologetically. Beyond her, the light fell in stripes on the floor that remained to be cleaned. Clare went through the light and shadow with Sophie. Light, shadow, light. Now Thomas appeared, entering the doors at the far end of the hall.

I was coming to find you, he said.

They went outside, down the steps. Thomas took Sophie's arm as if she were an invalid when she got into the car and sank down to the back seat.

Clare got into the front seat, glancing at her daughter.

She hasn't slept in days, Clare said.

Thomas pulled out of the hospital parking lot onto the street, and Clare saw how the world streamed past. A small truck overtook them, and she saw a man in the back holding several panes of glass upright. If he fell over, Clare thought, the panes would shatter. He had braced himself so he wouldn't fall. She felt herself holding the panes of glass. The truck veered gently to the right and the man leaned with the motion. The truck vanished, the man with the panes of glass disappeared.

CLARE GAVE SOPHIE A SLEEPING PILL, a large pill that was transparently green, an oversized emerald. Temazepam. Not just to help her go to sleep, but to keep her sleeping for a while.

Sophie slept. And Clare lay on the bed beside her. The blinds had been pulled, but the daylight still got through at the edges. Clare lay still. Gavin was turning toward her as he went out the door. See you later. It was winter. No, it was spring. He was standing in a doorway, the doorway at home in Nova Scotia, with its festival of May trees behind him, wild apple blossoms in a scattering of pinkish white. He was in shadow, but everything behind him was crazed with spring.

She woke again. Time had no edges at all, but it was still day, that much she knew. Her head was loose and fuzzy, and she was confused by the way she felt when she sat up, as if she'd left her head on the pillow. She hadn't taken a sleeping pill. But where was she? She was with Sophie, yes, and Sophie was still fast asleep, and they'd left Felix behind in the hospital. When she went to the bathroom she crashed into the door. She flushed the toilet and washed her hands and went back to the bed, where she lay on her back and listened to Sophie's soft, breathy snores. But she would have to get up, have a shower, put on clean clothes. She sighed.

THEY HAD WAITED FOR HER before eating. All the places were set. She realized she had slept all day, that they were sitting down to dinner.

Clare, said Monica. We're having – Hortensia, come away from Jonathan, please. You're bothering him.

Binta sat across from her, but this was a different Binta, in a starched white blouse. She beamed at Clare. Thomas gave the blessing, asking God to look after Felix.

When the chicken was on her plate, surrounded by an array of fried plantain slices, and green beans shining with butter, Clare ate a little, then set down her fork and put out her hand for her water glass, knocking it over. She didn't catch it before several ice cubes glided out, before the water made a damp stain on the tablecloth. There had been lemon slices in the water and one yellow wedge lay beside her plate.

God isn't up there looking after Felix. Clare righted the glass, putting her napkin under the tablecloth so the wetness wouldn't leave a mark on the table. You can ask all you want, but I just don't think it'll help.

Thomas looked at her.

I know that's what we all want, what you're praying for, but it's a septic infection. Sepsis. She shook her head. I've seen something like this before, back when I was nursing. I don't think he'll make it.

God works in ways we do not know, said Monica. He works –

I'm sorry – please – I'm sorry.

Clare got up from the table and went swiftly down the hall, before she stopped halfway along. It was a painting of pears in a blue bowl, pears that seemed to have been cut out of gold paper. They gleamed; the bowl shone. Something about the pears and the bowl wasn't right, but she didn't know what it was. She put a hand against the wall. A den opened off the hall across from the painting, and in it were two armchairs, a lamp with its shade poised over them, a soft Turkish rug, a glass-topped table, shelves of books. If she could have made an alternate life for herself, it would have been that den with the chairs and lamp, a longed-for life with Gavin in it. A trap door opened under her feet, and the chairs and lamp, the soft rug, the glass-topped table collapsed into the hole. But she was still there, and she felt the hard firmness of the wall under her fingers as she studied the painting of the five golden-brown pears, yes, five of them, inviting a person to pick them up, in the sturdy glazed ceramic bowl, which seemed substantial, with a daubed highlight of pale blue on the side of the bowl that caught the light. The painting was set off by a wooden frame made to seem antique. Gavin was never going to be with her again, and she would go on loving him, stupidly loving him. But she couldn't bear for it to happen to Sophie.

She kept going along the hall to the threshold of the kitchen, where she found a woman sitting on a stool, leaning against the counter.

You are welcome, said the woman, speaking formally. But then, of course, Clare was a guest.

Veronica, Clare remembered. Veronica was the one who had made the succulent chicken, the fried plantain. She'd finished her work, and now she was resting, rolling a couple of pills in her palm.

Clare went and sat on a stool by the counter.

How do you live, Veronica? said Clare.

Veronica made a grunting sound and shook her head as if Clare had said something vaguely comical. She put her hand on Clare's.

Veronica put the pills beside a glass so they wouldn't roll across the counter. She got up from the stool and went to the fridge, pulling a tub out of the freezer and scooping something into two bowls. She stuck a spoon in one and a spoon in the other, and put the bowls down on the counter, standing away from it to rub her back. She motioned for Clare to eat.

It is good, she said.

It was homemade ice cream. It was sweet and slightly tart at the same time; the most delicious ice cream that Clare had ever eaten. Veronica grinned at her, grinning so a gap was visible between her two front teeth before she came around and sat companionably next to Clare at the counter, eating her own ice cream, rolling it over her tongue, simply taking her time tasting the subtle flavour before she swallowed it. They ate together in silence.

SHE FOUND THOMAS IN THE DEN she had passed earlier, sitting at the glass-topped table, papers in two neat piles. She stood at the threshold.

He got up.

I was rude, she said. I'm sorry.

Do you think it matters? he asked. Clare.

I don't have –

I keep thinking about how I left you there. Jacob and I ran away.

I was glad you did. I wanted so much for you to get out of there. I wanted you to run and run and run. She came into the room and sat down in an armchair.

He went back to the glass-topped table and leaned against it. He rubbed the sides of his face. When we were young, I almost hated you. Why – I don't know.

You did?

Yes, and even when you were older. Maybe more, then. This family that had taken me in – a white father, white mother, white sister. I was the only one who wasn't like any of you. I didn't belong.

Her father held Thomas by one hand and Clare by the other. The three of them watched as if it were a play. A man had climbed up on a rickety ladder to stuff a flaming bundle into an open window, and below him, another man, held by the crowd, tossed something inside another window. The boy on the roof would be caught up there. Flames and tendrils of smoke curled out of the gutted openings that had been windows.

Why are they doing that? asked Clare.

Her father picked her up again, but she was too old for that. She could smell his shirt, the clean smell of the cotton, and another smell, under the clean smell, that was a little sour. He patted her back once, twice.

Nearby, the bougainvillea flowers were red, red, red, each one a little trumpet, all of the trumpets falling over an open shack where men were working on a car, and dust lifted up as a lorry went by – a lurch, honks, another lurch, more honks – so they couldn't see the church. But it was burning now, and they could smell the smoke from where they stood, far away from it.

She was beautiful, our mother, he said. Her hair, do you remember how it curled around her face?

Yes, said Clare.

She was like an angel. She used to kiss me goodnight. Thomas, she'd say. We love you so.

When they could see it again, the boy had climbed up to the wrought-iron cross at the top of the church's facade. The roof's pitch was not steep; he stood on the ridgepole and from there he pulled on the cross. Smoke billowed up and he was part of the smoke, but soon he reappeared, and the crowd yelled as he pulled, back and forth, back and forth. Thomas said in his high-pitched voice, He's going to break it.

I was jealous of the way she loved you, said Clare.

They could all see how hard he was working to break it.

Their father didn't say anything, but he watched, and Clare looked up at him, because it was time for them to go, but he wouldn't go. He waited until the boy had bent the cross completely, so it looked like an elbow. The crowd cheered wildly. He sat on it and waved a length of cloth in the air.

She died, and it was terrible that she died, he said. I thought no one would ever say that again – Thomas, we love you so.

But you hated us?

I said I almost hated you.

You were always Thomas-who-could-do-anything. And look at what you did, how much harder you worked than I did.

I had to.

She waited.

I had to work hard, harder than anyone else. In Edinburgh I felt completely alone.

You were there for years. Longer than I was.

Where else could I go?

You didn't want to have anything to do with me. Gavin or me. We wanted you at our wedding and you wouldn't come.

No. He put his hands in his pockets. I couldn't face you. Who was I? I had no idea. I came back here looking for anyone in my family – you know that. I found cousins on my mother's side and I had no real connection with them, but I thought maybe I could stay in Nigeria. It would take time to get set up, but it seemed to be the right place.

You were one of the reasons I decided to volunteer to be a nurse in that clinic. Oh, Thomas, don't let it –

I'm just saying it took me a long time. He sat down in the desk chair, leaning back and speaking to the ceiling. It's not you. It's not your fault.

She shut her eyes. She was the one who had wanted to keep driving through the night when they could have stayed in Onitsha.

You're all I have, Thomas, she said. You're my brother. I have you and I have Sophie.

We should leave, said her father.

And they left, so quickly that Clare couldn't keep up with her father's strides. Thomas trotted behind, but he wasn't as fast, and Clare was the one who stopped and urged him on. Poor little thing, Clare's mother had said about Thomas. Take care of him. Through the cramped alley of the tailors they went, as the tailors and seamstresses worked their old-fashioned sewing machines, lengths of fabric in the stalls behind them. Red, brown, blue, white. Clare looked back, but she couldn't see the crowd, or the church, or the boy riding the cross. A part of her wanted to see what would happen next, but her father was taking them away, and now she wouldn't know.

She could hear the clatter of plates in the kitchen. Someone calling in the driveway, Jonathan calling Andrew.

Why fast fast? called a man.

But their father didn't answer him, didn't slow down.

I'm scared for Sophie, Clare said. She hardly knows what's happening; she doesn't know what's up, what's down. I say the wrong things, I try to comfort her.

Sharp tang of urine from somewhere, quick jump over a gutter, around the corner where the leper stood, begging with his knobbled hand, and then to the shining hot car and its sticky plastic seats, parked at God Help Good Man Roadside Mechanic. Her father was with Clare and Thomas, but his eyes still roamed the street. She stroked his hand and he looked down at her, as if he didn't know who she was.

Is there anything we can do? asked Thomas. Anything I can do?

She rubbed her fingers on the armrest of the chair. The material was soft, satisfying to touch.

Talk to her, said Clare.

26

THE APPEAL WAS NOT GOING WELL.

The lawyers appealing on behalf of A'isha had a series of arguments: that citizens had no right to apprehend the appellant at her home and take her to be arrested; that the appellant had not had access to counsel from the beginning; that she had made a confession without understanding how it would be held against her; that she did not comprehend what zina meant; that the charges against the appellant were unclear and unspecific about the alleged offence; that the appellant had not been allowed to call upon any witnesses; that the judge should not have acted alone in the lower court in which the case was tried, but here A'isha lost track of what they were saying.

When she bent her head down, the sweat dripped onto her lap, onto the good wrapper, a waxed cotton that had belonged to her mother, with its golds and greens that made her think of being with her mother in the shade of the acacia tree, with its bowed-down old branches and fringe of leaves. Know your strength, her mother had said. But A'isha was afraid.

She wanted to fan herself, but she didn't dare; she didn't dare to wipe her forehead or her neck. She tried to concentrate. The lead prosecutor was a crested cuckoo; he strutted in front of the judges, taking up each argument that Farih Hussaini had constructed with Danladi so carefully, and destroying one after the other, not that A'isha understood all of the proceedings. Farih had said that A'isha should not look directly at the judges, but she wouldn't have dreamt of it. She kept her head lowered, in a way that let her observe the prosecutor through her eyelashes.

The citizens *did* indeed have the right to take a person forcibly to the police, especially one seen to be a perpetrator of wrongdoing, wherever that person might be, he said.

And, he continued, the laws of shariah superseded all others, including the constitution of Nigeria, which stated that anyone who saw a wrong being committed by anyone at any time could, and should, make efforts to stop it.

This was someone who felt himself to be right, truly right.

The charges – he said.

The confession – he said.

The pregnancy itself – he said.

A'ISHA HAD HEARD THE MEN COMING. She'd heard them banging at the grillwork protecting the windows; they broke the flimsy lock on the door and barged through, taking the door right off its hinges. She covered herself hastily with an old wrapper, one that had been on the bed. They'd come to kill her. No, they were not there to kill her; they'd come to take her to be arrested. They'd told her they were taking her to the police to be arrested on the charge of adultery. If they weren't going to kill her at the house, she thought, they'd kill her at the police station. But then there was the problem of the men not being able to rouse anyone at the police station, and they'd had to take her to the chief of police. He was not pleased.

They tried again at the police station, which also housed the jail; they beat on the door, and this time it was opened. The lights were turned on. It was at the police station where they had asked her all the questions, where they told her she had been arrested, and by that time she was so very tired, deeply tired, and dirty too, especially her feet, since she hadn't had time to put on anything better than slippers. She hardly cared she'd been arrested. They kept telling her she had committed adultery, and that she must confess to it. One of them pointed to her belly, round and full; it was clear that she had committed adultery, wasn't it? She was unmarried. Her husband had died a long time before. Wasn't it the case that she had been free with men since that time?

She protected her belly with both hands, leaning over, and hating the smell of them, their loud voices. Thirsty, she was so thirsty. One of policemen was a friend of her brother, the youngest brother who had a shop in Abuja, but she'd forgotten the friend's name. What was it? She looked at his boots, trying to remember. They confused her with their questions. So she said what they wanted her to say.

Yes, she'd committed adultery. Yes.

She was admitting to zina?

She didn't understand zina.

They talked among themselves; one of them, not her brother's friend, seemed to be taking her part, but he was called out by the others. He shrugged and drifted over to the wall. Now maybe they would let her sleep. They took her to a jail cell that stank of shit, with a cluster of other women and a clogged drain: ten, maybe a dozen women were inside a cell that was big enough for two. No one made space for her, but she couldn't sleep standing up, and at last a scrawny woman shifted closer to someone else, simply by inching her buttocks over. Come here, she said. A'isha had to sit beside her, with her arms around her knees; the floor was damp.

Was it Audu? Was that his name?

SHE GUESSED THAT WAS what they meant when they talked about her confession. And this confession was what the cuckoo talked about now, as if he knew. He called her the appellant. She had given up all her rights to counsel when she confessed, and, he said, no witness was ever called upon in such cases of zina, because there was no need. It was true she had been pregnant, and this pregnancy was all that was necessary for conclusive evidence of her misdoing; she had given birth to a child, a girl, and that was a fact, yes, *that* was a fact that could not be disputed. But A'isha was certain that this man, this prosecutor, had never had to sit himself down on a floor that was wet with people's urine, let alone try to sleep there.

The courtroom made A'isha think of her primary school, though it was grander, of course, but nothing special once a person walked through the entrance, once a person was sitting down. The chants of the primary school came back to her; she could hear all of them crying out an English rhyme in unison: Baa, baa, black sheep, have you any wool? The courtroom had not been cleaned thoroughly, and reddish sand was flecked across the concrete. Yes, sir, yes, sir, three bags full. And it was here, in this place that should have been scoured, made to be pristine, it was here that important people like this man in his two-toned shoes made of tan leather and dark leather, this prosecutor, with his complete faith in himself, could help decide whether she would live or die. Her life was in his hands, just as if it were no more than a bit of sand. How could a person's life weigh so little in another person's hands? She was sand on the floor.

Her mother had told her things to give her courage, but now her mother was gone. Her mother was a wavering candle. Sometimes A'isha felt her close by, but mostly she was just not there. She was not there when A'isha had come back after the funeral; she was not in the hut. Her eyes, which had followed A'isha, followed Safiya – what had happened to those eyes? A'isha couldn't recall the pretty shape of her mother's eyes, her nose, her mouth. Would her mother ever appear the way she'd been? Or would A'isha always be trying to piece her together?

She urged herself to focus on what was being said. The grounds for the appeal were being dismissed by the judges, since zina was a word that needed no explanation, since the lack of specificity about the time, date, place, and person with whom the offence was committed was irrelevant, since pregnancy itself was conclusive evidence, and A'isha found herself wondering about the judge who was speaking, about the way his voice seemed to ravel and unravel, so she could hear some, but not all of what he was saying. She chanced a look at him. He had glasses, but they bothered him. He took them off, put them on; they did not seem to fit him correctly, or perhaps they pained his ears. He took up each point and cast it aside, holding, he said, to the law. The appellant could not withdraw her confession. The court confirmed the sentence, which would be carried out once the appellant had weaned her child. Counsel for the appellant would be allowed to appeal, a second appeal, but it must be carried out within sixty days. The judge took off his glasses. And that was the end of it.

A'isha had sixty days to be with Safiya.

WE WILL DO BETTER NEXT TIME, said Farih. These judges, they simply want to uphold the previous judgement.

But A'isha wasn't listening. She should have known how it would go at the beginning; she shouldn't have allowed herself to hope. Her life was sand, nothing more. As Farih spoke,

A'isha felt the sand rushing through her body, from the top of her head down to her feet, the way part of it slid easily and left another part behind, and then all of it gave way. She was made of sand.

It will be heard in the Court of Appeals next time, said Farih. That will be quite different.

How could it be different? wondered A'isha, but she did not say anything.

A'isha, are you listening?

A'isha was feeding Safiya. They were in her uncle's compound after hashing out the appeal at the home of Alhaji Hassan. Farih had taken A'isha to her uncle's and then she didn't want to abandon her. A'isha wanted to say to Farih that it would be all right, that she would be all right alone with Safiya. She was hungry and wanted to cook, but first she fed Safiya as Farih talked.

Don't be downcast. You are something of a celebrity, Farih went on. Did you know that? People have begun to discover you. People have set up a Facebook group for you and it has thousands of followers. At the Spreading Acacia, I can't tell you how many people have been calling, asking how they can help.

How can they help me?

We tell them they must let us do the work. But really, this has become a full-time job, just talking to people about you.

I don't –

And you remember that reporter for the BBC?

Mr. Beck.

Fabian Beck did a story about you for the BBC, about what you were contending with, how difficult your circumstances have been. He mentioned the mob at Hassan's house – I read this article myself. He has been following your story from the beginning. He has been in Nigeria a long time, and so he understands the situation. They are talking about you all over the United Kingdom, all over the world, in fact. Today there were many reporters, as you saw. Did you know?

A'isha had thought only of the fact that they lost the appeal. No, she hadn't paid attention.

You have no idea how big this has become, Farih went on, excitedly. You have thousands of people supporting you – so many people, ordinary people. They are sending donations on your behalf to the Spreading Acacia.

A'isha tried to imagine thousands of people, but all she could think of were the men who had been shouting her name outside Alhaji Hassan's house. A – isha Na – sir. A – isha Na – sir.

They are discussing your cause on talk shows in America; this is what my daughter tells me. She's at university in Washington. Georgetown University. She knows what is happening.

You have a daughter?

Yes. She's a little older than you. She tells me about what's going on, what's in the news. There has been an article about you in *The New York Times* and another in *The Washington Post*. It has been on CNN. Of course, this kind of support in America did not help us win the appeal today, but in the future it could.

The future, thought A'isha. Sand, and sand, and more sand. The way the horizon was obscured during harmattan when a reddish haze hung in the air, the way the sun was gone, replaced by the reddish nothing. The grit of it on the tongue; the way it made a person want to spit. Anyone could taste it, the future.

Where is the other reporter? asked A'isha. Sophie.

Sophie MacNeil? She may have returned home.

A'isha was sorry about that. They had chased her away. Like a bird, Sophie MacNeil had come, like a bird she had flown;

that was how it went. She tried not to feel anything, but Safiya pulled at A'isha's breast, a quivering pull, the edges of her lips working to get at the deep sweetness of her mother. It left her empty. Why had A'isha felt that there was something in Sophie MacNeil that was like herself? She knew nothing about her. They came from different places; they spoke different languages; there was nothing that made them alike. A'isha had only spent a few hours with her, but even so.

We needed her article, though, the first one that caused all the trouble. People accused her of being an outsider, even a spy. It's true she was not Nigerian. But no one would have known about you, A'isha, if not for her. It got the word out.

Safiya did not want to suckle anymore. A'isha placed her against her shoulder and thumped gently on her back.

What is the name of your daughter? asked A'isha.

My daughter? Farih was fiddling with her mobile.

Yes.

She is Magajiya. Most people call her Maggie, over there, I mean.

What does she study?

Well, chuckled Farih, putting down her mobile. She wanted to study all sorts of things, but she has narrowed it down. She is a girl who could do anything, so she dabbled for a while. But now she is studying politics, policy, governance – why governments do what they do, that kind of thing.

She can study those things?

Oh, yes. They have a range of offerings. It is a university that was started by the Jesuits, and it has quite a global community. But it's strange to think of her in such a place.

A'isha didn't know what Farih meant by Jesuits.

Was she afraid to go there? asked A'isha.

Oh, when she first went, she called all the time. She was terrified. Of course, it *is* terrifying, going to another country. But she's not afraid now.

You must be proud, said A'isha, cradling Safiya in her arms. She would sleep now that she had fed.

Yes, very proud, said Farih.

Does she know her strength? Maggie? Magajiya?

Farih laughed. I wouldn't put it that way. She's a good one for being interested in clothes. When she was a girl, she was always painting her fingernails and toenails different colours – yellow and orange, yellow and purple, pink and purple, you know, with dots, with stripes. Then she would take it all off and start over. I despaired!

Farih grew quiet, pondering the question. Does she know her strength? I think she learned to be strong by going there. She is learning. She's young. It takes time.

Mmmm, murmured A'isha, shifting on the bench. I don't have time.

27

YOU'VE BEEN INSIDE FOR DAYS, said Clare. You haven't eaten.

I'll eat soon. Sophie sat up, leaned against the wall.

The sheet had fallen on the floor, and Clare picked it up, tossing it back on the bed. You can't just give up. She went to the window and raised the blinds, letting the light flood the room.

Sophie shut her eyes.

What are we doing here if you've just given up? I'll make arrangements for us to fly home.

No, said Sophie. The light was full on her face and she looked gaunt. No, she repeated.

Clare threw up her hands. Why? You haven't even called Grace, you haven't got in touch with her. You don't seem to be thinking of Felix, so there's no reason to stay. It's not fair to Thomas and Monica.

I'm thinking of Felix all the time. I'm thinking that I should never have done the article.

But you did, said Clare.

Yes, I did. Sophie spoke slowly. It's one thing to write an article and another to think that you have blood on your hands. I have blood on my hands. I didn't see that coming. If Felix dies, I'll have another person's blood on my hands.

Clare saw the mechanic swimming on the ground toward the old woman with the fried cakes. He had almost reached her.

You didn't kill those people, said Clare.

Would they have been incited to violence if not for me?

You give yourself too much credit. Anyway, you spoke the truth.

Maybe the truth wasn't mine to tell. Sophie shook her head. Maybe if I hadn't got in the way. It was A'isha's story, not mine.

She wanted you, Sophie, or she wouldn't have let you do it. Clare sat down on the bed. Charles, at the newspaper, he wanted you to do it.

I think he regretted it.

We tell stories that have to be told. This had to be told. A young woman who has never lifted a finger against anyone else, and yet here she is convicted of a crime. Who is going to speak for her? Do we say that only this person or that person is the one to tell her story? And you, you're cast into the outer darkness for speaking up? Don't let the naysayers get to you, Sophie. You're paralyzed, you're afraid.

I am. I'm afraid of so many things.

Don't be. Come on, we're going to get you something to eat.

Sophie swung her legs over the side of the bed. She sat, staring at the wall in front of her, and Clare thought she would never move. But she got up.

ARE YOU SURE YOU WANT TO DO THAT? said Thomas.

How can I leave without knowing? said Sophie.

They were sitting outside on the patio, a place that had always appealed to Thomas, because it was enclosed by croton plants. Some leaves were deep crimson-orange spears, and some were green, but there were markings of red and orange across the shiny green.

I'm not sure it's a good idea, he said.

She scuffed one sandal against a patio stone. I should at least find out how she's doing.

You might not be welcome. It hasn't been an easy time of it, especially for A'isha, and if you appear –

Don't you think I know what I've done? Serena told me what a mess I'd made.

Through the slats in the patio roof, Sophie could make out creampuffs of cloud moving overhead. Wind, pushing them along.

Her father was sitting at the kitchen table with his head in his hands.

That child had to be strapped to a bed in a room that was like a prison cell, said her father. His body spasmed with every convulsion. His own mother wasn't allowed to go near. I could go to him, but not his mother.

Sophie watched a bird with a yellow breast flit from branch to branch of a nearby umbrella tree.

Wagtail, said Thomas, following her eyes.

Help me. This is what Joseph was crying out. Help, said her father.

It wasn't your fault, said Sophie. It wasn't your fault that Joseph died.

You didn't know how people would react to that article, said Thomas. Yes, someone who is not a Nigerian might not have been the ideal choice to write it. Fair enough, but you did it out of a sense that the punishment didn't fit the crime.

I should have thought it through. Felix warned me.

You feel responsible.

Yes, for all of it, but especially for Felix. I'm angry he went there at all. I blame him; I blame myself. Here I am close by and I'm not at the hospital, I'm not anywhere near him. But even if I tried, well, only family are allowed to see him and I'm not family. Sophie raised her glass, sipped from it. Her hand was trembling.

Someone had given the boy's mother a glass of water and she was standing by his room, in front of the bars. Joseph screamed, and she dropped the glass of water. Water is terrifying for someone dying of rabies, said her father. Joseph screamed and screamed. Her father sighed. The whole of my life has been given over to helping people, to healing them, and for the most part I did a good job. For the most part. Except when I hear Joseph in the middle of the night.

The wind riffled Sophie's hair.

You should be clear about one thing, said Thomas. Felix is in the hospital because he made a decision to go to Minna.

Sophie could hear the wagtail's *seeoo, seeoo.*

He didn't know what he was getting into, she said. He thought he knew, but we all think we're invincible.

He didn't know what he was getting into; you didn't know what you were getting into.

I'd never do it now.

What if someone needed you?

No, I –

Not so long ago I thought I'd never see your Aunt Monica again, said Thomas. Or the children. I was a coward in that moment, I can tell you.

You had a gun to your head, said Sophie.

I thought that at least I'd loved the people I loved. Your mother was kneeling near me, and I hoped that I'd go first, not her. I didn't want to go last. That's what I mean about being a coward.

No one would want to have to go through that. It's only human.

A thousand things flit through your head. When Hortensia was born, and how she wailed. Monica, when we first met, when she was wearing that dress with a pearly belt buckle. A doll that I took from your mother when we were children. It all came to me in a rush.

Sophie set down the glass of water on the table by her chair.

I wasn't afraid of it for myself, but I wanted to be able to tell them, to tell Monica, not to be sad. It would be such a small thing, dying.

No big deal, she said.

He laughed.

I was a coward, I'm still a coward, she said. It was almost a relief when Serena told me I wasn't wanted. To leave, to get out of there.

And you took her at her word.

I had to. She took a breath. But I want to see A'isha.

THE COMPOUND WHERE A'ISHA LIVED didn't look like the same one Sophie had visited with Felix. It seemed smaller, with fewer outbuildings, and the thatch of two of the huts had been blackened by fire. The guinea hens, disturbed by the car's arrival, flurried away past the house, the one, Sophie knew, that was occupied by A'isha's auntie and uncle, but A'isha herself was nowhere to be seen.

Sophie could see Felix standing beside the black car eating groundnuts; she saw him bowing to a man, elaborately greeting him as they met; she saw him playing a game with the children when he took yams from his car, sunglasses up on his head, but he wasn't there, and his car wasn't there, and there was only one child, who seemed to be tracing something in the dirt.

Thomas parked the car and Sophie got out into the solid wall of mid-afternoon heat, into the darkness before her eyes, a brief dizziness. She straightened up. Yes, A'isha, with Safiya, was with her auntie, hidden in the shadow of the porch. The child who had been scratching in the sand leapt to his feet, commanded by A'isha's auntie, and ran to the car. No one stopped Sophie. No one said, You're not welcome here. But she wanted it to be over, now that it had come, the meeting with A'isha, the meeting Sophie had asked for. The next day she would leave for Canada with her mother, if they let her go, if they didn't try to stop her because of a number in her passport. Or if the article she'd written remained a sticking point. But her uncle had said there was no legal reason for anyone to keep her in the country, and he would accompany them to the airport in case there was any difficulty.

Her uncle opened his door and stood by the car, stretching his arms.

There she is, said Sophie. With her auntie.

We'll come back for you in about an hour, said Thomas. Will that give you enough time?

Yes, said Sophie.

The little boy took Sophie's hand, as if to propel her forward, as if she belonged to him and should be introduced by him, but as soon as they got close to A'isha and her auntie, the child burst into giggles and ran away.

A'isha stood as Sophie came toward her. Safiya lay on a blanket at her feet, sleeping, one arm curved over her stomach. A'isha's auntie stayed on her bench, inclining her head to watch Thomas and Clare drive out of the compound. Sophie remembered how she had resembled a large red spider that first day she'd seen her, so long ago, it seemed.

Sannu da zuwâ, said A'isha's auntie.

Sannu, said Sophie.

You are welcome, said A'isha.

Sophie smiled at Safiya. She has grown. She's lovely.

A'isha motioned to a chair, and Sophie sat down.

I am happy you are here, said A'isha. You come again.

I'm glad to be here too. Sophie glanced at the place where she'd sat with A'isha, with Felix, under the green palace of a tree. I was sorry to hear about your mother, A'isha. I wanted to send you my sympathies. My condolences.

Condolences? said A'isha.

Your mother, said Sophie. I am sorry.

Sorry-o, repeated A'isha softly. And Mr. Felix? He did not come.

Felix was in the rioting in Minna. He was injured.

Uh-uh, tutted A'isha.

He was not fighting. I mean, he was not involved in the rioting himself. He was going there to see what was going on, a bystander. Sophie didn't know how to put it so A'isha would understand. He is in the hospital now. He has an infection. She didn't know how to stop explaining; she rushed on. He got the infection from cuts, from injuries, but they couldn't do much to help him, even after we took him to a different hospital. Sophie spread her hands.

He is hurt?

Yes, badly hurt.

Safiya woke and A'isha took her up from the blanket, comforting her. Safiya had indeed grown. Soon she would be of an age when she could be weaned. A'isha got up, spoke to Talata and gave her some coins, and then motioned for Sophie to follow her across the compound, to a bench next to the hut

Sophie had once entered to meet Nafisa. A'isha put her hand out for Sophie to sit beside her. Sophie remembered the cashew tree by the hut, how the sun poured through its leaves, as it did now.

Mr. Felix, said A'isha. *Uhhuhhh.*

A'isha put her small hand on Sophie's, a light pressure, and Sophie leaned back against the firm, warm wall of the hut. Safiya woke, and the shushing sounds A'isha made as she rocked her were soothing. A'isha wouldn't tell Sophie things would get better; A'isha was well aware that things could get worse. Hadn't Thomas told Sophie and Clare on the way to Paiko that the first appeal for A'isha had not gone as planned? Sophie had forgotten all about the appeal. She was ashamed she'd forgotten.

Talata brought bottles of water, slipping herself beside A'isha on the bench and returning some coins to her. Sophie was given one bottle, A'isha another.

Nagode, said Sophie. She gulped the water, a pure stream sliding down her parched throat. She could have drunk several bottles.

What will you do? asked A'isha.

I will go home to Canada.

A'isha shook her head.

Oh, you mean what will I do once I'm there? I don't know, said Sophie.

You must do your work. A'isha looked directly at Sophie now, patting Safiya's back. Sophie was reminded of the grip of Nafisa's hand on her own. You must do it.

A'isha's life, a string, could so easily be snipped in two, and yet she was thinking of Sophie.

The appeal did not go, A'isha said.

Yes, my uncle told me. I'm sorry.

They will try another time.

And you – how are you? asked Sophie.

I am well.

What else could she have said, thought Sophie. She wouldn't have said what it was really like, waiting.

I came to apologize to you. Sophie said. She watched Talata go across the compound. There were always chores to be done. Talata couldn't curl up on the bench beside A'isha and go to sleep.

Apologize, said A'isha.

I wish what I wrote had not caused you so many problems.

You did not make problems for me.

If I had not done it, people would not have come to your – to this compound. Sophie brushed her hand across her forehead.

Those men, they wanted to cause trouble.

But I wanted to come and tell you myself. I should not have written the article. I had this idea that it might help you, but it didn't.

Farih says you were the first.

I don't understand.

You come – you came, you and Mr. Felix.

Yes.

I wanted you to speak for me.

Sophie finished the last of the water in her bottle.

The daughter of Farih says the story about me has reached America, said A'isha. She says people are giving money to help me. It is good.

Sophie sat with her hands in her lap. Yes, it's good. She was thinking out loud. I mean, if your story goes international it could help with the next appeal, A'isha.

Safiya gurgled at A'isha and she bumped her up and down on her knee.

Farih says that because of so many people knowing my story, Nigeria will not want the shame.

The shame of carrying out the sentence? Yes, she could be right, said Sophie. What do you think?

All is the same here. It does not change.

You don't see how this could help you? said Sophie.

A'isha made a little movement with her shoulders, almost a shrug.

Sophie leaned forward. A'isha, if enough people believe that you've been wronged, if enough of them, all around the world know about you, then something might happen.

UNCLE THOMAS AND CLARE had returned. Sophie saw her mother get out of the car, shading her eyes with a folded newspaper, and she felt a sweeping rush of gratitude. Her mother, her deep concern. She watched as her uncle went to greet A'isha's uncle, and how her mother and uncle were ushered onto the porch and given chairs. Sophie's mother fanned herself with her newspaper.

Talata came across the compound and spoke to A'isha.

You have been invited to take a meal with my auntie and uncle, said A'isha. I am invited also. It will be after sundown.

An electric fan was put outside to cool the visitors and keep the mosquitoes away. Two tables were put together, chairs of varying shapes and sizes were gathered, and Talata set lanterns and a few candles on the tables in case the power went out. She gave everyone plastic glasses and spoons. Sophie's Uncle Thomas was given beer in a large green bottle with a star on it, which he divided between Clare, Sophie, and himself.

A'isha, next to Sophie, was quiet; Safiya slept. It had been dusk for mere moments, or so it seemed, then a flare of sky, and darkness dropped over them. There was a wail from the kitchen outbuilding; the fan wound down; the power had gone out. But the egusi soup had been prepared. A'isha fixed the candles on a square of folded tin foil, melting the wax first so each candle would have a base. It made the tables festive. Sophie saw the merest edge of a new moon now as she shifted in her chair, and felt herself tumbling into the night sky, weightless.

A little over a week before, when the moon was waning, she'd pointed it out to Felix. They were driving to Lagos after she wasn't allowed across the border.

It's gibbous, he said. It must be in the last quarter.

What's gibbous?

Any moon that's half-full, less than full.

Waxing or waning, either way?

Either way, he said. You didn't know a moon could be called that?

It had been a long day, and they were both tired. The moon looked like a water-filled balloon, pale and distorted as she gazed at it through the car window.

He brushed a hand across her cheek. Things will get better, Soph.

He'd been beside her in the car, in the dark. So close, so alive.

The egusi soup was brought to the table in green glass dishes. There was enough pounded yam for everyone, and small dishes of water so they could clean their fingers. Sophie had eaten it before but had never quite got the knack of shaping the pounded yam to scoop up the egusi. A'isha showed Sophie how to do it, and laughed when Sophie ate it, carefully, her head bent over her soup bowl. There was palm oil in the soup that gave it an oily texture, and it was fiery with spices, but it was very good. The pieces of goat meat were tender and delicious. Sophie looked at A'isha, who had covered her mouth with one hand, eyes crinkled with amusement.

She grew serious when a visitor arrived and stepped from his car, arranging his clothes before joining them. It was Hassan Muhammed, the alhaji, the head man, and A'isha's uncle greeted him effusively, inviting him to the table. The best chair was brought from inside the house by two boys and put between A'isha's uncle and Thomas, Sophie's uncle. Hassan had eaten. But he would take tea, and after a long interval, Talata brought it to him in a cup that rattled on its saucer. It might have been the only cup and saucer the family owned. He made Talata nervous, thought Sophie. She must have boiled water over a kerosene stove, since there was no power. But by the time the tea came to the table, Hassan forgot to drink it. He was deep in conversation with Thomas. They spoke Hausa.

What are they saying? Sophie asked her mother.

But Clare couldn't hear them.

There was so little time, thought Sophie. Soon they would drive back to Abuja, and the next day she would fly to Canada. Yet now she was wiping her brow and finishing her egusi soup. She was sitting with A'isha, gathered together with her own family and A'isha's.

When it was time to go, Sophie reached out to A'isha and Safiya, and hugged them as one.

I will be thinking of you, said Sophie. Hoping for the best.

She saw A'isha didn't understand.

I hope everything goes well for you, said Sophie.

Yes, please. I pray to Allah, I pray.

You aren't angry? You can still pray?

Now always, I pray.

Goodbye, A'isha, said Sophie.

Goodbye.

Sophie, Clare, and Thomas walked to the car. It was cool. Above them, the glinting stars were shaken out, spilled across the clear air. The new moon, the deep blue of evening, the beginning of night. The past and the future were divided by the sound of the door opening and closing, by the car starting. Sophie was cleaved in two. She might never see A'isha alive in the world again.

28

BINTA LOVED HER DRESS, made by a tailor Monica knew. Binta had picked out the material with its print of birds dipping and circling and soaring over the blue waxed cotton. Now, wearing it for the first time, she thought the birds were lifting her off the ground. A different girl, Monica had said to Thomas, than the one who'd come to them. Soon they would tell her that the police had found and arrested Danjuma and B.B., the very police that Monica thought would do nothing. Should they tell her now? Binta knew that they thought they were speaking privately, but she overheard them.

Monica was helping Binta settle in, and Thomas had figured out a way to take her on as a helper, an assistant, as he called it, before she started back at secondary school. She had not finished school; she had never taken examinations, not received the Senior Secondary School Certificate. Thomas had an idea that she might make a lawyer one day: it was only a hunch, but hunches were, as his father had once said, the staff of life. Binta didn't really know how people studied to be lawyers, or what they did after they became lawyers, or why they needed briefcases packed with papers to be read, but the staff of life made her curious. Was it something that lawyers were given?

Monica had made sure Thomas was dressed up too, in a good suit, and the silk tie with a pattern of gold keys, though before he left with Binta, Monica told him she knew that the first thing he would do was to take off his jacket.

I can't do business with my jacket on, he told her.

Well, don't stuff the tie into your pocket.

WHEN THEY ARRIVED, Hassan was already seated in a chair on the terrace outside his house, under the awning, where cold drinks of lime cordial and soda awaited them. He was especially pleased by Thomas's gift of a goat. It would be saved for a feast.

Tani was about to beckon Binta inside the house, but Hassan gestured to her. Binta could stay. Thomas had been offered the place of honour at the head man's side, and Binta, to her surprise, was given a chair on his other side. She watched Thomas bow to the men who had collected in a circle to ask Hassan for advice about a family dispute, discuss a scholarship for a student, resolve a matter of a well that had been dug in the middle of a property line.

Thomas asked about their health; they asked about his health.

He asked about their families; they asked about his family.

Farih is coming, Hassan told Thomas. She will be the glue for us.

But you must not say, he added quietly to Binta, that I called her glue. She would turn into a lioness.

Binta imagined a lioness with her teeth bared.

You have decided? Hassan asked Thomas as he batted his woven whisk at a fly.

Yes, Alhaji, said Thomas.

Binta scanned the other men: one guzzled thirstily from his glass, another scratched his vast belly. None of them was as respectful as Thomas.

You do not have a reputation for pro bono work, said Hassan.

That is true. Up to now.

Binta was offered an orange soda and bobbed her head in thanks. She considered the words pro bono. She shifted the glass from one hand to the other.

Hassan chewed on a fig reflectively. You envision yourself working together with the others?

Farih Hussaini will be my guide, said Thomas. I have thought of another who may help. Yakubu Muhammed.

I had not thought of Yakubu.

However, I myself am not Muslim.

Hassan laughed. You do not need to be Muslim to help us.

Binta sipped her drink; both of her hands were freezing cold, but the rest of her body was warm. She watched as Thomas slid off his tie and crumpled it up. Now he would put it in his pocket. Binta smiled as he stuffed it in, exactly as Monica had predicted, so the tail of the tie, with its pretty gold keys, straggled out of the pocket.

Hassan grew serious. There will be those who will ask questions. There will be those who want to harm you, even want to kill you. Churches have been bombed in Abuja, and this is the very place where you are living.

I have talked about this with my wife.

But, frankly, you may be putting yourself in danger.

My own niece put her life in danger.

Yes, she did. Then there was the business of the fatwa, so you are aware of what may happen.

I am well aware.

Thomas was so quiet, like a little boy at school. He was looking intently at his shoes, the very shoes Binta herself had polished the evening before.

If my family is threatened, said Thomas, I will cross that bridge when I come to it. Perhaps I would need to reconsider.

Binta thought of him crossing a bridge and looking down at the water, considering and reconsidering.

Let us hope you will not have to, said Hassan. He leaned back in his chair. You will be under my protection, such as it is. You have met A'isha. You do not know that her stepfather married her off to a friend of his who had one foot in the grave. I intervened too late after he died. He drained his glass, set it down on the table. A'isha's mother died not long ago, as you know. Her death was a great loss.

Binta turned this over in her mind. Her own mother had been hit on the highway and carried home, where she died on her bed. Was her death a great loss to anyone but Binta? Afterwards, Binta had gone to live with her cousin, who liked his youngest wife best, his junior wife. Men could draw women like honey. How could they do that?

Ah, she has come. Beware the lioness, Hassan murmured.

Farih got out of the car, a Lexus, Binta noticed, since she knew a little about cars, and immediately Farih's glamour caused a commotion among the men. They slid their feet into shoes, adjusted their clothing, put down their drinks. Binta almost laughed out loud. But Farih paid no attention to the men grooming themselves; her eyes were on Hassan and Thomas. Her ivory-coloured dress shone as she moved toward them, and her pale-pink head wrap was twisted into a shape that resembled the open blossom of a flower. She was a queen. Binta revised her view: if men could draw women like honey, this woman could draw whatever she wanted. She *would* have whatever she wanted. This was the person Thomas must have been describing to Monica. The lioness.

I am behind schedule. Farih lowered herself gracefully into the chair provided for her. Binta observed how she managed it, one hand beneath the silky ivory dress. You must forgive me, said Farih.

Of course they forgave her. Who could not?

Come, said Hassan, we will go in.

And much to Binta's disappointment, the three of them vanished inside the house.

The sun was very warm, even under the shade of the awning, and one of the men who had been waiting to settle a matter with Hassan began snoring. It was a grumbling noise, occasionally punctuated by a clownish snort. Beyond the terrace in the compound, three girls dozed under a tree on a mat, their pale feet showing, and a woman picking insects out of a basin of rice let her hand fall idly on its rim; even the chickens were quiet, finished with squabbling. Dust furled and settled across the swept ground, and then all was still. Binta felt herself giving in to a sleepiness that crept up her legs, her thighs, her arms; she could not resist.

When she woke, she realized that her jaw had been hanging open. A small boy, seated on the step leading into the house, was gazing at her. Binta wiped her face with her kerchief. The men had gone, taking their claims and disputes with them, and there was only the child, laughing as he made a show of wiping his own face, mimicking Binta. Farih almost fell over the boy when she swept outside, and Hassan clapped his hands to make him scurry away.

Rasheed, Rasheed – off with you.

Binta sat up straight to cover her embarrassment; she hadn't meant to fall asleep. She wasn't a bush girl now.

LATER, WHEN THOMAS AND BINTA were leaving, Hassan came close to the driver's side of the car.

There will have to be a council, said Hassan. A meeting of elders. They will have to agree that Farih will take up the second appeal with your help and that of Danladi Baku, who worked with her on the first appeal, and perhaps Yakubu. It is a formality; I can assure you that they do not want harm to come to A'isha.

I will wait to hear, then, said Thomas. I hope I have the necessary mettle for this job.

It is said that unless we are afraid, we do not find courage, Hassan said wryly, lifting up his sunglasses so they were on his forehead.

If it is to be found at all, said Thomas.

Exactly so, said Hassan. He tapped the roof of the car in farewell.

SEVERAL DAYS AFTER the first meeting, Thomas went back to see Hassan with Binta and Yakubu. Hassan had invited Farih and Danladi Baku. Binta, too, was offered a chair in the circle, as if she herself were a lawyer. She sat very still. Her spine was iron. They had gone through the introductions; refreshments had been handed around, and Hassan went into the house and returned with the baby that was now being bounced on his thigh. The child was about eight or nine months old, with satiny brown skin and a chubby face. Hassan held her hands to keep her balanced, and she crowed whenever his leg gave an extra jiggle she wasn't expecting.

A grandchild, thought Binta.

This is Safiya, said Hassan. Safiya, I want you to greet some very intelligent people. He bounced; the child shrieked.

Hassan rose with Safiya in his arms and deposited her with Thomas. She gave him a puzzled look, then smiled rapturously as one hand went to his glasses, pulling them. He turned his head so she wouldn't yank them off, but now she tried the other side, grabbing his ear as if it were a toy. The others began to laugh as Thomas grimaced.

O-ho, she has you in her grip, said Hassan merrily.

She does, said Thomas.

Enough, now, Safiya, said Hassan gently, and she turned to him while Thomas retrieved his glasses. She climbed into Hassan's arms.

You have children, Hassan said to Thomas.

We have three at home. We are in the process of adopting another. Thomas did not add that this was Binta; she bowed her head so as not to look at him.

Praise Allah! So, you have an understanding of their deviousness, their caprices. I myself am father to seven, he boasted. And grandfather to five.

However, this one is not mine. He grinned and dabbed Safiya's nose.

He looked around at all of them more sternly. You should not underestimate the work you are facing, work that will require your complete attention.

Perhaps, thought Binta, these fancy lawyers had imagined Alhaji Hassan as a man from the bush, when he was not like that at all.

You may fail, but I hope you do not.

Safiya arched her back and began to cry, and Hassan handed her over to a girl who had appeared in the doorway of the house.

You must work only with one thing in mind. The benefit of that child, he said. And not only that child, but the child's mother. You must be very wise here. He tapped his finger against the side of his head. But you must be even wiser here. He tapped his chest.

BUT I HAVE NOT YET MET HER, said Binta that evening, as they ate dinner.

Monica sipped from her glass of water. It may be days yet.

Maybe we should get some medicine for Hassan's mother, said Thomas.

Oh, I was going to check. For pleurisy, is it?

Binta tossed her napkin on to the table. All of this will take a month! And meanwhile nothing is done for A'isha.

Eat your food, said Monica. Hortensia, what have you got on your fingers that you need to stick them into your mouth all at once?

They'll stay there, said Binta. There was a girl in my village who did that, and she couldn't get her hand out of her mouth. She tried and tried, and then her mother tried and then –

Monica smothered a laugh.

That's not true, said Jonathan.

Would I make up a story like that, Master Jonathan-I-know-more-than-you?

Hortensia's fingers promptly came out of her mouth. Her eyes were wide.

Yes, Binta, went on, looking at Hortensia. Her name was Efome.

Thomas got up from the table. Well, I don't want to have to excuse myself, but I must get to work.

Hours later, when Binta was going to bed, she saw he'd fallen asleep in his desk chair. She knocked on the open door to wake him.

Binta. He roused himself, collected the papers he'd been studying. I should be off to sleep, and you as well. Goodnight.

Goodnight, she said shyly.

Binta went to the bedroom she shared with Hortensia, where she undressed and folded her clothes in the dark. She lay down on the bed, but she couldn't sleep.

When Binta and Monica had gone to the Wuse Market to buy cloth, the sky was cool and fresh and blue. It was early, before the sluggish heat took the colour out of it, and all that Binta saw was new, a world made entirely new – the orange of a woman's headscarf, the green skins of the oranges piled in a basin, bottles of palm oil arranged on a shelf in a stall, a woman with a girl in her lap, plaiting her hair, a man taking another man's hand, lightly, in greeting, chickens stepping through the maze of feet and bicycles and motorbikes. A bus had broken down across from the market, and the passengers streamed out, some hoisting belongings onto their heads, some swinging them at their sides.

Binta and Monica were among them, dodging passengers who were disembarking, trying to get out of the way of a man carrying a huge woven basket on his head. One handsome woman, with an elaborate flowering arrangement of braids, had lost the heel from her shoe, and Binta helped her find it. She couldn't fasten the thin spike of the heel to the shoe; the woman would need to find someone who could fix it properly. She thanked Binta, picked up her bags and suitcase, and hobbled off with one shoe on and one shoe off.

Monica smiled at Binta; Binta grinned back.

They came to the section of the market where material was sold, and Binta reached out to touch the printed cotton, the rolls of gold and green, pink and yellow, silver and blue. She settled on the material with the birds in the air, soaring and dipping, because she was thinking of the airplane that Sophie and Clare had taken on their way home a week before. Had they been frightened, flying over the ocean?

It had been hard to decide between the cloth with the birds and the cloth with the flowers, and in the end, Monica bargained for both and bought them.

RASHEED WAS TOLD to get another chair and he raced off.

You have met her, Hassan told Thomas. Her father thought she was simple, but that is not so. She hides herself well.

It was some time before A'isha appeared, with Safiya, to greet Farih and the men seated in the shade. Hassan motioned for Binta to take the one vacant chair, but Binta remained where she was. If anyone took the chair it should be A'isha. A'isha's hijab was a little askew, as if she had been caught unprepared. It was the face of a girl like herself, thought Binta, but not a girl; she had the dignity of a woman, and because of that she reminded Binta of a woman of Monica's age.

A'isha greeted Hassan respectfully, whereupon he got up, taking Safiya and wheeling around in a circle until the child giggled.

A'isha, said Thomas, standing up. I am glad to see you again. He spoke in Hausa.

She lifted her eyes briefly.

I will be one of those who will represent you. I am hopeful that we can win this next appeal.

Hassan gave Safiya back to A'isha. She looked from one to the other, jiggling her baby in her arms. Binta could not be sure if there was a smile on her lips.

Mr. Thomas, said A'isha, speaking in English. You are welcome.

And this is Binta, said Thomas. She will be helping.

A'isha's eyes barely met Binta's, but there was a glint of curiosity, as if A'isha was interested in the indigo birds printed on the blue cotton. She wanted to see them, Binta thought, she wanted to see the swoop and spiral of the birds. Binta herself couldn't stop herself from looking down or keep from fingering the button at the collar. The tailor had worked swiftly. She wanted to say to A'isha that it had been a gift, that she hadn't been able to contain herself and had uttered a shriek of delight when Monica had come back from the tailor's and unfolded the newly made blouses and skirts, shaken them out. Had anyone ever given her anything like this? Two sets of clothes. Monica and Hortensia had agreed on how nice Binta looked when she put them on, one set, and then the other, and showed them off. Monica said she needed a pair of shoes to go with them.

A'isha and Binta remained standing, waiting for the boy to bring the extra chair. They were about the same age. Binta could have been the one with a baby in her arms; she could have been the one needing help. A'isha's skin was sleek and clear, and her eyes were large; Binta wanted her to look up. Instead, A'isha concentrated on Safiya, whose brown arm hung free from her mother's cradling arms. Even in the shade, it was steaming hot, and Binta shifted her weight from one leg to the other as she felt the material of her dress sticking to her skin.

A'isha should live; she shouldn't die. It roused a fierceness inside Binta that she hadn't known was there – the way A'isha stood, with her right hip slightly tilted, and how she first looked at Binta, as if questioning her, or the way Safiya's arm drooped sleepily, or the way that Thomas sat in the chair, one leg forward, one leg bent, listening to the man on the other side of him. Hassan took a spoon from his drink, which was tea, yes, she'd heard him ask his wife for sweet tea, with two spoons of sugar. She watched as he put the spoon beside his glass cup on the table, heard the sound it made as he set it down. All of this flashed through her and was gone.

I am glad to meet you, said Binta. You and Safiya.

29

IF THIS APPEAL DOESN'T DO ANY GOOD, if it doesn't change anything, at least I've given myself to Safiya, at least I'll know that. I tried to be a good daughter, a good mother. I want to think about that and not pay attention to the counsels for the prosecution, one of them coughing now, so that the one beside him unwraps a candy and gives it to him. I can hear the unwrapping of the candy as if it is exploding in my ears.

I am on the other side of the courtroom, in the Court of Appeals, with the counsels of defense, close to Farih Hussaini. I can almost feel her body vibrating beside mine. But I don't want to hear what they are saying, what they have been talking about for hours. I don't want to be in this room, trying not to listen and listening because I must. There are Farih's beautiful shoes to look at instead, her shoes with the gold loops. When she shifts her feet, the gold loops glisten, and this helps to calm the fanned-up feathers of panic, as if there's a bird in my chest, trying to get out. Maybe there really is a bird inside.

I can't bear to look at the face of the Grand Khadi as he reads the judgement. I can't bear to hear about zina, but then I find myself listening to him. He is saying that the police should not have charged me with the offense of zina. He is saying this, and I almost lift my eyes, but instead I keep them on Farih's shoes, and the gold loops, one looped with another. I think about how they were looped that way, how someone did that.

He is saying more, that the act of zina must be openly witnessed by four people, and that because four people have not witnessed it, the accused, the appellant, should be discharged and acquitted. Farih touches my arm, with a touch as light as the tip of a wing. I want to ask about discharged and acquitted, but the Grand Khadi has gone on to the next point, and anyway, I can't speak in this court, and I wouldn't speak even if I could.

I glance up, so that no one will notice, and I see the way he is intent, the way his face is set. His voice is a voice I can listen to. It is low, but it can be heard in every corner of this room, and he is making a rope with it, a good, strong rope. I hold on, I listen, I don't try to make him smaller in my mind. He says that discharging the man accused of being with me – Musa is the man he means, but he doesn't say Musa's name – that discharging the man while convicting the woman was an error and should not be sustained before the court. It was an error.

A mistake, something wrong. It was wrong for Musa to make me fall down with the basin of water in my hands. I close my eyes. I am lying still and looking up at the underside of the tin roof and the warm water making my clothes damp, and I am lying still, listening to Safiya's first cry, after she came out of my body, and I am lying still and not sleeping after my mother's burial, after she was wrapped in white.

But what Musa did was wrong.

The Grand Khadi says it was an abuse of law for a judge to sit alone at a trial, to preside over a trial when it has been stipulated in the penal code that a judge and two members should sit at the trial court. And he is saying that it was not valid, my confession was not valid, because it was not repeated multiple times, and also, that I was not allowed to withdraw my confession.

And he is still talking, but my ribs are opening. I can feel them opening from the bone that runs down the centre of my chest. They open, but not in the same way as a door. They open in the way the body opens. I can feel this happening, though my eyes are closed.

I hear some of the words he is saying, some of the bits and pieces, but not all. He is speaking of an accused person, he is speaking of the Qur'an. He is saying that the trial court records were unclear, and that where there are doubts, they should be resolved in favour of the accused.

My ribs are opening. Something wants out.

I hear him saying that the burden of proof should be borne by the prosecution. I hear him saying that the court has heard in favour of the accused, the appellant, and that this is the decision by which the counsels of law must abide, that A'isha Nasir is discharged and acquitted forthwith, that it is the will and decision of the Court of Appeals that she should go free.

30

AS SOON AS THE DOG JUMPS OUT of the car at the beach, trailing his leash, Sophie sees how the world has opened up. It has been months since she returned to Canada with her mother, but almost two years have passed since she has been at this beach. Sky, a roll of dunes, dashes of blue ocean where the ridges of sand and marram grass dip to reveal it.

No, she cries. Cuba, *wait!*

But Cuba is off down the weathered boardwalk, the uneven boards, with the burgundy leash flipping behind him. No one else is around; it's chilly. Cuba comes lolloping back and Sophie releases the catch on the leash, bundling it up in her pocket. She comes to the end of the boardwalk where it slopes down to the sand.

It's more than just chilly. The wind is biting, and waves pile one on top of the other, racing onshore, white flicked back from each roll of blue green. It makes her want to run. She turns east and the dog runs with her, galloping in and out of the water, making the seagulls fly up in a flurry of white and grey. The wind drives and drives and drives the tide, whipping it onward. The waves swing curving bodies into the home stretch, plunging forward on the sand. When the water draws back, the stones in the damp, purplish-brown sand are slick, and each one is sharp and clear and polished, each has a shadow.

She walks all the way to the eastern tip of the beach, where the dunes rise up in high mounds.

Thunder of waves against sand. A tern swoops low for something invisible on the beach, soars up; a flock of gulls putter around half-buried shells near a tidal pool. She walks on to the place where the water sucks through a channel at the mouth of the estuary, the current a muscle, surging up, higher than the rest, a thick muscle. The light is strong, heady. She could be tipped over; she is insubstantial. No, she isn't going to think about Felix. She won't. She sits where she can be sheltered from the wind, sheltered but thinned to gauze, less than she was before.

This is the place where she and her mother came, in the sheen of early morning, to scatter her father's ashes. Her mother wanted to scatter them at this hooked end of beach, and it had to be morning, and it had to be August, on the day of their anniversary. Clare anticipated everything, with a full plastic bag for Sophie, one for herself, and another with the tops of cut flowers that could be tossed with the ashes. She and Sophie were careful about the direction of the wind. Sophie put her hand into the bag and drew out a handful of brown-grey ash with bits of sparkle, the tiniest fragments: all that remained of a body that had been her father. Mostly it was the same colour as the sand at her feet, but it felt different, not what she expected. She held the ashes cupped in her palm. Her father. She didn't want to give anything up to the water, but her mother showed her how to throw some of it away from her, with flowers in it, so it would fall on the surface of the water, and they could watch the bobbing heads of carnations. She tossed her father's ashes here, where the channel from the estuary met the waters of the Northumberland Strait in this strip of wild water, right at this spot. The water twisted away, fled away. One thing poured into the other. Her father's ashes went out, rising on the swell of current, they must have risen, mixed with the water, the blossoms, going away and away, curling and spinning away.

SOPHIE GETS UP, watching the dog as he bounds to the shore, zigzagging near the edge of it, the lip. She wonders if some trace of her father remains in the water, the sand, the air. Does he exist somehow, or is he entirely gone? The wind is fierce; it carries the day with it, light streaming over her. Caught in the gusts, her hair waves around her head, and she digs in her pocket for her old, soft hat, one her grandmother knitted, pulling it over her head. It's the tail end of April, almost May. The wind shouldn't be harsh; it should be mild.

A'isha. Her uncle told them he'd call when he knew the outcome. The second appeal meant months of preparation for him. Sophie wants to know the verdict; she doesn't want to know. She's afraid to know. Across the channel is a reddish-brown strip of beach, Ferry Beach, and beyond that an island spiked with dead trees, and, farther east, the indistinct hills of Cape Breton's western shore, that blue coast, always mysterious, not quite there, as if hovering just above the earth. She saunters west, away from the estuary, back the way she came. The long curve of beach looks wintry, and there are patches of snow in the high ridge of dunes, a thin crust of ice over a tear-shaped pond in the sand. She kicks aside ragged heaps of eelgrass left after storms, and makes her way to the water's edge, where the waves surge in, cold and greenish blue. Farther out, the water is much darker, a deep navy blue, but here it's altogether different. She shivers. It's freezing, with that bracing wind, and though she knows she'll need a hot shower by the time she gets home, she doesn't move. It mesmerizes her. A'isha is alive, still alive. Soon the news of the second appeal will come. The tide swirls in, gathers itself, pulls back, and sweeps in again, but it's too cold to stand in one place watching it.

Cuba, she calls. Cuba!

The wind takes her cry, and she knows the dog won't hear. She scrambles up the dunes, but she sees nothing except a ragtag of gulls blown above her, crumpled paper thrown into the blue. No dog anywhere. No, she's wrong: down on the beach is a familiar plume of yellow-blond tail. He's tugging at something. She circles back, sinking in the deep sand of the dune wall as she descends and chases the dog away from whatever he is intent on ripping apart.

Hey, Cuba, get away from that!

He has a dark piece of it in his mouth.

Get over here!

He comes reluctantly, the dark piece dropped, ready to wheel and go back to what he found.

No.

The thing is partly hidden under eelgrass. A seal, a deer? It's hard to tell. Yes, a seal. There's a bit of flipper. Something has been at it, and the seal seems to have been eaten away. A skull, bits of skin, or fur, and the socket where an eye used to be, before it was a mutilated carcass. Like nothing else, that stench. The sweet-sick smell.

Cuba noses toward it, eagerly.

No, she says.

Her eyes blur with tears from the wind, and the seal slips from its place as if it's moving. In that moment, Cuba disregards her. She doesn't see him go to the seal again, but now he's yanking at it.

No! she cries.

Cuba lets go, slinks away. She rarely speaks so sternly to him.

The seal is dead. It can't move. It's nothing but a sack of leather-like skin, and bones, and putrid organs, and eyes that aren't there.

She leashes Cuba.

Down the beach is a loose group of people, three or four. They must have come from the boardwalk together, maybe headed in Sophie's direction. She hopes they'll go the other way, toward the hill at the far end of the beach, a green flank sometimes topped by wedding tents in summer. From that hill she has seen pods of minke whales in the water below, their smooth, dark bodies slipping over and under the surface.

Death takes creatures like the seal and turns them into distortions of themselves. It took her father and turned him into something like sand and he'd fallen through her fingers. The dog yanks on the leash and Sophie pulls back. It was a mistake to go to Nigeria in the first place. Yank and pull. She left Felix there and came home, another mistake. And it had been a mistake to have been so full of belief that she could write about A'isha, who lived in another country, another world.

Two of the people are going the other way, and they have a dog, no, two dogs. Was it a mistake about A'isha? Yes, they have two dogs, a light one and a dark one. A big one and a small one. They're chasing each other, scuffing the sand, digging at it and racing away, as if slingshotted. She's glad the couple are taking the dogs to the western end of the beach, that rougher part, strewn with rocks. How could she have known what would happen? Felix. No, she won't – she isn't going to think about Felix, how she –

One person remains at the water's edge, not far from where the lifeguard's tower is placed in the summer months.

Cuba wrenches her wrist, hauling on the leash.

At night she lies in her bed without sleeping, thinking of him, tossing, not thinking of him. It's true she abandoned him. She goes to the grocery store and finds herself turning over a Spanish onion; she wanders down an aisle with no idea what she's searching for. The ache catches her as she reaches for a bag of coffee beans, dark-roast Colombian, on sale. She picks up the bag, holds it in mid-air. When she puts gas in her mother's car, she's no longer staring at the hat-shaped hill called Sugarloaf, she's in the hospital and Grace is holding her. The driver in the car behind her honks, and she's startled into taking the nozzle out of the gas tank, ripping the receipt from the slot. She drives away and parks on the far side of the gas bar, turns off the car, leans back against the headrest. Sugarloaf. Something inside her is pierced, and beyond that hole, that Felix absence, is the blue afterworld, the far-off place that can't be reached.

She wonders if she can let Cuba off the leash, whether that solitary person will mind, because the dog is bound to investigate, bark, sniff for a treat. Some people like dogs and others want them gone.

She lets Cuba off the leash.

THE MAN WEARS A BORROWED HAT and scarf, and with the hat pulled down and the scarf wrapped around his face, only his eyes and nose are visible. His down jacket, thin and easy to pack, is meant to be warm, meant to withstand any weather. He feels the wind penetrating it. To stand here, wind assailing him, is not the smartest thing to do.

He sees that the woman has let the dog off the leash and

knows it will come to him. This is what dogs do. She and the dog are still some distance from him, and he shifts his gaze away, away from the white hat, away from the blue jacket. He concentrates on the water, counting the beats between each curl and drop, each foamy drift of spent wave. So damn cold.

One, two – his mind slips off and he brings it back. One, two.

A ribbon of kelp at his feet, and a mound of stuff, heavy and thick and tangled. He touches the tip of his German shoe to it, his glossy leather shoe that's entirely unsuitable for walking on a beach.

She's closer, the dog is closer.

The dog begins to bark, galloping over to him, barking and wagging its feathery tail. It won't stop barking until the man bends over, rubbing between its ears, and then it wants to play, whirling and whirling around him in a frenzy of exuberance.

Cuba! calls the woman. I'm sorry, I should have had him on the leash. Here, I'll get him away from you.

It's all right.

No – he'll jump all over you. He has no sense, really. He's never had any sense – Cuba!

Soph, he says.

She lets the leash drop on the wet sand, a lopsided figure eight. The froth of a wave slides over it.

He moves back. His shoes are wet, his ridiculous leather shoes that aren't meant for beaches. It's me, Soph.

The dog barks again, running one way, then the other, leaving the marks of its claws drawn deeply into the sand.

Your mother told me you'd be here, at Pomquet, and then she found neighbours of hers who could take me out here, because you have the car.

I do, she says. I have the car.

I came by bus from the airport, and then taxi. I had a time of it, finding the house, but the taxi driver asked around. I didn't know your mother's place was outside town, and the driver didn't know the name of the lane, but everyone knows everyone else here, or at least they know someone who knows – I mean, it's not a big place. I guess I don't have to tell you that.

He's talking too much. He needs to sit down, lie down on a bed where he can rest. His mother had said it was too soon to go halfway around the world, he'd do himself damage, but he didn't listen.

They're over there. He waves his hand. The neighbours – Ally and Ryan. She's pregnant with their first. I think maybe you know them.

She glances at the far end of the beach where the figures pick their way around boulders. The two dogs can no longer be seen.

It's so cold here, he says. The wind – I thought it was supposed to be spring in Nova Scotia.

It's you. Her eyes fill. Is it you?

NOTES AND ACKNOWLEDGEMENTS

The seeds for *Speechless* were planted many years ago when I volunteered with CUSO (then known as Canadian University Services Overseas) as an English language and literature teacher in Nigeria. In the first year, I taught at a school for boys in Niger State. In the second year, I worked at an Advanced Teachers College in Benue State. In those years, I learned much about the rich and vivid culture of Nigeria from those who extended such a warm, generous welcome.

The characters and story depicted in *Speechless* are fictitious, though there were several famous cases in Nigeria that helped lay the foundation for this novel. My invention of A'isha Nasir was greatly aided by a conversation with Hauwa Ibrahim at the Harvard Divinity School, and further helped by some details in her book, *Practicing Shariah Law: Seven Strategies for Achieving Justice in Shariah Courts.*

I have taken liberties with my depiction of the border crossing at Imeko in Chapter 13. Generally, foreigners like Sophie MacNeil would cross the border from Nigeria to Benin at Seme.

***

Novels take a great deal of time to write. I am deeply grateful to the Canada Council for a research and creation grant that gave me time to write *Speechless,* and for a Canada Council travel grant that allowed me to take up a brief residency with the Osu Children's Libraries in Ghana. My thanks also go to Nova Scotia Communities, Culture and Heritage, which awarded me grants on two separate occasions to write *Speechless*. I also received an invaluable Access Copyright Foundation grant to do research at the Library of Islamic Studies at McGill University in Montreal and at the Harvard Divinity School, Harvard University, in Boston.

***

Jackie Kaiser, of Westwood Creative Artists, went the extra mile with this novel to help it find a home. Thank you, Jackie. I am fortunate to have discovered Freehand Books and to have worked with a truly wonderful team including Kelsey Attard and Anna Boyar, with editor Naomi K. Lewis, and with copy editor Emma Skagen. As well, I am most grateful for Yemi Stephanie's comments on all matters to do with Nigeria.

As I mentioned, Hauwa Ibrahim was a great help to me in the writing of *Speechless*. I am also indebted to Richard Kearney of Boston College. Linda Darwish, of St. Francis Xavier University, assisted me with answers about Islam.

Kathy Knowles, Director of the Osu Children's Library Fund, supported me in many ways during a residency in Ghana, where Joana Felih, Vivian Amanor, and Martin Legend were all very helpful.

Imam Abdallah Yousri, at Ummah Masjid in Halifax, NS, was very gracious in answering many detailed questions. He spent a great deal of time going over Muslim funeral practices.

Special thanks to Dr. Elizabeth Brennan and Dr. John Graham-Pole for answers to medical questions.

I am also grateful to Atinuke Adeoye for her assistance.

In terms of details of life in Nigeria from the perspective of volunteers, I was helped by Alison Mathie and Paul Marquis.

Sections of *Speechless* were written at the Abbaye Notre-Dame de l'Assomption in Rogersville, NS. My grateful thanks go to Sr. Kate Waters.

Without Valerie Compton's encouraging reading of this novel, I might not have revised it as I did. Warmest thanks also go to Carol Bruneau, Alexander MacLeod, Liz Philips, and Johanna Skibsrud.

My heartfelt thanks to Janet, my mother, and to my sisters, Jennifer and Sue, and their families. And to my own family – Paul, David, and Sarah – my most loving thanks. I could not have done this without you.

ANNE SIMPSON has published two novels, *Canterbury Beach* and *Falling*, longlisted for the International IMPAC Dublin Literary Award and winner of the Dartmouth Book Award for Fiction. She has also written five poetry collections, of which *Strange Attractor* is the most recent. She won the Griffin Poetry Prize for *Loop* in 2004. Her book of essays, *The Marram Grass: Poetry and Otherness*, examines poetry, art, and philosophy. Simpson has worked as a writer-in-residence at libraries and universities across the country. She lives in Nova Scotia.